Asian and Pacific Short Stories

Asian and Pacific
Short Stories

compiled by

The Cultural and Social Centre
Asian Pacific Council

CULTURAL AND SOCIAL CENTRE
FOR THE ASIAN AND PACIFIC REGION
Seoul, Korea

CHARLES E. TUTTLE COMPANY
Rutland, Vermont and Tokyo, Japan

Representatives

For Continental Europe:
BOXERBOOKS, INC., *Zurich*

For the British Isles:
PRENTICE-HALL INTERNATIONAL, INC., *London*

For Australasia:
PAUL FLESCH & CO., PTY. LTD., *Melbourne*

For Canada:
HURTIG PUBLISHERS, *Edmonton*

PJ
441
A8

Published by the Charles E. Tuttle Company, Inc.
of Rutland, Vermont & Tokyo, Japan
with editorial offices at
Suido 1-chome, 2–6, Bunkyo-ku, Tokyo

Library of Congress Catalog Card No. 73–93869
International Standard Book No. 0–8048 1125–3

First printing, 1974

Printed in Japan

Photosetting by Thomson Press (India) Limited, New Delhi

Table of Contents

Preface

IN MAY 1969, the Cultural and Social Centre for the Asian Pacific Region held its first seminar on the promotion of cultural cooperation among the member nations of the Asian Pacific Council (ASPAC). Among the recommendations of the seminar was that the Centre sponsor the publication, in the English language, of representative literary works from each of the member nations.

The literary works of a country are a mirror of that country's culture and civilization. Since the Centre was founded in order to promote mutual understanding and cooperation in the cultural field, we felt that a series of anthologies of the member countries' literature would go a long way toward achieving our objectives.

This collection of short stories from the writers of nine countries is the first in what we hope will be a series of anthologies of contemporary Asian writing: future volumes will collect the work of poets, playwrights, and other writers.

The stories in this volume—two from each of the nine ASPAC member nations—were selected by the member governments with the collaboration of each country's P.E.N. Club. (The P.E.N. clubs are groups of writers in each country, who are affiliated as a body with the International P.E.N.) The P.E.N. clubs in these Asian nations have been instrumental in encouraging new writers and providing an outlet for their work. In addition, they have been emphasizing the importance of making the literature of Asian nations more widely available, in translation, to the rest of the world. For this volume, the P.E.N. clubs of the Republic of Korea, Thailand, and the Republic of Vietnam themselves commissioned the translation of stories which had not previously been translated into English.

With this volume, a step has been taken in bringing together works of writers as different in their backgrounds of culture and tradition as the countries in which they live. As the Chinese proverb goes, "A journey of a thousand *li* begins with a single step."

At the Centre's seminar, one of the participants declared: "The business of cultural relations is like forestry. If we do not plant trees today our grandchildren will lack forests to use and to enjoy. If we do not now develop cultural relations between nations as wisely and as broadly as we are able, our children and grandchildren will not have the human resources without which international peace and cooperation and human freedom cannot be preserved."

In publishing this volume, you might say that the Cultural and Social Centre has attempted to plant the trees. May our readers use and enjoy the forests.

MARIO T. GATBONTON, General Editor
Cultural and Social Centre, ASPAC

Acknowledgments

Angus & Robertson, Ltd. for "The Tractor," from *Short Stories of Australia—the Moderns,* and for "At the Galahad," from *A Bachelor's Children.*

Mai Ya Publications, Inc. for "The Ivory Balls," from *The Ivory Balls and Other Stories.*

Greenwood Press for "Grandma Takes Charge," from *Contemporary Chinese Stories.*

The Japan P.E.N. Club for "The Death Mask," from *The Japan P.E.N. News No. 23.*

Yoichi Nakagawa for permission to publish "The Moustache."

Korean P.E.N. Centre for "Seaside Village," from *Modern Korean Stories and Plays.*

Hwimoon Publishing Co. for "Shadow," from *In the Depths.*

Heinemann, Ltd. for "Poonek" and "The Jade Bracelet," from *Twenty-Two Malaysian Stories.*

Longman, Paul, Ltd. for "Along Rideout Road That Summer."

Landfall for "The Bulls."

Syracuse University Press for "The Sea Beyond," from *New Writing from the Philippines*.

The Bookmark, Inc. for "The Day the Dancers Came," from *The Day the Dancers Came*.

P.E.N. Thailand Centre for "The Grandmother" and "Champoon," from *Thai Short Stories*.

Vietnam P.E.N. Centre for "My Milk Goes Dry" and "An Unsound Sleep," from *Poems and Short Stories*.

The Tractor

[AUSTRALIA]

by Peter Cowan

SHE WATCHED him coming back from the gate, walking towards the slightly ornate suburban-style house she felt to be so incongruous set down on the bare rise, behind it the sheds and yards and the thin belt of shade trees. Yet he and his family were proud of it, grateful for its convenience and modernity, and had so clearly not understood her first quizzical remarks that she had never repeated them.

He stood on the edge of the verandah, and she saw in his face the anger that seemed to deepen because he knew the feeling to be impotent. She said :

"What is it?"

"Mackay's two big tractors—that they were going to use for the scrub clearing—they've been interfered with. Sand put into the oil. The one they started up will cost a few hundred to repair."

"But no one would do that," she said, as if already it were settled, her temporizing beside the point.

"We know who did it."

"But surely," she said, "he didn't come right up to the sheds—as close as that to the house—"

"No. They left the tractors down in the bottom paddock. Where they were going to start clearing."

"And now—they can't?"

"Now they can't. Not till the tractor's repaired."

She looked towards the distant line of the low scrub that was deepening in colour as the evening came. She said :

"That is what he wanted."

"What he wants is to make as much trouble as he can. We haven't done anything to him."

"You were going to clear the land along the bottom paddock at the back of Mackay's. Where he lives."

"Where he lives?"

"You told me he lived in the bush there."

"He lives anywhere. And he takes the ball floats off the taps in the sheep tanks and the water runs to waste, and he breaks the fences when he feels like it, and leaves the gates open—"

"You think he does this deliberately?"

"How else?"

"Oh," she said, "yet it is all so ruthless."

"You mean what he does?"

"No. You only ever think of what he does."

"Well, I'll admit he's given us a few things to think about."

"Clearing with those tractors and the chain," she said. "Everything in their path goes—kangaroos—all the small things that live in the scrub—all the trees—"

He looked at her as if her words held some relevance that must come to him. He said :

"We clear the land. Yes."

"You clear it," she said. "It seems to be what is happening everywhere today."

"I don't know what you mean, Ann," he said.

She got up from the chair by the steps. "Perhaps he feels something should be left."

"Look," he said, "maybe you teach too much nature study at school. Or you read all this stuff about how we shouldn't shoot the bloody roos—so that when some crazy swine wrecks our property you think he's some sort of a—"

"Some sort of a what?"

"I don't know," he said, aware she mocked him. "Better than us."

"No," she said. "Perhaps just different."

"Different all right."

"What are you going to do?"

"Get the police," he said. "They don't take much notice most of the time, but they will of this." He looked at her as if he would provoke the calm he felt to be assumed. "We'll burn him out if we can't get him any other way."

She looked up quickly and for a moment he was afraid.

"You wouldn't do that."

"He's gone too far this time," he said stubbornly.

The long thin streamers of cloud above the darkening line of scrub were becoming deep and hard in color, scarlet against the dying light. He watched her face that seemed now calm, remote, as if their words were erased. She was small, slight, somehow always neat, contained. Her dark hair was drawn straight back, her brows clearly marked, lifting slightly so that they seemed to give, sometimes, humor to her serious expression, her firm, mouth.

"I'd better go, Ken."

"The family expect you for tea."

"It's Sunday night. I've to work in the morning. I have some things to prepare."

"Look," he said. "If it's this business—"

"No. I'm just tired. And I've assignments to mark."

"All right," he said.

As they drove she watched the long shadows that spread across the road, and over the paddocks from the few shade trees, the light now with a clarity denied through the heat of the day. She would have liked to make some gesture to break the tension between them, to explain to him why she had been unwilling to stay and listen to the inevitable talk of what had happened. But to tell him that at such times she became afraid, as if she could never become one of them, certain that the disagreements which were now easily enough brought to a truce must in the end defeat them, would not lessen their dissension. He said suddenly :

"You're worried about it, aren't you?"

She knew that he referred to themselves, as if he had been aware of her own thoughts.

"Yes," she said. "Sometimes."

"It could be all right, Ann. You'd come to like it here."

"In so many ways I do."

"It's nothing like it used to be. This light land has come good now. We've done well. We've got everything —you wouldn't be without anything you'd have in the city."

"I know that, Ken," she said.

"But you're not sure of it."

She thought that he perhaps deliberately tried to provoke an issue on the material grounds, as if these at least were demonstrable of some conclusion, that he was lost, unwilling, in the face of their real uncertainty. He was more perceptive, she knew, than he cared to reveal, but he had a stubbornness she felt it was perhaps impossible to defeat.

"Not sure of some things. You must give me time, after all. I—hadn't thought to live here. It's different for you."

The few high trees stood out darkly above the low thick scrub, and beyond she could see the roofs of the town.

"This other business will probably be over next week, anyhow."

She supposed he deliberately minimized this which perhaps he did not understand, preferring evasion, the pretense that when it was settled it would not matter. He was so clearly afraid that she would escape. She reached out quickly and touched his hand.

He stopped the car before the house near the end of the main street where she boarded. Further down, near the club, she could see the cars parked, and people moving without haste along the pavements.

There was no wind, and in the darkness the street was hot, as if the endless heat of summer was never to be dissipated. As he closed the door of the car he said:

"I have to go out to the paddock on the way back. It won't take long."

She made no comment and he said, as if to prevent her censure:

"I've got to take some stuff from the store out there."

"They haven't found him?"

"No. The police think he's moved out. But we know he hasn't. He makes fools of them in the bush. They've been looking since Sunday, but they've given it up now. Anyhow, you could walk right past him at three feet. And there are no tracks."

"To be able to dodge them like that he must know all this country well."

"I suppose he does."

"Almost—more than that. He must understand it."

"He doesn't seem to do anything else all day."

She smiled. "Well, do you?"

"I'm not sure what you mean by that. You mean we don't understand it?"

"Perhaps in a different way. You're making it something you can understand."

"Here we go again." He banged his hand against the steering wheel. "We never take a trick. Why don't you go and live with this character?"

She laughed suddenly. "I'm sorry, Ken. How long has he been here? That's a harmless enough question."

"He's been round about here something like ten years. I remember when I was at school. He's mad."

She said, "All those who oppose us are mad."

"Well," he said, "we're going to get him out this time. We're taking shifts down at the tractors, and we've got a watch on a camp of his we found."

"A camp?"

"Made out of boughs." His voice was grudging. "Pretty well made. You could live in it. We flushed him out, because he left some food, and a radio."

"That's not in keeping—a radio."

"It doesn't work. May never have been any good. But it might be only that the batteries are flat. We'll find out. But he could have camps like that all through the bush. We'll be lucky if he comes back to this one."

They turned off through a fence gate, and down along a track that followed a side fence. He switched off the car lights and drove slowly.

"He'll hear the car," he said. "Still, the lights are a giveaway."

Suddenly they were close to the dark thick scrub, and then she saw the forms of the tractors, gaunt, high, like grotesque patches of shadow. Two men moved up to the car. One of them started to say something, then saw her, and paused. He said :

"He came back, Ken. Got the food. We never saw him."

They carried rifles, and suddenly she began to laugh. They looked at her with a surprise that had not yet become hostility.

"It—it just seems funny," she said weakly.

"It's not funny," Ken said. She was aware of their anger.

"We'll get him," the tall man she recognized as Don Mackay said. "We'll get him this time."

She was reminded suddenly of the boys at school in the playground at the lunch period, confronted by some argument physical force could not immediately solve. Even their voices sound alike, she thought. Perhaps it is not so serious. But when they had taken the box he held out to them, and as they stepped back from the car she saw again the guns they carried, and the parallel frightened her.

"How long will they be repairing the tractor?" she asked.

"End of the week." His voice was brusque. She knew she had belittled him before his friends. She moved closer to him as he drove, and he looked briefly at her small, serious face shadowed in the half-light of the car.

"We'll go through there next week. I wish he'd get between the tractors when they're dragging the chain, that's all."

"Is he armed?"

"Yes," he said. "He is. He's lived off the land for years. And by taking food. He might be dangerous now."

She said slowly, "I wonder what made him begin to live like that?"

"No one will know that."

"You'll have to take care."

He nodded. "There'll be a few of us there to watch for him."

"Actually he hasn't ever threatened anyone, has he?"

"No. But he's never damaged anything big like this. And the police have never bothered about him before, either. You can see why. He's made fools of them."

"And of you."

"All right. And of us."

"Oh, Ken," she said. "I'm sorry. It's—it's just that I wish somehow you could just let him be."

"And have him do what he likes?"

"Well, he's not done anything much."

"Only wrecked a tractor."

"He would hate tractors," she said, as if she no longer spoke to him.

"Well, it's a reason why we can't leave him there."

"I suppose," she said, "you have to clear that land?"

"Of course. We clear some land every year. It's a tax deduction. And we need it the way taxation is."

"So there can't be anybody who wants things to stay the way they are for a while?"

He looked at her strangely. "Stay the way they are?"

If it was not what she meant she could not perhaps have found words that were any more adequate. It was not a simple thing of statement, of definition. She saw with a sudden desolating clarity the gray sprawl of suburbs crossed by the black lines of roads, the clusters of city buildings that clawed up like a focus, the endless tawdry overdecorated little houses like the one he and his family had placed on the long low rise of land from which almost all else had been erased. As though, she thought painfully, he hated this land she had herself, incongruously enough, come to feel for in the brief time she had been close to it. And it was perhaps worse that he did not see what he was doing, himself a part of some force beyond him. Duped with pride. It was as if she had made some discovery she could not communicate to him, and that set them apart. She said desperately:

"Do we have to change everything? Wipe out everything so that everlastingly we can grow things, make things? Get tax deductions? You don't even leave a few acres of timber, somewhere for animals and birds—"

"Animals and birds," he said. "You can't stop progress."

"The unanswerable answer," she said. Before them the shade trees showed briefly as the road turned near the farm. "So we must all conform."

He slowed the car for the house gate, and in the headlights she saw the facade of the house as if suddenly they had turned into a suburban street. As he stopped the motor the silence held them. For a moment they did not move, then he drew her against him, his arm about her shoulders, the gesture token of a security they might both have willed, denying the words with which they had held themselves separate.

"Maybe," he said slowly, "it's because you're so crazy I have to have you. You—you're different—"

"I'm sorry, Ken. Because I'm afraid I do love you—I suppose I have to have you, too."

"And you'd rather you didn't."

"Perhaps," she said, "I would rather I didn't."

"It's a mess, isn't it?"

"It might sort out," she said, and she laughed with him. At the house the front door opened briefly, the light shining across the entrance porch as someone looked out at the car.

In the weekend she had arranged to stay at the farm, and she expected him to call for her soon after breakfast. She put her small case on the verandah, but she went back inside. Idly, rather irritated at his lateness, she took out her paints and began to work on the flower illustrations she was making. She had begun to paint the native flowers, their grotesque seeds and leaves, to use for her teaching, but the work had begun to absorb her, and she spent whatever time she could searching for new examples. Many, at first, she could not identify. Now, though she had told no one, she had begun to hope the paintings might be publishable if she could complete series of different areas. It was midmorning when she heard him outside. In the car as they drove he said:

"Some of the fences were cut, out by Hadley's boundary. We've been too busy this week to look down there, and the sheep had gone through into the scrub. We got most of them back."

"You lost some?"

"Some."

"I'm sorry," she said, as if somehow it were her fault.

"He knows we're going to clear that land, and he's out to do as much damage as he can first."

She had no wish to draw him, as if she deliberately sought their disagreement, but it seemed she must form the words, place them before him, his evasion too easy.

"You're sure about it, Ken, aren't you? That he's just getting his own back? That it's as simple as that?"

"It's obvious. He's done pretty well, so far."

"And that's the only side there is to it?"

"What else could there be? He can't expect to stop us."

"He might know that."

"Well—that proves it."

"No—perhaps we've all got to make a gesture of some sort. For the things we believe in."

"You put it your way if you like. But what I believe in is using that land."

"Yes, Ken."

"We can't all be dreamers." And then, as if he refused to be further drawn, he laughed. "It's funny the way I've got caught up with one. Perhaps it will sort out, like you said. You do the dreaming. I'll do the work."

She ran her hands lightly over her arms, smiling at him. "You think we might convert one another?"

"It's a risk we'll have to take."

"Yes."

"I'll be out a bit this weekend, Ann. We've got to stop this somehow. While we've a few sheep left."

He went out late in the afternoon for more than an hour, and she helped his mother in the kitchen. The older woman had a quietness and a kind of insight that she found attractive, and they had always got on well together, though sometimes the girl was irritated by her acceptance of the men's decisions and views, as if this was something she no longer questioned—or perhaps, Ann thought, she had never questioned.

When Ken came back she heard him talking to his father on the verandah, and then the older man's voice raised in disagreement, though she could distinguish only a few of the words. She went out through the kitchen door and the men stopped talking. As she came towards them Ken said :

"We've found one of his camps. Ted and Don found it, but this time they turned off and kept away. They didn't go near enough for him to realize they'd seen it. We made that mistake last time."

"Where is this?" she said.

"It's new. So he may still be there. It's down in the paddock off the side road to Mackay's. Straight in from the dam. About half a mile north."

"There."

"Yes. By the new land. Where we were going to build." He looked at her as if she might have contradicted him. "When we were married."

"What will you do?"

His father said, "I told them to get the police."

"He walked away from the police last time." For a moment his eyes met the girl's. "And us. All right. We were no better. And the reporters came up from town. Photographers all over the place. A seven-day wonder for the suburbanites."

"It's not something that happens every day," she said. "Naturally, it was news."

"They'll make it news again, if we let them. But this time it will be different. We won't do anything until tomorrow night. That way he won't be suspicious if he sees our tracks near the camp. Then Sunday night we'll make a line north of the camp, and if the wind's right we'll burn back towards the firebreak along the paddock. He'll have to break out through the paddock. We'll have a chance that way."

"I think it's too big a risk," his father said. "You'll burn the whole of that country. You can't do it."

"We're going to clear it, anyway."

"You can't start a fire like that."

"If we try to close in on the camp he'll hear us."

"You could still get him. There's enough of you."

"He'd go between us in the bush. No matter how close we were. You know that. No one's been able to get a sight of him in the bush. The police had trackers there last week. They found plenty of tracks. But he kept as far ahead or behind them as he liked. No," he said, "he's made fools of us long enough. I think we've got a chance now."

He turned suddenly towards the girl, and she stood beside him, not moving. It seemed to her that his words had a kind of defiance, as if he did not himself believe them, and she thought that it was not simply that he doubted their ability to carry out the plan, but that he did not really believe in the idea of the fire himself. That if she or his father did not further pursue it he might be glad to drop it. But she could not be certain, and before she could speak, he said, as if he had intended to prevent her words :

"Let's forget this now, Ann. We'll go over to Harris's after tea. They've a bit of a show on there for May's birthday."

Almost all those she had come to know seemed to

have found their way to the party. And all of them discussed the hermit, as they called him. She realized it was general knowledge that he was expected to be caught soon. She listened to the undercurrent of derision that the police with all their resources had been mocked by this man it seemed none of them had seen, as if in this they were on his side. Some of the older people she spoke to claimed to have caught glimpses of him when, some years earlier, he had taken food quite freely for a time from the farm houses. Some claimed to know his name. But it seemed to her, as she mixed with them and listened to them, that none of them really cared. She felt they simply accepted the idea that he must be denied, driven from cover, and killed if necessary, as they might have accepted the killing of a dingo or a fox, a creature for them without motive or reason. When she tried to turn their words, to question them, they looked at her with a kind of surprise, or the beginning of suspicion, in doubt of her as a teacher of their children.

And she saw that quite quickly they exhausted the topic, turning to the enjoyment of the evening, as if already the whole thing was disposed of. In the end she thought it was their lack of involvement, their bland rejection of responsibility, that irritated her to the point of anger, so that she was forced to hold herself from rudeness.

It was late when they returned, and in her room, after she had changed, she stood for a time by the window in the darkness. There was a small moon that seemed scarcely to break the dark ground shadow, and beyond the paddocks she could not see where the scrub began. Her sense of anger had given place to dejection and a kind of fear. She tried to imagine the man who in the darkness slept in what they had described as his camp, something she could picture only as a kind of child's cubby house in the thick scrub. But she could form no picture of him as a physical being, only that it seemed to her he must possess imagination and sensibility beyond that of his pursuers, that he must be someone not difficult to talk to, someone who would understand her own feeling about these things for which he was persecuted. And who might even, she thought, be glad to know, however briefly, that they were shared. She was aware of a sense of disloyalty, but the image persisted, and it was suddenly monstrous that the darkness of the scrub should be swept by the glare of fire, as she would see it from the window where she stood now, the man stumbling from it in some unimaginable indignity. Whatever doubt she had of the men's intention to carry out their plan, it seemed now in the darkness only too probable that in anger they might do what she, and perhaps they themselves, feared. And it was impossible. Her hands felt the cold of the sill, she was aware of the faint wind that blew in through the window, cool upon her skin, and she could hear it in the boughs of the few shade trees behind the house.

On Sunday, in the afternoon, Ken left to make arrangements with the other men. His parents were resting, but she knew they would not question her going out; they were used to her wandering about the farm, looking for the plants she wished to paint. She went down through the yard gate, across the paddock towards the track that led out to the belt of scrub and timber. It seemed, in the heat, further than she had expected.

She walked along the side fence, where the brush

began, feeling that it would hide her if any of the men were watching. If she met them she would say she had come to look for Ken. She could see the dam ahead, the smooth red banks rising steeply, to one side a few thin trees, motionless in the heat.

At the dam she paused. The side track to Mackay's had turned some distance to the left. In front of her, facing north, the scrub was thick, untouched, and she was suddenly reluctant to go beyond the fence on the far side of the dam.

She pushed the wires down and stepped through. She began to pick her way through the scrub, choosing the small, almost imperceptible pockets where the bushes were thinner. It was only after a time, when she could no longer see the dam or the trees beside it, that she realized her method of walking had led her away from a straight line. She had no clear idea how far she had come. She went on until she was certain she had covered half a mile, but as she stopped it was suddenly clear she could have deviated in any direction.

The bushes grew upward on their thin sparse stalks to a rounded umbrella-like top, the leaves tough, elongated, and spindly. They stretched away like endless replicas, rising head-high, become too thick for her to go further. As she looked about it seemed improbable she had come so far. In the heat the scrub was silent. Along the reddish ground, over the fine stems, the ants moved, in places she had walked round their mud-colored mounds. She looked down at the ground, at the hard brittle twigs and fallen leaves, some of them already cemented by the ants. In a kind of fear she began to walk.

A short distance to the right a thin patch of trees lifted

above the scrub, and though she thought it was the wrong direction she began to push her way towards it. The trees were like some sharp variation in the endless gray pattern of the brush that rose about her.

Beneath them the bark and leaves were thick upon the ground. She stood in the patch of shade, and she tried to reason that she could not have come far, that she could find her way back if she was careful. And in the silence she thought again, as she had the night before, of the man she had come to warn. It had seemed that if she could explain to him, he must understand, and that perhaps he would go. She had relied on there being understanding between them, that at least in these things they must feel alike. So that it had seemed her words would have effect. Now, in the heat and the silence, it was a dream, holding in this place no reality. She could never have thought to do it. And it was here he had spent ten years. It was like nothing she could encompass. She felt a sharp, childish misery, as if she might have allowed herself tears.

It occurred to her that if she could climb one of the trees she might gain an idea of direction. But the trunks were slippery, without foothold, and at the second attempt she fell, twisting her leg. She leaned against the trunk, afraid of the pain, trying to deny it as if she would will herself to be without injury which might imprison her.

She was not aware of movement or sound, but she looked up, and turned slightly, still holding to the smooth trunk. He was standing just at the edge of the clump of trees. He might have been there all the time. Or been attracted by the noise she had made. She said weakly :

"I—didn't see you—"

His face held no expression she could read. His hair was gray and short, and she was vaguely surprised as if she had imagined something different, but cut crudely, and streaked across his head by sweat. He was very thin as though all the redundant flesh had long ago been burned from him, his arms stick-like, knotted, and black. His hands held a rifle, and she had a sudden fear that he would kill her, that somehow she must place words between them before he took her simply as one of his persecutors. She said quickly:

"I came to warn you—they have found your camp— tonight they mean to drive you out towards the paddocks—"

But they were not the words she had planned. His eyes gave her no sign. They were very dark, sharp somehow, and she knew suddenly they were like the eyes of an animal or a bird, watchful, with their own recognition and knowledge which was not hers. The stubble of beard across his face was whitish, his skin dark from the sun.

"I—if only you would go from here," she said. "They only want you to go—they don't understand—"

The words were dead in the heat and the silence. She saw the flies that crawled across his face.

"I wanted to help you," she said, and she despised herself in her terror. Only his hands seemed to move faintly about the rifle. His stillness was insupportable. Abruptly she began to sob, the sound loud, gulping, ridiculous, her hands lifting to her face.

He seemed to step backwards. His movement was somehow liquid, unhuman, and then she thought of the natives she had once seen in the north, not the town natives whose movements had grown like her own. But with a strange inevitability he moved like an animal or the vibration of the thin sparse trees before the wind. She did not see him go. She looked at the boles of the trees where he had stood, and she could hear her own sobbing.

Some time in the afternoon she heard the sudden sound of shots, flat, unreal, soon lost in the silence. But she walked towards where the sound had seemed to be, and after a time, without warning, she came on to the track that ran towards Mackay's place. She had gone only a short distance when she heard the voices, and called out. The men came through the scrub and she saw them on the track. She began to run towards them, but checked herself. Further down she saw a Landrover and one of the policemen. Ken said :

"We missed you—we've been searching—it was only that Ted saw where you'd walked down the fence—"

She said, "The shots—I heard them—"

"We were looking for you—we didn't see him. He tried to get past us, then shot at Don—we had to shoot."

She did not speak and he said, "We had to do it, Ann. We sent for the police. But where were you? How did you get out here?"

There was nothing she could tell him. She said : "I was looking for you, I think."

The Landrover had drawn up beside them, and the driver opened the door for her. They moved back down the dry rutted track where the thin shade had begun to stretch in from the broken scrub.

At the Galahad

[AUSTRALIA]

by Hal Porter

FINALLY, BORED with the higgledy-piggledy autumn beach, the now-on now-off sunshine, and the hard-eyed importunities of seagulls, I walked to the Galahad Hotel for a drink. There, risking a fractured pelvis on the immensity of the black-and-white-tiled foyer, I ran into Rupert Gaar-Smith. About us bronze nudes upheld spheres lit by forty-watt globes. Gaar-Smith had an air of distracted importance; his large eyes rolled like a gelding's.

We were of an age, and old acquaintances; thirty-odd years before we had lived opposite in a Gippsland country town. Boyhood proximity and many accidental encounters such as this one had produced a seeming friendship, though now we were older we hardly liked each other. We were not friendly enough to quarrel, but were always titillated by the way our paths kept interlocking at odd places.

My career had been patchwork; so had his. But our planes of experiment were well separated. He had been a Wurlitzer organist, an actor, a radio announcer, a dress-material salesman; once he had run a Collins Street *coffee shoppe* hung with Klee and Miro prints. God knows what else he'd done or would finish up doing, but I was surprised to find him assistant manager of a hotel, and such a hotel, and in that place.

That place was the seaside suburb where I had been skulking past the film-set scaffolding of Big Dippers and shuttered ice-cream kiosks. It was a suburb that had sledded downhill from fashionable elegance in late Victorian and Edwardian years to the tawdry and the downright criminal; it was now a Cannes to spiv, cat-burglar, confidence man, petty gangster's moll, pervert, and juvenile delinquent. Port Phillip waters nudging oranges and fishing net corks onto the beach exhaled that smell of decaying seaweed Edwardians called ozone.

The suburb, built-up as a sundae, breathed back the stench of hamburger, espresso, and fish-and-chip shops. Time had added some pseudo-Gropius flats, tiled bus-stop shelters, an outlining of neon, a glaciarium like a hangar, and a multi-colored coating of paint. This covered everything: balustrade, roof, Greek Revival, Belgian Gothic, Florentine Renaissance, stucco faces of rams and Mincrvas, molded-iron parapets, and Moorish arches.

Only the Pompeiian tiles, leading to basalt steps still edged with blackout-white, had missed this symbolic midcentury veneer. Only these and the Galahad Hotel.

The Galahad retained much of the top-heavy grandeur of its prime when Sarah Bernhardt had stayed there, Rudyard Kipling, Henry Handel Richardson, and squatters' broods with their immigrant nursemaids. Framed menus of Derby Day meals at Windsor Castle hung in the vast dining room, with its Carrara fireplaces, stained-glass windows of Malory knights and ladies, its life-size Majolica swans. It was one of those mansarded hotels in which marble statues of the Seasons and Virtues stood below huge oil paintings—Sunset in Egypt, Dawn at Ronda—and prints of setters by Thomas Blinks. There were pillars of liver-colored stone; corridors ended at looking-glass walls in which one sidestepped oneself just before the crash.

Rupert Gaar-Smith, theatrical of voice, jowly, in charcoal-gray and handmade shoes, too greenish-gold of hair for—forty-one? forty-two?—seemed pleased to see me: "You are manna," he said, as though to the gallery. "Manna! Your ear I must have. I must unburden ere I go quite em, ay, dee."

His manner was odd; the dressing-room affectations I'd heard before, but there was intensity in his wheedlings. "Spare me a scant half-hour. For the sake of our in-no-cent boyhood. My washstand, dear man, groans with expensive strong waters."

"Don't be a fool," I said. "I'd enjoy a natter. And free drinks."

"Oh, good," he said. Ringingly he called towards the reception desk, "Laura, my ducks ... oh, it's you, Miss Daly. Miss Daly, I am now off duty. Mr. Rockleigh is on. You'll find him in ... well, you know where."

Gesturing me on rather in the manner of the ghost in Hamlet, he said from the corner of his mouth, "In the saloon-bar is Brother Rockleigh," and led me to his room by corridors at first thickly wall-to-walled, next runner-carpeted, finally of linoleum glossy as a sergeant-major's boot.

His room, in the oldest part of the hotel, was large: marble fireplace, cedar armchairs, brass double bed like Salvador Dali's, tiled washstand serving as a cocktail-bar. He poured drinks, chattering on.

"Gin and tonic? Thank God you turned up. I can tell someone; get the thing off my chest. Two of the old girls. And each time I was on duty. Enough tonic? On duty both times, wot you. Very sinister. And all so ... so ... " He handed me my drink.

"How about," I said, "starting at point A?"

"Murder," he said.

"Go hon!"

"Murder most foul. Suicide. Jealousy, lunacy, the lot."

"The suspense," I said, "is killing me."

"Sit down," he said. "Do you know that five minutes before I met you I'd just seen off the second old witch to the morgue? Discreetly. Back-alley job: past the coke-heaps."

I felt I had raised an eyebrow.

"All right, all right. Toss that down." He poured more drinks. "I," he said, "am the only one who knows."

"Knows what?"

"Oh don't be tah-some! I'll start at point A; just give me a burl." He sat down. I could see him arranging his thoughts like a Conrad character; he drank; he began.

"This place is a madhouse—not just my opinion. In the hotel racket it's called Worthington's Circus. Papa Worthington owns it, lock, stock, fire-extinguisher to cellar, every cockroach behind the bain marie, every souvenired liqueur glass. Inherited in the twenties before this suburb got seedy. At least before the seediness started to show. He was the only son, spoiled—little Lord Fauntleroy. He's an old maid now; married to an old maid. Not pub-types like his mum and dad, who ran a pretty dazzling show.

"He's got plenty of loot; has shares in everything from here to Perth and is just not interested in being Mr. Ritz. The Galahad is merely home to him. So long as everything is as dear mum and dad left it, he's as happy as Larry. Who is Larry? All he and Mrs. W. do is travel and buy appalling objets d'art; their suite is the sort you'd expect Boris Karloff to live in. Don't worry me, is his idea, just keep on as Mum did.

"Perhaps he's right. It certainly means good food, linen sheets, cedar furniture, and no nasty questions about expense so long as it's nothing to do with Americanization, chromium, public-address systems, wireless, all that sort of thing. But he won't throw anything away: you know how the rich always break their fingernails undoing the string on parcels?

"Afterwards I'll show you disused nurseries, smoking rooms and music rooms all chockablock with Sheffield-plate teapots, Venetian-glass finger-bowls, Waterford jugs, candlesticks, hundreds of marble clocks, cruets, and tureens. One old writing room is packed to the ceiling with chamber-pots. And the patching and mending goes on all the time: lino., carpets, sheets, blankets, loose-covers. There's a carpenter-johnny wearing one of those baize apron things who's been patch, patch, patching for forty years. Look!"

He rose, opened the door to his bathroom: a deep bath set in mahogany, a wash-basin and lavatory-bowl with a design in Willow-Pattern blue.

"Early Doulton," he said. "Now look at the floor."

It was gleaming sheet-lead patched in twenty places with exquisite squares and rectangles of new lead.

"See? Papa Worthington doesn't want new things. Or new ideas. Why has he got Rockleigh, the near-dipso, as manager? And me as assistant? Because we're mild bunnies willing to jog along in the old way. A bright and shiny boy from the Hotel Managers' High School in Michigan or wherever would be out on his bee, you, em at the first peep about laminated wood or shilling-in-the-slot wireless sets."

"Point A yet?" I said.

"Have another drink, paysan, and don't ... be ... tah-some! I'm explaining the kind of hotel it is. Certain sorts of pubs attract certain sorts of guests." He was pouring drinks again. "This one's a leftover from what the Readers' Digest would call 'more spacious days.' So are the cruets and marble virgins. All leftovers." He sat. The drinks were strong. His voice had lost much of its back-row-of-the-gods pitch. "So are its permanent guests."

He drank again. "Leftovers! The place has about thirty of these permanents—like a ... a home for re-tired gentlewomen. Bishops' spinster daughters, Anglo-Indian widows, superannuated deaconesses—you know the type: eking out allowances, savings, legacies, bitching at the waitresses and chambermaids; always shooting the roller-blinds right up. Something's always too hot or cold. Or not early enough. Or late again."

I saw what he meant. I knew them: gunmetal-gray stockings; long, narrow shoes; crocodile-skin handbag containing scraps of a richer past; the brown snapshots of the 1920 tennis-party at Kuala Lumpur; the juiceless voices:

"Oh, Mr. Gaar-Smith, Ai don't want to make trouble for the gels. Yet Ai do feel that the gel on mai teble is not quaite ... well, frenkly, she's vedy sleck. Mai toast this morning was barely...."

I could see the obsessive glitter in aging eyes: food, the god of the lonely, the god of many communions. Tea in bed. Breakfast. Morning tea. Luncheon. After-noon tea. Dinner. Supper.

"Some of the old bags," he said, "eat more than a stevedore father-of-nine. Imagine a silvery-haired little-old-lady-passing-by." His voice became maliciously falsetto, he peered at an imaginary menu:

" 'Now, wetress, let me see. Ai'm not vedy hungry this morning. But breakfast is such an important meal; Ai'd better trai end nibble something. Cereals ... end fruit. What is the fruit? Oh, I'm vedy fond of pears; bring me three ... no ... four pieces. Kedgeree, this morning! Oh, Ai adore it. Kedgeree then—end on buttered toast, not drai. Perhaps, too, a steak, end tomatoes. Waitress, tel chef it's for me; he knows Ai laike it medium. Not too rare. Not all draid up. End I'll hev a fraid egg with thet....' Never fear, my boy, Mother Macree will get through the lot like a gray-nurse. She'll sit frail and fretting till morning-tea.

"Then she'll be ready to wait for tiffin. My God, they've got me saying it. That's what half of them call it: 'Ai thought the tiffin-gong was a little leet. Mai watch says three minutes past.' Tiffin! In this little Chicago, in 1956, with bodgies and widgies about to batter through the revolving doors with Coca Cola bottles! I need another drink."

I was beginning to understand how he felt as keeper of this genteel zoo of women with nothing to do except read Frances Parkinson Keyes, gossip, vilify, take purgatives, and eat.

It was in the dining room, beneath the stained-glass Burne-Jones Galahads, Geraints, Gareths, and Guineveres, that trouble began.

At a dominating table, attended by a waitress who served no one else, Mr. and Mrs. Worthington royally disregarded the world from behind an elaborate epergne. They were sacrosanct; the year could have been 1913. Almost equally sacrosanct were the spinsters and widows whose tables lined the walls so that intruding fly-by-nights, the mobile Present, occupying central tables, were hemmed in by the static and withering Past, each with her still-life on the cloth before her of bottles of digestive tablets, jars of anchovy paste, chutney, marmalade, or Dusseldorf mustard.

Some had sat at one table for twenty years. Solitary, with the unwinking eyes of barracuda, they assessed the intransigents from the vulgar world of nylon, jet planes, and divorce. I felt the pathos of these macabre spectators; how many hundreds—thousands—had they silently rejected beneath the lofty ceiling, with its double row of molded acanthus-wheels from which depended involved electroliers?

Most ghastly was his description of the corridor outside the dining room. It was customary for the manager on duty to unlock the twelve-foot-high double doors of plate-glass, sand-blasted and gold-leafed with art nouveau floridities, and with art nouveau handles. This happened when the gong had been beaten to silence.

But, long before, Gaar-Smith's old hags, bats, trouts, and faggots, the colonels' widows, and the daughters of judges who had died younger than their old-maid survivors, with powdered froglike throats, waited, spitefully examining the cloisonné watches pinned to their sapless breasts. This elderly queuing for food had, in that setting, a taint of unbalance. What were they really waiting for?

The stiff drinks were having effect : impartiality and objectivity were losing ground.

"Note and note well," said Gaar-Smith, pouring out the fifth—or was it the sixth?—gin and tonic, "that gent-on-duty unlocks door." His accent had lost its drama-school succulence, was down-to-earth and re-Gippslandized.

"Press on," I said. "You interest me, Mr. Gaar-Smith, sir."

"We-e-ell," he sucked at his drink, "some of the crazed old harpies get into their skulls the idea that certain tables are in better possies than others. Quite arbitrarily. Or because they hate someone. Then they'll scheme and lie like Lucifer. They'll do ... anything." He drank again, glared at nothing. "Anything," he repeated. He went on :

"About three months ago one of them went off to foist herself on a nephew in South Aussie for a couple of months—"

"Foist?" I said. "Don't be too tough. She may have been asked. Aunts are."

He fixed me with tipsy severity : "You don't know 'em. Tough as mallee-roots, a bite like a tiger-snake. No relative could put up with any of 'em for two hours. Why are they all here? Because none of their families can bear them. People don't hurl helpless old girls into the hard world. These aren't helpless. Far from it. They have the money; Worthington's mad; they're mad, and there's lots of lovely food. I wouldn't trust one of those. ...."

"Go on, go on," I said. "Very sorry. Go on."

"O.K. This old aunt, Beaufort by name, is—was—like something out of Barrie : all blue eyes, lavender-water, and bunions. So sweet; such pink little cheeks : 'Oh, Mr. Gaar-Smith, Ai'm so sorry to bother you, but you know Ai'm going away for two months. Now, about mai little teble. Ai've had it for faive years, end Ai'm most etteched to it. Ai expect it when Ai return. Ai'm certain you'll keep it for me.' And she gave me an envelope with four bob in it and—off to upset things in Adelaide.

"I, dear man, would have kept her table for her; the here-today-and-gone-tomorrows could have used it when we were in a hole, but only for lends, not for keepies. Yes, I'd have kept her bloody four-bob table for her—I'm no neck-sticker-outer. But I'm ess, ell, oh, double-you; and just a Gippsland moron; these dolls are supersonic. No sooner had Beaufort, frail as a leopard, tottered to her taxi than another old tartar was after me—pounce. The taxi hadn't even started. 'Oh, Mr. Gaar-Smith, so sorry to bother you but. ...'

"This killer's name was Carlyle, and she was after Beaufort's table.

"I can so-sorry with the best of them : 'I'm sorry, Mrs. Carlyle, but Miss Beaufort will only be away for a time and we've already arranged,' etcetera, etcetera, 'and I'm so sorry and I'm sure you understand.' Of course she was so sorry, too, but she understood, she quaite quaite understood. It was just that with her rheumatism, and her table was in such a shocking draught. ... Draught! You couldn't get a draught into that dining-room if you were paid to. But we'd played our little scene and I—poor deluded rustic—heaved a sigh of relief.

"As you observe, I have no illusions about these old cows, but I knew they didn't break the rules, at least not in such a way as to lay themselves open to rebuke or even comment. Cold war's the shot; they work underground, like ferrets; no loss of face, all decencies preserved on the surface. They'll commit hair-raising bitcheries, but protocol is observed and there'll be a foolproof justification; they'll refer you back to the nod they've been given with the speed of light.

"The next time I was on duty there was Underground Agent Carlyle at the Beaufort's table. She saw me gaping like a Tassie Shepherd who's just seen his baa-lamb gnawing away at a fox. She beckoned me over. Archly is the word, as archly as Clytemnestra : 'Ai expect you think Ai'm being a notty gel. Ai'm not, really.' She sipped some consommé, and I waited for revelation as she intended I should. Then, 'Ai heppened to see Mr. Worthington.' More consommé. Like hell *heppened to see*. Lay in wait like fly-paper. 'Mr. Worthington was asking after mai rheumatism, Ai explained about the draught. He ebsolutely insisted thet Ai hev Miss Beaufort's teble. Ai'm sure you understand.'

"I understood. I'm paid for just that. I didn't utter a peep. How could I? Worthington's so-and-so Circus, and Papa W. cracking his whip in fine confusion. 'Nother snort, old boy? All little Rupert Gaar-Smith had to do was await La Beaufort's return. That's all : the tumbril was on its way—look, lil' Rupe, there's pretty guillotine sparkling in the morning sunshine. . . ."

He was getting drunk. I too. Nevertheless, I could see

the humiliation brewing, the maddening impotency.

Miss Beaufort came back. Mrs. Carlyle, in legalizing her own action, had also legalized his defection. She had presented Worthington's fiat to him; he did the same to Miss Beaufort. She went an unusual color; he thought she was about to faint. He hoped she would carry the squabble to Olympus, go raging to Worthington. She did nothing but control herself to say flatly and softly:

"So that woman is to hev mai table. After faive years ... faive years. Thet woman." She closed her eyes—was she going to faint? She opened them again.

"We shell see," she said.

Next she began to walk away down the long corridor doubly reflected and lengthened to infinity in the walls of looking glass at each end. He could see their two selves repeated there endlessly, diminishing away forever, the golden fence of brass standard ashtrays vanishing to nothing. A few paces and she turned, came back to him—lavender water, blue eyes.

"They all seem to wear those blue eyes," he said thickly, "with a whitish ring at the edge of the iris, like ... like. ..." But gin had drowned the simile.

She looked at him with those imperfect eyes:

"Mr. Gaar-Smith, Ai feel you hev let me down bedly. It is only raight for me to ask you return the gretuity you hev decaidedly done nothing to earn."

Gratuity? Gratuity?

At first he did not understand, and then did. While she waited he groped in his pockets: no silver. The smallest money he had was a ten-shilling note, which, as he held it oafishly, she took. "Ai hev no chenge," she said. "Ai shell send it down to you." At the next meal

time a waitress brought him six shillings neatly enclosed—not in an envelope; in a square of brown-paper.

A week later Mrs. Carlyle was found dead on the
tiles at the bottom of a stair well.

She had apparently fallen from five floors up through
the worm-eaten balustrade.

"I wash ... I was on duty." He was getting very
drunk. "About an hour before tiffin—luncheon—was
correcting error in French on all the menus when
housekeeper told me. Now 'member ... re-member
this: housekeeper, carpenter, and I were the only ones
in Galahad who knew until hours-'n'-hours later what
had happened. Hotels smother these sorts of things
quick-smart. No fuss, no scandal, nothing nasty in
woodshed. Doctor, police, morgue-blokes all teed-up
pronto. Body whipped out back way! Ultimate verdict—
accidental death."

He drank. His funny-man's goo-goo eyes were
ludicrously tragic: "I know it wasn't. I know, boy, it
was not accidental. No one could imagine what sixty-
year-old woman doing up there in forbidden, disused
section, rooms filled with left umbrellas and portman-
teaux and furs. But old girls bit odd, eh? they said, Odd!"

"So Carlyle's smuggled out like a load of dirty
laundry; I wash shaky little paws, comb hair, down
tiny brandy and—Boom! Boom! Boom!—the lunch-
gong. Got it? See it? See it all? Old faggots in clean
pinnies lined up like orphans outside e-nor-mous
glass doors, waitresses inside fiddling with apronbows
and butter-knives, me advancing avec poise with key
to holy door ... walk, walk. You know, long way, like
Valli at end of 'The Third Man' ... walk, walk, walk.
Show mush go on! Reach door. Turn key. Hostess

inside swings doors open ... smile, smile. In the old otters file. In files Beaufort."

He stopped. While I waited he drained his glass and yet seemed to regain clarity and sobriety.

"Honest to God I wasn't even thinking of her. But I seemed to notice her specially; don't know why.

"She walked to the table she'd been using, walked firmly like—like Lady Hamlet. No, no; like Lady Macbeth and the dagger things. You know. She gathered her collection of bicarbs and doodads—and her table-napkin, and went straight as a die to her old table; Carlyle's table. She sat down, arranged her paraphernalia, and began to read the menu. It wasn't until she was through her entree that I realized what was wrong.

"I was shattered. I couldn't think what I ought to do. My hands started to shake again. Not hers, bruvver. She ate through four courses."

Then, fiercely, at me: "Get it? Get it?"

I got it. I was willing to half-believe what he fully believed: she had known, before entering the dining-room, that her old table would be empty, would be hers again and till the end of time if she and her money and the Galahad could last so long. However, it seemed common sense to suggest, even if it did make her behavior still pretty cold-blooded:

"Someone could have told her."

"No! Who? Who, man? Housekeeper? Carpenter? Not them. And no one else knew."

"Somebody who saw the body being whipped out; a kitchen-boy lurking behind the coke-bunkers."

"No. Nobody. Anyway, covered up—head to foot. Oh, I knew there'd be explanations like yours. 'S why I kept my trap shut. No one else noticed Beaufort back at her own table. I practically convinced me I was loco. Prac-tic-ally. Not any more. Not after today."

"Today?"

"I told you, child, there were two stiff-uns. Beaufort deadibones in bed this morning. You should have heard the Latvian chambermaid screaming like an ambulance! No note on pillow. Overdose sleeping pills. Accident! Of course. Why should shweet, lavender-scented, well-heeled old bod commit suicide?"

He began to giggle drunkenly. "Accident my truss! Must have had conscience after all ... conscience, eh. ... ? Believe now?"

It didn't matter if I did. I'd served my purpose: the parcel of unwanted knowledge had been divided in two.

Before I could answer him a gong began, primitively, reverberating through rooms of leftovers: umbrellas lost for decades, candlesticks no one used, clock that had stopped on some sunny day a long time ago.

"Dressing-gong!" said Gaar-Smith, and stumbled to the washstand for another drink.

As the gong thudded like drums of death, I imagined puckered fingers lifting rings from china ring-trees, pinning on brooches of opals, lightly powdering collapsed cheeks.

Gaar-Smith was giggling, giggling, and horridly mincing about:

"Reahlly don't feel laike dressing tonaight ... not going to hev any dinnah tonaight ... someone else cen hev mai teble. ..."

I understood.

The Ivory Balls

[REPUBLIC OF CHINA]

by Peng Ko

AFTER TWILIGHT, the wind had begun to quiet but the snow kept floating ceaselessly downwards, unfeelingly, more and more heavily.

Looking through our window, I could see that the doorstep and the front garden were already covered with a sheet of white. Over the low wall, as far as the eye could see, fields and hillsides were also covered with white . . . a much more distant, vaster, and thus a more mysterious expanse of white.

I loved the outside world of ice and snow, but that was for tomorrow morning. For the moment, I loved the warm fire in the room even more. At night, we went to bed very early so as to save lamp oil. We seldom had a light in the room, so that the yellow, red, and blue tongues of fire darting out from the stove became even more colorful and attractive. The old tabby cat with her tail all curled up was snoozing at my feet, and I was also in a state of half-sleep, half-wakefulness as I sat beside my mother. The firelight threw our shadows on the wall, huge and flickering like monstrous spirits in a dream, dancing around us.

Mother sat in the shadows working on an old sweater of mine, putting in two new sleeves. She had always been an expert knitter, but tonight she kept murmuring to herself, counting the stitches, and often she would unravel a whole section and begin again. I could not see her face clearly but dimly felt that there was something wrong.

At that time, we were living on the flat ridge on the northern bank of the Hwai River. In front of us we could see the black cliffs of Ching Mountain, topped with a snowy hat. This was the first settled home we had had since the Lu Kou Chiao Incident* a year before when we had fled from Peiping. Here, we slowly learned to forget the hardships we had endured on our flight and to become adjusted once again to the routine of living that was always and ever monotonously the same.

For example, at that moment, we heard the chugging of the locomotive at the foot of the mountain and the shrill blast of its steam whistle. Ordinarily it should have been 8 :55—from what the grownups said, ever since the war started, the green steel-plated cars of the Lung Hai Railway had never been on time a single day—and if it were according to old custom, I should have been in bed and asleep long ago.

"Little Yuan, you better go to bed now." Mother had just finished a row and pulling her needle out, she stretched.

"I want you to come and sleep with me."

"No, I still have to wait up for someone." Mother rubbed her hands, then gently brushed off the wool strands that had stuck to her dress.

* The incident at Lu Kou Chiao (Marco Polo) Bridge on July 7, 1937, that sparked the Sino-Japanese War.

"Waiting for whom? So late." And I threw myself into her arms.

"Good child, don't be tiresome," Mother said, but at the same time, her hand did not stop caressing my face. "Mother has to wait for a guest from far away."

"Who? Is Papa coming home today?" I sat up in happy excitement. Father was in Sian for a meeting and had been gone several days already.

"All you remember is your Papa," Mother said laughingly. "It is a guest who first saw you several years ago when you had just learned to walk."

As a small child I had been in very bad health. Even when I was five years old I could not walk by myself, so that my learning to walk was a very big affair.

"Ma, tell me, who is it?"

"It's Aunty Liang. Do you remember her?"

I shook my head; I couldn't remember.

"Little muddle-head, didn't she stay with us in Peiping for one or two months, teaching you your characters, drawing pictures for you, and you can't remember anything?" Mother hugged my shoulders and murmured as if to herself: "Ai, there have been too many changes these past years."

I thought hard. It was like trying to find a loose photo in a disordered album of photographs—maybe it was thoughtlessly stuck in somewhere, maybe it was already lost. It was really much too difficult for a ten-year-old to try and remember someone of five years ago.

"What is she like, ma? Help me remember."

"What is she like?" Mother was also remembering. "The first day she arrived at our house she had on a black satin cape and you said she looked like someone on the stage."

I still could not remember.

"Oh, yes, you must remember her stole—a whole fox skin with two bright glass eyes, just like a real live fox. The minute you saw it you started to cry with fright, and she even laughed at you for not acting like a boy."

At this, I began to see some light. Yes, that fox with a long bushy tail, wide open mouth, and two rows of sharp white teeth—fearful looking. That's right, I had been frightened into tears by it.

"At that time, your grandmother was still living and she always used to say to me that among all of us younger wives, this Mrs. Liang had the most in every way, whether it was looks, manners, or gift of speech. Even old-fashioned as I am, I could not help but keep looking at her."

Suddenly, I seemed to remember a little; a tiny, graceful lady in a black cape, a pair of black satin, high-heeled slippers that were covered with shimmering brilliants, and with heels of a precarious height. In Peiping, in those days, this was really something new, especially in a home like ours.

Yes, her fox fur had scared me to tears, but her small mouth had curled in a smile: "Strange the first time, familiar the second time. Take it, dear. Look at it carefully and you won't be scared of it any more."

She had placed the fox in my hands and I didn't even dare to open my eyes. I still felt that it would come alive.

"Wasn't there also an Uncle Liang?" I said. I remembered that when I was crying, Uncle Liang had scolded her: "So childish, you'll never change!" I remembered that he was older than father while Aunty Liang was so very young, and when I had asked about this, Mother had chuckled: "There are plenty of husbands who are older than their wives, what is there to ask about?"

And now I said: "I remember Uncle Liang always wore a long gown, his hands tucked into the sleeves, and in his palms were two ivory balls, so smooth and round, that he kept twirling them around.*

As I remembered this, it seemed that it was because of these muscle-building ivory balls that I had always felt Uncle Liang was more approachable, that although he was already bald, he would like to play with a child like me.

"Is Uncle Liang coming today?"

Mother shook her head, gazing fixedly into the fire. After a short silence she said: "When Aunty Liang arrives, don't you mention Uncle Liang!" She repeated the order.

"What's the matter?"

"Children shouldn't ask too many questions about things they don't understand." Mother's voice was very solemn. "Do you hear?"

I didn't say a word. I thought to myself, Uncle Liang must be dead—like my uncle. My uncle had been an officer in the army and was killed fighting in Shantung. My mother had told me never to talk about him in front of my father. Once when I had wanted to eat some crisp dates, my father had said that if I ate too many it would give me indigestion, and I had said: "If you won't buy them for me, I will ask Uncle to buy them." The next day, Mother told me that because of what I had said, Father had not been able to sleep the whole

* In the old days, many gentlemen of leisure manipulated two spherical objects in their hands for the purpose of strengthening the muscles.

night. The affairs of grown-ups are really too much; really very queer.

I dozed off beside Mother, and when I woke I was already in bed. Aunty Liang had not come and Mother was still up. It was most probably very late. They really are good friends. I thought.

I called : "Ma!" and Mother came in from the sitting room. She adjusted the covers around me without saying a word, her fingers ice-cold.

"Why don't you go to sleep?"

"I will wait until the next train. She said that she would come today." Saying which, Mother turned over the corner of her quilt and lay down with all her clothes on. "The weather today is really unbearable. Tomorrow the road down the mountain will be covered with ice."

"Aunty Liang will be frozen to death." I said. "I remember she used to draw in her breath, sucking the cold air, saying: 'Everything about your Peiping is good, except for this cold which is hard to bear.' "

Mother's face was turned away from me and she made no other reply except an "Uh." She must be thinking of something again.

Just as I was about to fall asleep once more, the noise of people came drifting from far away in the garden; first was the sound of Lao King, the driver, yelling at the animals "Yu-u, O-o-oh," then the crunching of the wheels of the mule cart as it rolled over the ice. Soon, the cart stopped and the servant boy, Sun Te-hai, began knocking at the gate, calling : "Mistress, we have come back!" Mother did not wait for Old Sun Ma to get up but ran out to open the door. I scrambled up, heedless of the cold, and peered out through the window.

Sun Te-hai was standing by the door with a storm lantern in his hand. The guest stepped off the cart—this mule cart was the public transportation vehicle of our factory, as there were no motor cars where we were; neither were there any roads for cars. She climbed down so very slowly, just a blurred shadow with a tiny face. The people standing in the snow, the blue canvas-covered mule cart, and the mule that was stamping its forelegs, white vapor blowing out of its nostrils ... it all had a dream-like quality, as if they were not real at all.

The minute Aunty Liang got off the cart, she threw herself into Mother's arms. Most probably she was crying. Mother led her into the sitting room. I crawled into bed again, suddenly feeling very nervous and embarrassed, not exactly knowing why.

I guessed that Uncle Liang must be dead and gone but what was strange was that he was not a leader of soldiers like my own uncle. Would the Japanese also kill him? I could not reason it out.

Thinking of easygoing, happy-go-lucky Uncle Liang in his long gown, I could not help but also think of the two spherical pieces of ivory, pale yellow with a silky sheen and delicately lined. When you looked at them under the light they were as shiny as Uncle Liang's forehead. If Uncle Liang had died, I wondered whose hands were holding them now. Although I knew it wasn't right for me to have such thoughts at such a time and I was somewhat ashamed of myself, I still could not help wondering about it.

Aunty Liang was crying and sobbing in the sitting room, and I could not hear what was being said but suddenly I heard my name mentioned:

"Little Yuan? He must be seven or eight by now?"

"He will be ten after Spring," answered Mother. "When he heard that you were coming, he insisted on waiting up for you but when it became too late he couldn't stay awake."

"He is in school now?"

"He is in fourth grade already, in our factory dependent's school which is not bad, as most of the teachers are college students from Peiping and Tien-tsin."

"I'll go in and look at him," and they started to walk into the bedroom.

First came the light from a Priest's Hat Candle—this label was very expensive and seldom seen around our part of the country, and I felt the difference in its light as it fell on my face. I kept my eyes closed as I pretended to be fast asleep. A strange hand, thinner and colder than Mother's, stroked my forehead and cheeks. It was very ticklish. I forced myself not to giggle. I felt the loving tenderness of her touch and felt embarrassed at my pretense.

"He is not plump," Aunty Liang sighed. "In the twinkle of an eye, Little Yuan is already such a big boy. Look how long his legs are." She stroked my legs which were stretched out under the quilt. I was just wondering whether I should sit up or not when I heard her crying again. "Ai, I never would have thought. . . ."

What couldn't she have thought? Shouldn't I have grown up? I hated this sort of condescending talk from the grown-ups, and, in annoyance, I pulled my head under the quilt, disregarding them.

The next morning, Old Sun Ma woke me up to go to school. After hurriedly chewing a toasted bun and swallowing a bowl of hot congee, I rushed off to school. It was only after class began that I remembered what had happened the night before. I had not seen clearly what Aunty Liang looked like; nor did I know why she had been sobbing and crying.

At noon, when I went home for lunch, I finally met Aunty Liang. I had always been afraid of meeting strangers, but Aunty Liang did not seem at all strange to me; she took me in her arms and asked me about this and that, talking about so many things. She had on a black quilted gown that seemed to be rather thin and of poor quality and a short coat that was also black. I looked at her feet; there were no high heels now, nor were there any brilliants, only a pair of cloth slippers that looked as if they were made by her own hands. Even among the "big city people" who had come here to this country place, this kind of attire was considered very simple. There was a small room, off the sitting room, that Old Sun Ma had slept in, which was just big enough for one bed. This was now given to Aunty Liang, while Old Sun Ma went to sleep with our neighbor's maid.

Except for the word "thin," there did not seem to be another adjective to describe the present Aunty Liang. Most probably, she was still afraid of the cold. I later found out that she was from the south, and nine out of ten southerners could not stand the cold. Her face was white with a bluish cast, but her eyes were red-rimmed, so red that it made you uncomfortable to look at them. In no way did she seem to resemble the Aunty Liang of my memories. Time could not have made that much difference. No matter from what angle you looked at her, she had become a shrunken little old woman. The change was like a ripe red persimmon becoming a dried, frost-covered persimmon cake, and it was difficult to reason out.

She had lost her gaiety, and also her bold, straight-forward manner of talking. Maybe she had finished all she had to say, so that she just sat without moving, all day long. Even when Mother talked to her, Aunty Liang would often wander off the subject. Her manner of not being interested in anything around her made you sorry for her—just as for the old cat that could not catch any more mice, too old to care whether the mice jumped over the rafters.

This was during wartime, when things were becoming more and more difficult. Father used to work for the factory and had followed it when it moved to the north-west to begin all over again. The factory was financially in bad shape; at home, we often heard Mother say: "No money again." Sun Ma and her son, Sun Te-hai, were old servants of ours, but because Father had such a small income, we had found Sun Te-hai a job making molds at the factory. He had once been an apprentice for several years and knew something of carpentry. After work, he would come to our home and help out a little. The five of us, masters and servants, were really sticking together, just like one big family.

Old Sun Ma could, indeed, be said to be faithful and true to our family. It may have been due to her age, but she was more upset by our family's misfortunes than my parents were. I often heard her grumbling: "Your mother and father are too good, still acting like the master and mistress of the old days, with no thought for the future. Times being so difficult, how can they be as generous as before? Just see if when we ourselves are in difficulties, will anybody be half as warmhearted?"

Every time we had guests she would grumble: "Not earlier, not later, just when we are having a meal." Then she would go and sit on the little stool in the kitchen, angrily working on the bellows at the stove. It was not so bad with the guests who were there for the first time, but if they came often, like some of Father's students or subordinates who had no place to go on Sundays and would come over to our house to make up a table of majong (which, of course, would result in staying for supper, and also a midnight snack), then Old Sun Ma would certainly not condone it: "What kind of times are we living in; one whole chicken in a pot, four or five catties of meat in one meal; don't they know how much one catty of flour costs?" Sometimes, she would intentionally cook too little rice and put the burnt rice at the bottom of the pot in the guest's bowl. After the guest left, Mother would have to give her another talking-to.

It seemed that, this time, Aunty Liang meant to stay at our house indefinitely. After the third day, Old Sun Ma was the first to become impatient. "Who is without home, without work? How can anyone just stick in someone else's home and not leave?" Mother pretended not to hear.

While Mother was in the sitting room and could not overhear, I stealthily asked Old Sun Ma: "Who are you talking about? Is it Aunty Liang?"

"Huh, who else? Even though she is a good friend, there is no reason for this. During these troubled times, how can she just come into somebody else's home with no intention of leaving?"

"She doesn't have a home of her own?"

"That's so, she doesn't even have a home. Your

mother only knows how to be generous, but just think how many months or years she may stay."

"Where is her home?"

"She ran away; she doesn't want it any more!"

"Where is Uncle Liang?"

"Don't mention that Liang! He has become a traitor!"

"Traitor?" This term really scared me. Young as I was, I had heard it too often. Whether it was the grown-ups at home or the teachers at school, whenever the term "traitor" was mentioned, everyone gritted their teeth in anger. I remembered when we were on our way from Cheng Chou to Lo Yang, at the station in Lo Yang we saw a pale looking middle-aged man dressed in gray cloth gown who was surrounded by a crowd. Everyone was cursing him, hitting him, pulling at him; even the women were spitting in his face. The enemy planes had bombed Lo Yang that day, and during the alert somebody had seen this man sending up signals. I had asked Father what it was all about and he had said firmly, without any hesitation : "A traitor, he should be shot!"

But, how could Uncle Liang be a traitor? I felt it was very strange. Did he also send up signals when the enemy planes came to bomb? I asked Old Sun Ma, thinking that most probably she would not know either, but unexpectedly she said :

"Because he had this!" She stretched out her right hand with the thumb and little finger sticking up, and the other three fingers curled up in her palm while she pursed up her mouth, making a sucking noise: "Fu ... fu ... fu."

"What is this?" I did not understand.

"This is smoking opium!"

"Do all opium smokers have to be traitors?"

"We don't allow smoking here! They shoot anyone who smokes opium, so the opium smokers have all become traitors and gone over to the Japanese devils. He used to have quite a lot of property and had houses in all the big ports; also quite a lot of business. But because he has that habit he cannot stand hardship like your father does, so he does not dare to come out. He stayed in Peiping and became a traitor."

"How did you know all this, Sun Ma?"

"She herself told your mother; I heard her with my own ears."

"Then why did she come out? She is a traitor's wife then. . . . " I did not have the heart to say anything about taking her into custody. I now felt even more sorry for Aunty Liang; Uncle Liang was a traitor, and sooner or later he would not be able to escape what had happened to that man in gray I had seen; surrounded, beaten up, spat upon, and, in the end, shot to death.

I asked Mother about all this, but she scolded me not to talk nonsense; then she also scolded Old Sun Ma.

But this had left a ball of suspicion in my heart.

A child's heart cannot differentiate between right and wrong, good and bad; it can only be influenced by emotions. I knew that a traitor was a bad person but I could in no way think of Aunty Liang in relation to a traitor. Especially since Mother was always so good to her. Mother's judgment could not be wrong; there must be some other reason.

However, I was at odds with myself and filled with inner conflict, pulled back and forth between the two extremes of Mother and Old Sun Ma. Aunty Liang was no longer a person who was always happy; even with a little child like me, she seldom talked and laughed.

Father was busy moving equipment, purchasing materials, and hiring workers for the reopening of the factory. He was still in Sian and could not come home. Every time he wrote he asked Mother to tell Aunty Liang not to worry but to go on living with us, and as long as we were there, she was to make our home hers. If in the future she wanted to find a job, there would always be a way.

Aunty Liang had also mentioned finding a job but it was not easy to do so, as she had no special ability or experience. After a while, the matter was dropped.

It was very rare to have such a beautiful day during the last month of the year. I don't know why but I shall always remember what happened on that day. At noon, Mother, Aunty Liang, and I were seated in the doorway of the sitting room, sunning ourselves. The two grow-ups were mostly silent, their occasional remarks entirely disconnected and unrelated.

Aunty Liang kept praising the weather—the third time she had said the same thing. But this time she added : "I have never opened my little suitcase. Let me open it up and air it in the sun."

So I helped her carry it out; a small red leather case that was between the size of a large valise and an overnight bag, faded and worn with a much-travelled look to it but kept so clean that it was apparent that its owner prized it highly.

The suitcase was very heavy, as if it were filled with stones or pieces of iron. However, when it was opened it was filled mostly with pages torn from books, unmounted paintings and calligraphy, diaries and letters.

There were also large and small photographs, already turning yellow, on the backs of which were black scars where they had been torn out of an album. When she first opened the case a strong smell of mold assailed our nostrils. When Aunty Liang saw that there were bookworms crawling around, she picked them out like bedbugs and crushed them on the ground.

Besides the papers, there were some other articles wrapped in tissue paper, pieces of cloth, and cotton wool. Picking up a little bundle, Aunty Liang said to Mother: "Just looking at this makes my heart ache." It was a hypodermic needle, just like those the doctors used to give me my injections. "This was what he used when he was trying to break the habit. What with medicines and injections, he was almost on the verge of being cured, but he could not control himself, and then war had to come. . . ."

"This is really a calamity!" Mother said. "If it weren't for the Japanese, Brother Liang would not have begun on this stuff again. He is not a weak-willed person, and since he had made up his mind, he surely would have broken the habit sooner or later."

Mother tried to comfort her: "With you here, he must worry about you constantly. Maybe he will soon be cured and come and get you—it is not too difficult now to come out from over there."

But Aunty Liang just shook her head.

She rummaged around in the case again and took out a little package wrapped in silk. When she opened it, I felt a sudden stab of joy, as if I were seeing an old friend. . . . It was the two balls of ivory. Aunty Liang sighed deeply, murmuring as if to herself: "These were given to him by an Indian antique dealer on Tung

Chiao Min Hsiang who said that any couple possessing these would always be together, happy and contented. Really. . . ." She smiled, maybe at the Indian, maybe at herself; a ghostly looking smile that was close to crying.

"Don't keep looking at these things; go and rest for awhile!" Mother said.

Aunty Liang started to cry, sobbing brokenly: "It is so difficult . . . when a person wants . . . to do something good; truly . . . bad things are so easy . . . too easy, once learned, and whether you want to or not, you cannot change. He has always been capable. . . clever." She dissolved into sobs. Then, suddenly, she wiped away her tears and as if she had come to an important decision, she said to me: "Little Yuan, you can have these ivory balls to play with."

"Oh no, how can you?" Mother hurried to protest.

I was startled. This was something entirely unexpected. I had loved them too much and had coveted them for too long a time, but after all this while, I had never expected to set eyes on them again, let alone have them offered to me. I was greatly excited.

I jumped up and ran—stepping on the old cat that was sleeping by my feet, so that she switched her tail and screeched wildly. I did not pay her any attention but ran to the kitchen door as if I were running away from someone, shouting: "I don't want them!" Then, to strengthen my decision and to fight against my desire for possession, I added: "I don't want Uncle Liang's things; he is not a good man; he smokes opium, he is a traitor!"

Maybe my voice was too loud, although I did not realize it, but the effect of these words on Aunty Liang was like a clap of thunder.

I stood by the kitchen door so that I saw everything clearly. Her face instantly turned a pitiful white. She stood stupefied, then sank slowly into her chair, one of the balls still tightly clasped in her hand while the other one rolled, unheeded, onto the floor. Mother looked helplessly first at me, then at Aunty Liang.

For a moment, it seemed as if Aunty Liang were still trying to smile as though nothing had happened, but it was a fleeting effort, for I could see the tears begin to pour down her face.

Mother glared at me. She did not say anything, for most probably she thought this was too serious an affair to put right with just a few words of scolding. But I saw one encouraging smile turned towards me ... from Old Sun Ma, who was working the bellows in the kitchen.

After a long moment, a very embarrassing moment for the grown-ups and an uncomfortable one for me, Aunty Liang said slowly. "I think ... I should be going in another day."

Mother looked at her in astonishment.

"I received a letter from a friend who is the Dean of a middle school in Swan She Pu saying there is a vacancy there. I think that will be easy work and not too far from you. . . ."

Ordinarily, this would not have been surprising, but the two things happening one on top of the other seemed too much of a coincidence.

Mother was by then too embarrassed to try to say anything in explanation of my behavior, and I did not get a scolding.

The next day, after school was over, I met Lao King and his mule cart driving down the mountain road and saw that it was Mother with Aunty Liang. Lao King stopped the cart and lifted me in. I could not say why, but I felt miserable and did not dare to look at Aunty Liang's face.

During the ride, Mother kept finding things to talk about. She mentioned the letters of introduction she had given Aunty Liang; when she reached Pao Chi she should look up so-and-so and get a ride into Swan She Pu; in Swan She Pu there were this and that friend, all old friends from Peiping, etc. etc. Aunty Liang murmured some responses, but I felt her eyes on my face.

At long last we reached the station. The train arrived and Aunty Liang went to her seat. Aunty waved at Mother and me through the window. The station master rang his bell and the cars started to move. Suddenly Aunty Liang lowered the window and sticking her head out, cried : "Older sister, if you receive any news of his coming out to the free area, you must be sure to let me know."

Seeing her begin to cry, I also started to cry; I did not quite understand whether I felt sorry for her or for myself. I only knew that I was very unhappy.

On our way home, the mule cart seemed very empty but the atmosphere was less oppressive; Mother merely said : "Hurry home and have your lunch or else you will be late for school again." I wanted to ask her if Aunty Liang was angry with me, and also about the ivory balls, but I was afraid that it would make her really angry with me.

The train's whistle sounded from the distance; the mountains and valleys reverberated with the echoes. I turned to look but the train was already far, far away— on the other side of the plain. Mother sighed : "A man must not take the wrong road! Such a good wife! Ai-ya, how it has burdened her."

When we arrived home, Old Sun Ma came out to meet us with a letter from Father saying he was coming home immediately for New Year's. He also said that since we had Aunty Liang with us this year, we should have an even happier New Year. As I impatiently urged Mother to read the entire letter to me, I felt some special warmth in this familiar home of ours that I had never felt before; but at the same time, I also felt an indescribable sadness.

Aunty Liang, where would she spend her New Year? And that pair of ivory balls, and the shiny forehead of Uncle Liang that reflected the light just like the ivory balls. . . .

Many years have passed, but I have never forgotten this incident.

After the war was over, Uncle Liang was caught and imprisoned but he was not shot as I had feared he would be. We heard that after he was freed, he married again, the daughter of a businessman. When someone mentioned his first wife, he just smiled; when they asked any further, he said: "That woman, she is too old-fashioned."

In the beginning, Aunty Liang had kept in touch with my family. After victory came, she went back to her old home, south of the Yangtze River, but she was separated from her husband. People thought she must also be at some fault, no matter how little. Nobody knew or cared that she had sacrificed her happiness because she had stuck to her principles. Then, finally, we had no more news of her.

It seems that this is not a story with a beginning and

an ending; neither is it a story of "goodness always has its own recompense." Maybe it is only because I myself was involved in all this that I remember it at all. It really is without any special significance—just as many of the things that happen in life are disordered and meaningless. But every winter when the day is overcast and gray, I still think of what happened that day, of the snowdrifts, the sun, the cold wind, the roar of the train as it faded into the distance, the sorrowful face of Aunty Liang whom I had unwillingly hurt—and the pair of unfeeling ivory balls.

—TRANS. BY NANCY CHANG ING

Grandma Takes Charge

[REPUBLIC OF CHINA]

by Lao She

YOU COULDN'T blame old Mrs. Wang for wanting a grandson, for what was the use of getting a daughter-in-law if it was not to pave the way for a grandson? And you couldn't blame the daughter-in-law either. It is not that she hadn't tried, but what could you do if the baby didn't live after it was born, or was born without any life at all? Take the first birth, for instance. As soon as the mother became pregnant, old Mrs. Wang forbade her to do anything whatsoever, forbade her even to turn over in bed. You can't say that's not being careful. But after five months she had a miscarriage, probably because she blinked her eyes once or twice too often. And it was a boy, too! During her second pregnancy, she did not even dare to blink her eyes without due deliberation, or indulge in a yawn without two maids on either side to make sure that nothing went wrong. Indeed, carefulness pays, and the mother gave birth to a big, plump boy. But for some reason or other the child had lived barely five days when it took eternal leave of this world without so much as a cheep or without even a ghost knowing. That happened in the eleventh month. There were four open stoves in the nursery, without so much as a single pinhole in any of the windows. Not only was it impossible for any wind to get in, it would have been pretty difficult for the God of Wind himself to have found his way in. Moreover, the baby had piled on it four quilts and five woolen blankets. You can't say that he wasn't warmly covered, can you? But the baby died just the same. It was simply fate and no one could do anything about it.

Now young Mrs. Wang was again blessed. The size of her belly was astonishing, like stone rollers that road gangs use. Was old Mrs. Wang tickled! It was as if her heart had grown two little hands that kept on tickling her and making her laugh. Judging by the mother's size it would be a wonder if it did not turn out to be twins! The Goddess of Children had answered her prayers and was going to reward her with a pair of them. She was ready to do more than offer prayers and burn incense; she could hardly have refused her daughter-in-law if she had wanted human brains for dinner. For midnight supper she gave her stewed fresh bacon, chicken noodles, and such rich delicacies. The daughter-in-law was very obliging on her part. The more she lay motionless the hungrier she became. She would eat a couple of pounds of moon cakes for a between-meals snack, so that oil fairly oozed out of her down the pillow, and you could have swept out mincemeat and crumbs from under her covers by the bowlful. How could a pregnant woman give birth to a plump baby if she did not eat as much as she could? Both mother-in-law and daughter-in-law were agreed on that.

And of course maternal grandma was not to be outdone. She came every few days to "hasten the birth," and every time she came she brought at least eight trays of food. It has been discovered long since by philosophers that in-laws are implacable foes. And so the more things maternal grandma brought, the more convinced the other grandma became that the former was just trying to show off and shame her; and the more paternal grandma tried to press food upon her daughter-in-law, the more convinced maternal grandma became that her daughter did not get enough to eat. The result of this wholesome competition was a boon to the young woman, who ate and ate until her mouth was worn thin.

The midwife had been on hand for seven days and seven nights, but to no purpose. They had tried all sorts of weird prescriptions and quantities of pills and powders and incense ash from the temple of the Goddess of Children, but nothing worked. On the eighth day, the young woman couldn't even be tempted with chicken broth. She just rolled and groaned with pain. Old Mrs. Wang burned incense to the Goddess of Children, and maternal grandma summoned a nun to read the charm for hastening birth; still it was no use. Thus they struggled on toward midnight when the top of the reluctant child's head finally came into view. The midwife tried all her tricks but accomplished nothing more than to maul and bruise the young mother. The child just would not come out. The minutes, each as long as a year, dragged on until it was almost an hour, but still only the top of the child's head could be seen.

Someone suggested the hospital but old Mrs. Wang would not hear of such a thing, for that would mean that the mother would have to be disemboweled and the child "gouged" out by force. Foreign devils and foreign-devils-once-removed could do that if they wanted to, but not the Wangs. The Wangs wanted their grandchild to be born naturally, not "gouged" out by force. Maternal grandma didn't like the idea either. You couldn't exactly hasten the birth of a child. Even a hen has to take her time about laying an egg. Moreover, the nun hadn't yet finished incanting her charm, and to slight the nun was to be disrespectful to the gods. What was the hurry?

Another hour went by. The child was as stubborn as ever. The mother's eyes became glassy. With tears in her eyes, old Mrs. Wang made up her mind to save the child and forget the mother. You could always get another daughter-in-law; the child was more important. It was time to be resolute and pull the child out by brute force if necessary. A wet nurse would do just as well in case the mother died. She told the midwife to pull hard. Maternal grandma, however, had a different reaction. To her a daughter was a daughter, much closer than a grandson. It was better to get her to the hospital, without waiting for the nun to finish. Who knows what she was mumbling anyway? What if it wasn't the birth-hastening charm after all? Wouldn't that be wasting valuable time? The nun was dismissed, but paternal grandma was obdurate against "gouging." There was little that maternal grandma could do. A married daughter is like water that has been thrown out of the pail. As long as her daughter lived she was a member of the Wang family, and when she died she would still be a Wang ghost. The in-laws glared at each other, each ready to bite off a hunk of the other's flesh.

Another half hour went by, and the child was as

unhurried and reluctant to come out as before. The midwife decided it was hopeless and sneaked off at the first opportunity. Her departure weakened old Mrs. Wang's position and gave more weight to maternal grandma's plea: "Even the midwife has sneaked off. What are we waiting for? Do you want the child to die in the womb?"

The juxtaposition of "death" and "child" made a deep impression on old Mrs. Wang, but still "gouging" would hardly do under any circumstances.

"Lots of people go to the hospital nowadays; they don't always resort to 'gouging,'" maternal grandma vehemently argued, though she was not so sure of it herself. As for old Mrs. Wang, she naturally did not believe it at all; to her going to the hospital meant only one thing and that was "gouging."

Fortunately, maternal grandpa arrived on the scene, immediately improving the position and morale of maternal grandma. He, too, was for going to the hospital. There was little else to do after that. After all he was a man and in a matter of life and death a man's word carries weight, though childbearing is strictly a woman's business.

And so the in-laws, the young mother, and the grandson who had only his hair showing all went to the hospital in a motorcar. The in-laws shed tears at the cruel fate of the grandson who had to be carted about in a motorcar when he had just barely showed his hair.

Old Mrs. Wang exploded almost as soon as they got to the hospital. What, they had to register? What did they mean by registering? It was a case of childbirth, not as if they had come for their quota of rice at government price or to get a bowl of free gruel. Old Mrs. Wang

was outraged and declared that she would sooner give
up the idea of a grandson than to submit to such a
humiliation. But when she found that if she refused to
register they would refuse to let them in, she decided
to swallow her pride, hard as it was for her to do, for
the sake of her emerging grandson. If only her husband
were living—it would have been a wonder indeed if
he did not tear down the hospital then and there. A
widow couldn't do that; she had to put up with things
even though she had money. It was no time to ruminate
over her grievances; the most pressing thing was to
coax her grandson out. So she registered and was told
that she had to pay fifty dollars in advance. That gave
her her opportunity: "Fifty dollars? Even five hundred
is nothing to me. Why didn't you come to the point?
Why this nonsense about registration? Did you think
my grandson was a letter?"

The physician came, and again old Mrs. Wang
exploded. It was a man; a man was to act as midwife.
She wouldn't have a man attend to her daughter-in-law.
Before she had a chance to recover from this shock,
two more men came out and proceeded to lift up her
daughter-in-law and put her on a stretcher. She was so
outraged that even her ears quivered. Why, it was worse
than revolution and rebellion! What did they mean
by letting a crowd of men handle a young pregnant
woman? "Put her down! Isn't there anyone here who
knows what human decency means? If so, you'd better
ask a few women to come out. Otherwise, we leave."

It happens that she had to deal with a very good-
natured physician. "All right," he said, "put her down
and let them go!"

Old Mrs. Wang swallowed hard and what she had to

swallow burned her heart. If it were not for the sake of her grandson she would give him a few resounding slaps at least. But "an official in authority is not as important as a flunky in charge," and what could she do since her grandson had decided to be difficult? All right, take her and waste no more words. As soon as the two men put the daughter-in-law in the stretcher, the physician began to press her abdomen with his hands. Old Mrs. Wang closed her eyes to the horror of it and cursed maternal grandma in her heart: "It's your daughter and you let a man press her belly without uttering a word of protest! Oh, the indecency of it!" She was about to say something aloud when her thought again turned to her grandson. For more than ten months he had never suffered any indignity or discomfort. Would he, with his tender skin and bone, be able to stand the physician's rough handling? She opened her eyes and was about to warn the physician when the latter anticipated her by asking: "What have you been feeding the mother? Look at her! I don't know what to do with people like you. You keep feeding the mother everything you can think of until the child is so large. You would not come for check-ups. Then you come to us when everything else fails." Then without waiting for old Mrs. Wang to say anything, he said to the two men, "Carry her in!"

Old Mrs. Wang had never suffered such a humiliation in all her life. It was as if the Goddess of Wisdom herself was being taught how to be wise! That was not the worst of it; there was not a grain of sense to what the man said. If a pregnant woman did not eat nourishing food how was she to bear a child, how was the child to grow? Did the physician thrive on northwest wind when he was in his mother's womb? But Western-style physicians are all foreign-devils-once-removed and you couldn't reason with them. She would take it out on maternal grandma; wherewith she glared at her. The latter was too busy thinking about her daughter to mind. She tried to follow the carriers. Old Mrs. Wang followed suit, but the physician turned around and said to them: "Wait here!"

Both women's eyes turned red with indignation. What, they would not let them in to watch? How were they to know where they were going to take her, and what they were going to do to her? After the physician left them, old Mrs. Wang unloosed the acrid smoke of her rage on maternal grandma: "You said they would not have to 'gouge' him out, but see now, they would not even let you go in and see what's going on! Why, they may even have her quartered twice over. It would serve you right to have your daughter cut up like that. But if anything should happen to my grandson, I shall not live; I'll match my life against yours!"

Maternal grandma was frightened. What if they really did cut up her daughter? It was not beyond these foreign-devils-once-removed. Didn't they exhibit a human leg and a torso in glass jars the last time the medical school was opened to the public? "Now you are blaming me! Who was it that kept on stuffing my daughter from morning till night? Didn't you hear what the doctor said? It was you who insisted on stuffing her. Now see what you have done. I have seen a lot of people in my time but I have never seen a mother-in-law like you!"

"Yes, I have fed her well, but that's because I wasn't sure that she ever got enough to eat before she was married into our house," sneered in-law Wang.

"And I suppose it's because we never gave her enough to eat in our own house that I had to bring eight food trays every time I visited my daughter at your house!"

"Now you have admitted it yourself. Yes, eight trays. Yes, I have stuffed her and you haven't!"

Thus the in-laws battled on, neither willing to weaken. Their jibes and retorts were highly original and effectively delivered.

The physician came back, and said, as paternal grandma had anticipated, that an operation was necessary. The term "operation" had an unfamiliar ring, but there was no question as to the implication; it meant that they were going to cut her up. If they operated, the physician said, they might save both mother and child; if not, both would probably die. The child was hours overdue and was definitely too big to come out without an operation. But a member of the family must sign before they could operate.

Old Mrs. Wang did not hear a word of what the physician had said. She was saying to herself that she would not stand "gouging."

"What are you going to do?" the physician said impatiently. "You must decide right away!"

" 'Gouging' won't do!"

"Are you going to sign? Hurry up and make up your mind!" the physician again urged.

"My grandson must be born the natural way!"

Maternal grandma became anxious: "Would it be all right if I signed?"

Old Mrs. Wang flared up at maternal grandma's presumptuousness: "She is my daughter-in-law! Who are you?"

The physician became more and more impatient. He

shouted into old Mrs. Wang's ear: "This is a matter of two lives!"

" 'Gouging' won't do!"

"Then you don't care about a grandson?" the physician adopted a new line of attack.

For a while she was silent. Many ghosts presented themselves before her, and all of them seemed to say: "We want someone to keep burning incense to us. We are willing to compromise on the 'gouging' issue."

She surrendered. Of course the ancestors must have an heir; let them resort to "gouging" if necessary. "But just one thing, it must be alive!" She had hearkened to the ancestors' wishes and given her permission to the physician to cut open her daughter-in-law and "gouge" the child out, but she must make it clear that she wanted a live baby. What good would a dead one be? As for the mother, it didn't matter so long as the grandson lived.

Maternal grandma, however, was not so indifferent to the patient's fate: "Are you sure that both mother and child will live?"

"Hush!" said paternal grandma.

"I believe that there will be no danger," the physician said, wiping his forehead. "But the birth has been very much delayed and we can guarantee nothing. Otherwise why should you be asked to sign?"

"You wouldn't guarantee anything? Then let us not go through all this for nothing!" Paternal grandma was very responsible in her attitude toward the ancestors; it wouldn't do anyone any good if only a dead child came out of all this horror.

"All right, then," said the physician, suffocating with exasperation, "take her back and do what you like. But remember, two lives!"

"What if it were three lives, since you would not guarantee anything?"

Old Mrs. Wang suddenly decided that perhaps she had better let them try. She would not have thought of this if the physician had not started to walk away. "Doctor, doctor, come back! Supposing you try what you can." The physician was so exasperated that he hardly knew whether to laugh or cry. He read the release to her and she signed it with a cross.

The grandmas waited and waited for they did not know how long. It was not until almost dawn that they succeeded in "gouging" the child out. What a big baby it was, fully thirteen pounds! Old Mrs. Wang was overwhelmed with happiness. She took maternal grandma's hands, laughing with tears streaming down her cheeks. The latter was no longer her enemy but her "dear elder sister." The physician was no longer a foreign-devil-once-removed, but a benefactor of the Wang family. She wished she could reward him with a hundred dollars at once. If he had not resorted to "gouging" her nice fat grandson might have suffocated. How would she then face her ancestors? She wished she could kneel down then and there and do some good old kowtowing, but they did not have any shrine for the Goddess of Children in the hospital.

The baby was now washed and put in the nursery. The grandmas wanted to go in and take a look. Not only to take a look, but to pat and fondle the child with their wrinkled hands that had not been washed all night. The nurse would not let them go in; they were only allowed to look through the glass partition. There was their own grandson inside, their very own grandson, and yet they were not even allowed to touch it! Paternal grandma took out a red envelope—which she had planned to give to the midwife—and handed it to the nurse. She would surely let them in after that! But nothing seemed to go right; the nurse actually refused to accept the gift! Old Mrs. Wang rubbed her eyes and contemplated the nurse for a long while. "She does not appear to be a foreign-devil girl," she said to herself, "then why is it that she would not accept a gift? Perhaps she is shy and feels embarrassed." She had it! She would strike up a conversation with her. Everything would be all right after she had broken down her shyness. She pointed to the row of baskets in the nursery and asked, "I suppose they were all 'gouged' out?"

"No, only yours. All the others were born naturally."

"Nonsense," old Mrs. Wang said to herself. "All those who come to hospitals must be 'gouging' cases."

"Only when you feed rich and fattening food to the mother is it necessary to operate," the nurse said.

"But would the child be so big if the mother didn't have enough to eat?" said maternal grandma, standing on a united front with old Mrs. Wang on the issue.

"A big, fat baby is better than a skinny monkey, though one may be 'gouged' out and the other born naturally," old Mrs. Wang said, beginning to feel that none but "gouging" cases had any business to come to the hospital. "And who ever heard of natural cases coming to the hospital? That would be as unnecessary as letting down the pants in order to break wind!"

But they remained on the outside of the nursery for all the talking they did.

Old Mrs. Wang had another idea. "Maid," she said to the nurse, addressing her as if she were a servant girl, "give the baby to us and let us take him home. We have a lot to do to get ready for the Third Day bathing ceremony."

"I am not a maid and I cannot give you the baby," said the nurse, none too politely.

"He is my grandson! You dare to refuse me? We can't invite guests to the hospital and do things properly."

"The mother can't nurse the child right away when we have to operate; we have to feed the child."

"And so can we! I am getting on toward sixty and I have borne sons and given birth to daughters. I should know more about such things than you do. Have you ever borne any children?" Old Mrs. Wang wasn't sure whether the nurse was married or not. Who could tell what these white helmeted women were anyway?

"We can't give you the child without the doctor's permission, no matter what you say."

"Then go and get the doctor and let me talk to him. I don't want to waste words with you!"

"The doctor has not yet finished; he has to sew up the incision."

This reminded maternal grandma of daughter, though old Mrs. Wang was still too full of her grandson to give any thought to her daughter-in-law. Before the birth of her grandson, her daughter-in-law always came to her mind when she thought of her grandson, but now that her grandson was born, it was no longer necessary to think of her daughter-in-law. Maternal grandma, however, wanted to see her daughter. Who knew what a big hole they made in her belly? They would not let anyone into the operating room and there was nothing for maternal grandma to do except to gaze at the child with old Mrs. Wang from the distance.

Finally the physician came out and old Mrs. Wang went up to parley with him.

"In operating cases it is best for mother and child to stay in the hospital for a month," the physician said.

"Then what are we going to do about the Third Day and the Full Month?" old Mrs. Wang asked.

"Which is more important, their lives or the feasts? How can the mother stand the strain of entertaining before her incision heals?" the physician asked.

Old Mrs. Wang undoubtedly believed that the Third Day celebration was more important than her daughter-in-law's life, but she could not very well say so with maternal grandma listening. As to how her daughter-in-law was to receive the guests, that was easily managed : she would let her receive them lying in bed.

The physician still refused. Old Mrs. Wang got another idea. "I suppose it is money that you are after? All right, then, we'll pay you, but let us take mother and child home."

"You go and take a look at her yourselves, and see if she is in a condition to be moved," the physician said.

Both grandmas hesitated. What if she still had a gaping hole in her, as big as a wash basin? Wouldn't that be horrible? Love of her daughter finally enabled maternal grandma to summon up enough courage to go in, and there was nothing for paternal grandma to do but to follow.

In the sickroom daughter-in-law lay on the bed, propped up on a reclining rest, her face like a sheet of white paper. Her mother cried out, not sure whether her daughter was dead or alive. Old Mrs. Wang had more fortitude and shed only a tear or two, which were immediately followed by an indignant protest : "Why won't you let her lie down flat and proper? What kind of foreign torture are you subjecting her to?"

"It would put a strain on the stitches to have her lie flat, understand?" the physician said.

"Can't you bind her up with plaster tape?" Old Mrs. Wang could not get over her distrust of the physician's ideas.

The physician would not even let maternal grandma talk to her daughter, which made both grandmas suspect that the physician must have done something or other to the patient that he was anxious to hide. It was fairly evident that she could not be moved out of the hospital for a while. In that case they could at least take the grandson away so that they could plan on the Third Day festivities.

Again the physician refused. Old Mrs. Wang became desperate: "Do you observe the Third Day bathing ceremony in the hospital? If you do, I shall invite all our friends and relatives here. If you don't, then let me take him away. He is my first grandson. I can't live and face people if I do not celebrate his Third Day appropriately."

"Who is going to nurse the child?" the physician asked.

"We'll hire a wet nurse!" old Mrs. Wang said triumphantly.

The baby was brought out and surrendered to her. She began to sneeze as soon as she got into the car and sneezed all the way home, each sneeze being well aimed at her grandson's face. A man was sent out immediately to find a wet nurse. Grandma kept the baby so that she could sneeze into him. Yes, she knew that she had caught a cold, but she would not relinquish her grandson.

By noon the infant had received at least two hundred sneezes and was beginning to develop a temperature. That made old Mrs. Wang even more reluctant to give it up. By three o'clock in the afternoon, the child burned like fire. By night they had hired two wet nurses, but the grandson died without having had one swallow of milk.

—TRANS. WANG CHI-CHEN

The Death-Mask

[JAPAN]

by Yasunari Kawabata

HE DID not know how many other men she had loved before. It was obvious, however, that he was certainly her last lover, for her death was near.

"If I had known that I would die so soon, I would rather have been killed that time," she said lying in his arms and trying to smile gaily as if remembering her many lovers.

She could not forget her beauty even in her last hour. She could not forget her many love affairs. She did not know that those memories made her look even more forlorn.

"All men yearned to kill me. They didn't say so, but at heart they wanted to. . . ."

Now that she was dying in his arms, he was probably happy with no worry of losing her compared to those poor men who had loved her and who had to tell themselves that the only way to hold her love was to kill her. The fact was that he was a little tired of holding her. She was no longer able to sleep peacefully without the feel of a masculine touch on her neck or breast, even on her sickbed. She had always longed for passionate love.

When she realized that her last hour was near, she said, "Please hold my feet tightly. I feel lonesome there." She often felt lonely at her feet, as if death were stealing up from them. He held her feet tightly as he sat at her bedside.

Her feet were as cold as death itself. Suddenly, his hands betrayed him and trembled strangely. Unexpectedly, his hands had felt her very womanhood in those tiny feet. Her cold feet gave him the same pleasure as he felt when his hands touched the warm, sweaty soles of a woman's feet. He was ashamed of himself thus almost to profane her departing soul. But wasn't the entreaty to have him hold her feet a last demonstration of her coquettishness? He found himself becoming afraid of the woman in her which verged on shamelessness.

"You've been dissatisfied because there is no need any more to be jealous of our love, haven't you? But when I die, you'll be jealous of someone, I'll bet."

With these words, she breathed her last. Surely, she was right.

An actor of modern drama who came to the wake made up her face. He did it trying to revive her vivid beauty in the days when she was in love with him.

Then came an artist who covered her whole face with plaster. The actor's make-up was very effective in bringing her face back to life again. It looked as if the artist were trying to stifle her to death out of jealousy toward the actor. Apparently, the artist was trying to make her death-mask for a keepsake.

Since it was all too clear that the competition for her love would not end with her death, the man realized that it was merely a fleeting triumph on his part to have her die in his arms. So he went to the artist's home to take the death-mask away from him.

The death-mask looked like a man and a woman at the same time. It also looked both like a little girl and an aged woman. Suddenly, he said in a low voice as if his passion were dying out, "That is she, and yet not she. Beyond that, I can't tell the sex."

"That's right," said the artist sadly. "Generally speaking, one cannot tell the sex of a death-mask unless he knows whose it is. Beethoven's face, for example, would seem somehow womanly when looked at closely. I thought, however, that her death-mask would turn out to be womanly because she was more like a woman than anyone else. But, after all, she could not overcome the force of death. Death puts an end to all distinction of sex."

"Her life was a life of tragic joy that she was born a woman. She was too womanly even at the time of her death. If she has now been entirely freed from the tragedy," said the man, "we could go ahead and shake hands beside this death-mask. It bears no distinction of sex, does it?" He extended his hand as if awakened, refreshed, from a nightmare.

—TRANS. BY GEORGE SAITO

The Moustache

[JAPAN]

by Yoichi Nakagawa

ON NEW YEAR's Day, Mr. Ezure was walking along the approach to the Meiji Shrine. He had on gloves of perrin and his big moustache was carefully groomed, trailing on his cheeks like white clouds.

Then there came a triumphant general with a cane. His moustache, too, was exceedingly big and stuck out sharply into the air, grazing his mouth.

Approaching Mr. Ezure, the general addressed him.

"Well, I've often heard of you. You're Mr. Ezure, aren't you?"

"Yes, Your Excellency. I have always been mistaken for you. It may have given you some trouble, I'm afraid."

"Never mind. I've long wished to see you."

Mr. Ezure, too, was an aged reserve soldier, a corporal or something, and when he faced the general, his spirit fully expressed in his moustache made him clearly equal to the general.

He often appeared in Ginza Street when he was neatly dressed and dropped in at Shiseido, a cosmetics shop, where he had a chat with the manager.

He had been a Christian since his youth, and sometimes went to church. And yet, strangely enough, he would put on a vest lined with an obscene picture. In his day, he kept no less than three mistresses, and he enjoyed giving the same dresses to them that he gave to his wife.

But it was his belief that women should be kept well-off, and when he became short of money he broke off with each one of his mistresses and began to live with his wife alone.

At fifty-six, he was grief-stricken when he lost his wife, and since then his only joy was to go to the Ginza and walk there.

Old men are forgotten by young women in any case. Therefore they always try to make their lives worthwhile through some hobbies. But Mr. Ezure soon found that his greatest joy was in the company of a pretty woman. He then thought that he must always be clean in order to do so. In fact, while walking with a girl, he looked bright and was always seized with an impulse to buy her whatever she wanted.

He would stop at Eriji, a draper's, in order to select and buy some neckbands for his young companion.

"What is this one?"

"Well, it's called Kawai-komon. This scattered-figure pattern will be very becoming to this lady, I think."

"Kawai-komon, did you say? It sounds nice. This will do."

He put it against the girl's bosom and looked at it in a very satisfied way.

"Is it a little too sober for you?"

The elegant girl, whom he had found somewhere or

other, kept silent, standing before the mirror so that she might be complimented.

Slowly twirling his moustache, he bought the neck-band with a beaming face, and went out to the pavement again. People respectfully watched the old gentleman with the big moustache exquisitely accompanying the pretty girl.

But on parting from her after taking something at Fugetsu, a tea house, he was disheartened as if possessed by some devil. Then he trudged home alone and unlocked the door of his little old house, at which time he became quite another man.

For in the house his idiotic son of thirty-nine was always waiting alone for him. No one would have expected this of a man who had such an excellent moustache.

Then he took off his affected leather gloves. Then his wrinkled hands were revealed, roughened here and there into white by water-eczema.

This was because he did the cooking for his son and himself. Then he began cooking at once. But he couldn't do it well, and walked to and fro again and again in the room, which made him tired. It was strange how such a man as he was so perplexed, but every time he cooked he was always at a loss and walked nearly four kilometers in the house. His habit, however, was to do the work even if he was tired, and he turned on the gas and cut up the vegetables. Being tense outside his house, it might have been that he involuntarily began to relax inside.

"Hey, won't you eat, Shige-ko?"

Shige-ko, facing his father with his excellent moustache, began eating a late supper rather cheerlessly. He, too, seemed to have the nature for a moustache, and he already had some dark hair around his mouth like an Ainu.

Mr. Ezure's house, at the innermost recess of Koma-gome Street, became so quiet late at night that the owl's hooting in the forest nearby sounded quite weird. Strangely enough, however, Shige-ko was always against moving from this house. Therefore, Mr. Ezure had been living for nearly twenty-five years in this dark house where his wife and daughter had died. It not only became old and rotten here and there, but was quite desolate, being a womanless household.

"Did you have a good time?"

The idiot asked a boyish question.

"Yes, I have collected some money from my debtors."

Mr. Ezure still continued money-lending in those days.

Mr. Ezure, staring at his son, would think he'd like to outlive his son, somehow or other, in order to take care of him. Especially when he returned home, he felt pity and love for this son waiting at home so obediently.

When he was a sergeant-major, Mr. Ezure was once addressed at grand maneuvers by His Majesty. He was praised for his fine attitude, and it seemed to move him so much that still now he boasted of it to others as the greatest honor in his life.

His moustache was not so big in those days. And yet his attitude was full of strength, which strangely attracted people the same as nowadays. But as he grew old, the form and color of his moustache became more refined and suitable to him. For instance, when he went to Hokkaido as a member of some tourist party, all the officials of the Sapporo Municipal Office came to greet him, taking him for the principal guest. Again, when he once visited the Shochiku Theater, all the actresses gathered around him and offered their name-cards.

It was natural, however, that his tragedy should lie in the very fact that his exceeding prominence sometimes slighted his superiors among soldiers or officials.

This was not very pleasant for his superiors. So he wished to get out of this tragic situation at all costs. Because of this or that, soon after coming back from the army, he hit upon becoming a usurer with a small fund of money.

This job seemed suitable to him, and he succeeded in it at every turn. Above all, his big moustache made him appear to be a rich man, and also made it possible for him to threaten his debtors.

Since then he had done his best to increase his wealth, and for the same purpose he learned how to repair watches. Owing to his greediness as well as to his native skill, he quickly cultivated this technique. And every time he mended a gold watch, he used to scrape off some gold from the interior of it.

Using a black monocle with a magnifying glass in it and looking downwards, secretly in the interior of his house he scraped off as much gold as possible from the watches. Sometimes he even scraped off gold from coins and saved it in a celluloid box.

But recently, when he mended watches for young girls or widows he never scraped off any gold.

"I won't scrape gold off from your watch while mending it," he would say, as he talked to them of the past and of his passionate youth.

He wanted to collect money from his debtors quite regularly, all the more because it was his nature to be true to his promise; when he became angry, he shouted in a loud voice as he had been trained to do in the army. Then his big moustache would tremble as if it were charged with electricity, which always frightened the debtors.

"Why can't you pay such a small amount of money as this? You helpless fellow! You'll die a beggar unless you change your mind."

He was strict with his debtors. He not only shouted; he also knew how to collect his money.

Being a man of vehement temper, he continued to be hostile to any person whom he had once hated. Once he became angry, he could not restrain his anger at the person, and he would not enter his house again even on business, but would send a proxy there.

For all that, he sometimes cancelled a bill when there happened to be a pretty girl involved. As he grew older, perhaps he yearned for beauty more than anything, as well as firmness, because he must have been aware of his shortcomings in these areas, and of his utter loneliness.

Old age usually makes people think of ways to stay healthy. He felt that this was a sad thing, but he began to make regular use of garlic so that he might outlive his foolish son. Then he went for walks with young girls.

When he was in high spirits he used to say that he would like to blow out his brains in a coffin which he had had made previously. For there would be no one to take care of him should he happen to fall ill.

When he was in a good humor, twisting his moustache, he would say to his friends that he had two or three children borne by a woman other than his deceased wife. But he didn't seem to have a mind to search for them himself, and somehow or other the woman didn't come to depend on him.

Well, his fine moustache obliged him to put on only first-class garments. When he was in European clothes, he always wore homespun made in England. While wearing Japanese clothes, he made habitual use of Yuki silk and always wore a *haori*, or coat, embroidered with the emblem of a wheel of arrow feathers.

But it was not only to clothes that he had to pay attention. When he was out, in order to adapt himself to his own moustache, he made every unconscious effort to express all his virtues and strength, putting a great strain on all his senses.

He was fond of a sea-otter fur wrap, which became him very well on cold winter days. His personality sometimes seemed so gallant and even so artistic that you might wish to put him always beside the general. His hands, however, sometimes became itchy under his gloves.

"Dear Tane, won't you go to the Hotel Atami with me?"

On that day he was with a girl in European clothes. She was in a dress with a lovely cape-collar.

"Yes, I may go with you."

Well, this girl was the kind who would go anywhere with him, which rather pleased Mr. Ezure.

"I'd like to show you the garden there." After a pause, he went on, "Hama married a diplomat the other day. She rose in value because of walking with me."

He always felt a certain mysterious power about his moustache. He had a queer belief that his girlfriends married fairly well. Or it may have been that he was just fond of announcing such a thing.

And yet it was a fact that his person was so full of dignity and beauty as to allow him to have belief in his power. But his power at once went away from him on his way home when he descended the slope near his house.

Was it because of his son, his home, or his old age? It goes without saying that he heartily loved his son and home; nevertheless, something strangely different appeared in his person.

This melancholy side of such a high-spirited man provided an example that everything has its reverse side.

Perhaps his whole person took off its fine external appearance just as his hands did when he removed his gloves of French make.

Then under his grandeur there appeared an aged man, wretched and unattractive as water-eczema, stubborn and gloomy, who only thought of scraping gold watches. He was a man who bought oranges and rice-crackers in the neighborhood when his son asked for them. He became just gloomy enough to neutralize his triumphant figure in the streets.

But this transformation represented the strange dual human mentality which we should not define merely as vanity. In his case this change was so natural and fatal that it appeared to possess even some beauty of instinct.

At such a time, he was apt to deem it a punishment for his selfishness that he was left behind with this grown-up child by his late wife.

When he made the same gay kimono for each of his three mistresses, he sometimes had his wife sew them, and this made her weep. Remembering the long life of joy and sorrow passed with his late wife, he sometimes couldn't help feeling pity for her.

Then Shige-ko, the idiot, suddenly took hold of him by the arm and began to question him.

"Are you a dog or a man? If you are a man, I'll set you free. What are you—a dog or a man?"

"Oh, Shige-ko, I'm a man. Take your hands off. Off!" Panting under his son's powerful hold, he pulled down his moustache and began losing his dignity.

He knew very well that at home he was helpless, however loudly he might shout, or even if he made his moustache tremble.

He did his best to convince his foolish son that he was a man, filled with misery and deep affection at the same time. He could do nothing but smile faintly, shaking his moustache.

In his absence, his son would sometimes draw out of a chest of drawers his old vest lined with an obscene picture.

When alone, Mr. Ezure put this vest on with a curious expression on his face. In the vest he felt happy recollecting various things from the past. He wished to go out in this vest as in former days.

On a fine morning in May, he was to have a photograph taken with the general at the aviation-hall, their big moustaches ranged side by side. And it occurred to him that he should put on the vest this morning.

"Your Excellency, I was happy to see you the other day."

"Thank you for coming today."

Then the two went up to the roof, stood together before the camera, and straightened themselves up, boasting of the only two excellent moustaches in Japan.

"Isn't mine a little bigger?" asked the general.

"Before coming here I trimmed my moustache a

little lest it should be bigger than yours. Ha, ha, ha . . ."

"I see. I also trimmed mine, though. But surely no one else in the world has a moustache like ours. Ha, ha, ha . . ."

The general looked happy, too.

Their moustaches trailed like white clouds, buoyant under the clear May sky.

"But my moustache has prevented me from doing anything wrong all through my life, because it has always made me conspicuous," complained the general reminiscently, though full of pride.

"Is it also the case with Your Excellency? My moustache has also given me more trouble than good luck."

"Well, are you ready?" the photographer gave a warning. For a moment the two men put on very grave looks. But as the photographer wouldn't take the picture, the talkative general resumed.

"The bigger a moustache is, the better it is. But the long whiskers which I have sometimes seen hanging to the belly are barbarous."

"Ready, gentlemen?" The photographer made a low bow and stared at them.

Entering another room, Mr. Ezure abruptly and without a word showed the general the inside of his vest.

The general kept his eyes on that curious design for a while, then laughed aloud.

"It's wonderful. You are a very interesting fellow. Won't you come to my house now and then?" he said.

After that Mr. Ezure went straight to Ginza Street. Walking pleasantly along the antique road paved with red bricks, he felt his existence superior, splendidly bright and high, and this filled him with pride.

Soon he ran into Tane, whom he had met the other day. Walking with the girl, he thought himself the kind of man who, however miserable he might become in the future, would always appreciate beauty more than anything else.

That evening he took Tane in European dress to the Atami. But he was so happy with Tane that it was as though he had enjoyed her body too much for his old age.

But the next morning he awoke feeling well, and walked about on the lawn facing the sea, accompanying the girl as if he were some aristocrat.

The next day he went home.

Going home, he changed into another man as usual. The following day, however, his change was unusually great : he took a nap from which he never awoke.

When Shige-ko touched Mr. Ezure's body, it was cold and wouldn't move however hard it was stimulated. Only his white moustache projected sharply in the air as usual. Frightened, Shige-ko ran off to call the neighbors.

The neighbors came; then friends and relatives gathered. Entering his house, they found that the interior was very dismal—something which, because of his fine bearing, they had not imagined possible. The house, disarrayed by Shige-ko, strengthened the misery the more, and made people wonder if this was his real life.

But on that very day the photograph arrived which showed the figures of the two high-spirited old gentlemen with moustaches before a disused airplane on the light concrete floor of the roof. Moreover, one of them was the famous general. They stood as if commanding all the sufferings of life. There was a strange haunting quality in the artistry of the picture.

Unwrapping the parcel, one of the relatives whispered with an air of respect.

"Well, what magnificent persons they are!"

Soon they all gathered around the picture and were at once released from their miserable feelings; they began praising the moustache of the deceased man again.

—TRANS. BY CHIEKO MOROZUMI

Seaside Village

[REPUBLIC OF KOREA]

by O Yong-su

THERE IS a small seaside village called "H" on the coast of the Eastern Sea. On a windy day, the whistle of a faraway train can be heard from the west, and the stone walls of the village houses are washed by occasional high waves. The walls are constructed of round stones heavily crusted with oyster shells. The small grass-roofed houses, about twenty or so, look like a cluster of mushrooms.

If there are any differences at all between it and other seaside hamlets, it might be said that there are too many widows in the village. The old people of the hamlet attribute this fact to the divided western mountains and the rough waves. Anyway, they believe in geomancy.

A small dragnet watch tower stands on the coast to spot the schools of sand eels. The village is noted for its kelp, and most of the men engage in various types of deep-sea fishing according to the season. At low tide, the wives gather seaweed or dig clams and at other times tend their small vegetable patches. Life is just like that of any other seaside hamlet.

It was the beginning of summer. One night, the gong was heard pealing loudly from the watch tower. The villagers were aroused suddenly in lively expectation. Whenever a school of sand eels was spotted, they signaled with a gong or cymbals. And then all the village rushed toward the watch tower and hauled on the ropes of the dragnet. Various kinds of fish were given to the helpers as a bonus according to the size of the catch. This was their toil. Whenever they went out to pull in the dragnet nobody forgot to bring a basket or a dish. Most of them were womenfolk. It was the most prosperous and lively season of the year for the village.

Hae-sun, a widow, twenty-three years old and the youngest of them all, was busy changing into her old clothing.

"Young widow! Won't you join us?" Suki's mother called at Hae-sun's door.

"Oh! Yes. Wait a minute. . . ."

"Everybody has gone already. Come quickly! What's the matter with you?" Suki's mother called again.

"What's the big hurry? Do they give bonuses first to the ones who arrive first?" Hae-sun said, coming through the twig gate.

"What a girl! you . . ." Suki's mother said shaking her fist at Hae-sun, "All you need to put on is a skirt when you are . . . you are just wasting time."

"But it's disgraceful to wear only a skirt, sister; are you really wearing only a skirt?"

"It's night! Nobody can see what we are wearing. Anyway, we'll be thoroughly wet and it's bothersome to wash our clothes all the time, you know."

It was true that their clothes always got thoroughly wet when they pulled on the rope. The hamlet was short even of drinking water, and it was not easy to find water for washing. The wives were in the habit of coming out at night barefooted and wearing only a skirt. And, consequently, the men tried to make fun out of it. Well, nobody knew exactly whether or not the wives liked the mischievousness of their men.

Hae-sun and Suki's mother hurried to the watch tower, walking over the sand on the sea shore. The wet sand felt cool to their bare feet. The earlier arrivals were already pulling on the rope. Hands were clinging to the heavy rope like the legs of a centipede.

"Dehya deya!"

They pulled the rope, shouting alternately from side to side. By and by the rope grew tight, closing the loop. Hae-sun and Suki's mother joined in hauling in the net. The guide was shouting orders, signaling with a lantern off shore. The men who were taking care of the slack rope led the pulling hands by chanting "dehya." The sand eel brokers were already busy speculating here and there. A fire had been built under a big iron pot and water was boiling with a hissing sound. The closer the dragnet came, the faster they shouted, "Dehya deya."

"Dehya deya; dehya deya!"

The sand eels were splashing and jumping, gleaming white, on the sands. When the sand eels were tightly enclosed, the water mounded up in heaps, and in places the net was broken by the weight. That night, also, there was a heavy catch of sand eels. The guide ceaselessly signaled with the lantern. The pullers were breathless with excitement.

"Dehya deya; dehya deya!"

At that moment, Hae-sun's hand on the rope was

clasped by a strong hand. Her hand was helpless. She could not withdraw it. The rope pullers became more breathless as if they had taken fits. At that moment, Hae-sun's waist was embraced by a strong arm. Hae-sun jerked herself away instantly and moved away to another place. Now the net was almost landed.

"Yase, yase!"

This was the moment for the men to jump into the water and drag in the bottom of the net. Somebody thrust his hand under Hae-sun's skirt. Hae-sun, in her frenzy, ran away, shaking off the hand. The sand eels were writhing about pell-mell, gleaming white on the sands. The women were busy collecting them into their baskets. The dragnetting was over.

The sand eels were scooped up into the baskets by a piece of net and then were dumped for selection into a big cement basin. The big ones were sold on the spot to be salted by the dealers, and the rest of them were thrown into the boiling iron pot to be sun-dried afterward.

Hae-sun was handed a basketful as a bonus. She was uneasy while returning home bearing the heavy basket on her head. Her thoughts were occupied with the strong hand rather than with the eels. Who was he? Was he the broker who gave her a larger bonus than she deserved? Someone might have noticed it! "What a disgrace!" she thought.

In the presence of the other wives, Hae-sun was as uneasy about her big bonus as if she had committed some crime. She tried to drop a little behind the other women, but Suki's mother noticed this instantly.

"How did you get such a big bonus?" she asked, nudging Hae-sun's side.

Hae-sun could not answer. She had accepted it as it was handed to her. That was all.

"Pish! I know! You smart girl!"

The wives sniggered meaningfully. It seemed as if they knew something. Hae-sun felt her cheeks burning.

"Sister! Would you like to have some of my eels?" Hae-sun said as they reached Suki's house.

"I may be slapped by the man who gave them to you," Suki's mother said. Nevertheless she held out her basket. Hae-sun poured more than half of her share into the basket.

Hae-sun washed her legs and lay on her mat, but could not fall asleep for a long time. Her thoughts were occupied again and again with the strong hand that felt like the hand of Song-gu. Hae-sun tried many times to shake off the thoughts. She invited sleep by closing her eyes but it was useless. Just like forbidden fruit, the harder she tried to forget, the more vividly the thoughts returned to her. For Hae-sun it was like feeding kindling to live coals. It was a night of restlessness and agony.

Light filled the window. Hae-sun opened it and looked out. The moon was shining on Sari Island. Hae-sun gazed at the fragments of the moon's reflection shattered by the waves.

"Is he alive or dead?" she wondered.

Her eyes were filled with tears. She sighed deeply. And then she lay down, resting her head on her pillow. She fell asleep caressed by the moonlight.

Somebody shook her shoulder. She was afraid to open her eyes but found her mother-in-law looking at her. Hae-sun got up instantly, arranging her breast tie.

"Oh my goodness! It looks like I've been drowsing," Hae-sun said, confused.

"You'd better lock the door first, then sleep," her mother-in-law said, gently as usual.

She pitied her widowed daughter-in-law, and Hae-sun was sad to see her mother-in-law missing her son. They helped and consoled each other just like real mother and daughter. That night, however, she could not help turning her face away from her mother-in-law to hide her blushes. Once before when she was going out in the evening, she had been told by her mother-in-law to lock the door fast, then sleep. Hae-sun remembered the words too well to be able to excuse herself that night. Her mother-in-law knew everything in detail.

Hae-sun was the daughter of a woman diver. Her father had been a vagabond fisherman named Kim. Her mother could not leave the hamlet since she was with child. Hae-sun had been born in the village. Following her mother's life, Hae-sun had been raised on the sands, toughened by the monsoon or soaked by the salt water while she was playing with shells. She had known how to dive since she was ten years old. When she was twenty, she had been married to Song-gu. Having seen her daughter married, her mother had gone back to her native island, Cheju.

"I haven't been able to set foot on my native island for twenty years because of you. Now I can go light-heartedly. Don't seek your mother any more, since you have a husband to rely upon," her mother had said.

Her mother sailed aboard a fishing boat. Song-gu, whose sole dream it was to marry Hae-sun, loved her so much he would not let her work at sea. He was a born hard worker with a faithful heart. Though his earnings were not really sufficient, he could just manage to feed

four mouths including his widowed mother. It hurt
Hae-sun to see him toiling all alone. If she had been
allowed to work in her diving suit, she would not have
fallen behind Song-gu as a wage earner.

"Ah! It's the diving season!" Hae-sun said one night.

"Want to cool yourself, eh?" Song-gu teased her.

"I'll find a little earshell tomorrow."

"You must go over Kal Rocks to find earshells,"
Song-gu said anxiously.

"Oh! Yes! There are many big earshells there," she
said excitedly.

"Don't go!"

"I will!"

"I won't let you go."

"I've nothing particular to do in the house," she
protested.

"Just relax yourself."

"No, I'll go tomorrow, anyway."

When she was in such a mood, Song-gu used to drag
her down with his strong arms and then hug her soft
waist until her bones cracked.

It was the mackerel season. An eight-man crew of
villagers sailed off aboard Ch'il-song's fishing boat.
Whenever sailing for deep-sea netting, the crew was
organized chiefly by the villagers. Having sailed out
early one day, they came back together the same day
of the next week. Consequently, many babies were born
in the same month in the hamlet. There were five babies
who were born in the same month in "H" village.

It was fine weather. The wives were busy around the
fishing boat arranging their men's fishing tackle and
other accessories. The men occupied themselves with

retelling what they had told their wives in bed the night before. The sails were up. The boat began to slide out on the ebbing tide, blown by the southwesterly wind. The men took their positions, lifting the sculls on board.

Man-ni's father, about to light his pipe as he stood on the bow, began to shout his boy's name through his cupped hands. He hurried toward the stern as if he had something serious to say. Instead of his son, his wife rushed splashing into the water. Holding up her skirts, her ear cocked towards him.

"You do just as I told you," the man shouted.

"Do what?"

"What I told you last night!"

"Oh, yes, of course!" the woman said.

Standing against the mast, Song-gu was gazing at the corner of the village where Hae-sun was standing by the stone wall with her hands on her hips. Being a new bride, she was too bashful to come down to the shore to see him off. Song-gu made up his mind firmly, by some means, to buy a wardrobe for her at the end of the season.

The boat was offshore already. None of the men on their way to sea felt the slightest uneasiness; nor did their wives who had come out to see them off. All were full of cheerful expectation. They loved the sea and trusted it. Having lived on the sea all their lives they did not need the help of any weather forecast. Their knowledge of the weather was gathered from experience, and their confidence in their judgment was absolute in spite of many disasters. After they had selected the sailing day, the boat's owner washed his body clean and offered a sacrifice to the Goddess of the Wind and to the Dragon God. They prayed for an abundant catch.

It was fine weather. They were on the ebbing tide and furthermore the sails were filled by the southwesterly wind. They had nothing to worry about. On the far-away horizon clouds were floating like a flock of sheep where the sky melted into the sea. They sailed until the boat looked like a speck in the distant sea.

While most of the men were out to sea fishing, the village was peaceful and dull. Occasionally the old men took their grandsons with them and sat in the cool shade of the boats or beside the rocks. That was about all they did.

On the third day Old Man Yun was aroused by the feeling of something unusual, and he went out to see Old Man Pak. Old Man Pak, too, was going down to the beach with the same feeling of uneasiness.

The two old men sat on the sand beside a rock.

"Look at the tail of that cloud!" Old Man Yun opened his mouth first.

"Uhm!"

The column of cloud was moving like a dark flame towards the northwest from the southeast.

"Look! Look at the color of the water!" Old Man Yun said again, excitedly.

Old Man Pak had already seen everything even before he was told to. It was an omen of something menacing, no mistake. A slow billow beat the shore. That was not a mere wave. Whenever it came, it sent forth a strong salty smell. There could be no mistaking their feelings.

"They went toward Taema, eh?" Old Man Pak asked, though he knew the answer.

"Well, they are just following a school of mackerel. They hadn't any set course. They might have gone to Ullung Island."

The two old men had nothing further to say. The sun was already covered by the dark cloud. Even the wind had stopped blowing. The oncoming waves were growing higher and higher. Whenever the billow broke, there was a strong salty smell. The two old men stood up without exchanging a word and then set out, each to his own home. Their experienced judgment had always been right. The disaster most feared by the two old men presented itself at last. It was a dreadful night!

The jet black night. The heavy rain driven by the hurricane! The roaring sea! All that could be seen were waves like mountains. It seemed as though the age-old wrath of the infuriated sea exploded all at once, crushing the water savagely with his white teeth.

The roaring waves swallowed the stone walls beyond the sand and demolished several houses. The villagers gathered in the ancestral hall on the hill.

Day dawned. The hurricane passed and the roaring of the waves ceased. All were quiet as the day began. The hamlet that morning was beyond description.

One man died that night. He was Old Man Yun. According to his daughter-in-law, Old Man Yun came out of his stone walled garden, leading her and her son. But for some unknown reason, he went back into the house, telling her to go ahead. After that nobody knew what happened to him.

The old sea was rippling on the sand as though it knew nothing of the past calamity. The sun was hot and the sky sapphire-blue. But the mackerel boat did not show up again. The village sank into bottomless grief. Two days later, the owner of the watch tower came back with a newspaper and read the news that many fishing vessels were missing. The village gave itself up to uncontrollable sorrow. Grievous crying was heard from every house. Two more days passed. At last they wearied of crying. It was not a problem that could be solved by crying.

"They cannot be dead," said the wives drawn to the shore by vain expectation. Anyway, they had to live. They lived by the sea and died by the sea. Hae-sun had a stronger faith in Song-gu's return than any other wife. Meanwhile three mouths had to be fed. Hae-sun went to the sea in her diving suit.

The wives picked seaweeds and dug up clams. But occasionally, as though they were reminded, they stood up and gazed out at the horizon with hands shading their eyes. When they spotted a sail passing far off, their hearts would thump like drums in their expectation.

It was the sand eel season, but there was no dragnetting. The watch tower had been standing there roofless since it had been blown away. The owner was in no mood yet to repair it. During the summer nights, deprived even of their dragnet fishing, the wives used to gather on the sand. The woman who had come back from the village fair told about the prices and what she had heard on her way back. This was news and joy for them. They did not realize the passing of the night, burying their feet in the cool sand.

"What a soft pillow!" Suki's mother said, laying her head on Hae-sun's lap.

"Where is the owner of the pillow?" someone said.

The wives sighed softly.

> "Eheya deya! Eiya deya!
> Sails on an ebbing tide.
> Away they went
> blown by the southwesterly wind."

Suki's mother began to sing, looking into Hae-sun's eyes.

> "Eheya deya!
> Come back riding on a coming tide
>   blown by the easterly wind,
>   Eheya deya."

The wives began to chant all together, but were soon choked by their emotion.

"You bunch of mischievous widows! What are you up to?" It was none other than Ch'il-song's mother.

"That would sound much better if you weren't a widow yourself," Man-ni's mother said.

"Well, that depends. I'm a forty-year-old widow, you see? But you lousy widows! Why don't you sleep? You are missing men, aren't you?" Ch'il-song's mother said, sitting on the sand with her legs stretched out.

"You'd better not argue with us. They say a woman widowed in her teens can last without a man, but a woman widowed at forty ..."

"Oh! Shut up, you sluts! I'll round up a bunch of men for you. You can do whatever you ..." Ch'il-song's mother said.

"Oh! Sister! Don't worry about us, you do whatever you wish to do."

They laughed hoarsely.

The summer had gone while they were passing the time thus. They wasted away that autumn season which should have been full of various fish. They were busy for a time picking and cutting various seaweeds—sweet, prickled, green, and brown. It was already the kelp season.

During the kelp season, Hae-sun was more valuable

than gold to the whole village. The best kelp is found always down on the bottom, a fathom and a half deep. There was no one but Hae-sun who could dive that deep in the cold season. The kelp that was brought up by Hae-sun was bunched into a braid by the waiting wives and then laid on the rocks to be sun-dried. By the end of March, the kelp season was over.

One night, Hae-sun fell asleep like a log after a day's hard diving. She didn't know exactly when it was, but she was aroused by a certain sense of pressure with which she was familiar. It was done already. She tried to scream, but she was almost breathless and her tongue dry. She clasped at his coat desperately. However, her body was dragged back into the misty memories of Song-gu. She released the coat in spite of herself.

"What is this? Am I a . . . ?"

Hae-sun was astounded at herself when she came to her senses. As though she had wakened from a dream, she seized his hair and held his head against her breast. The man was reaching for the door with his foot.

"Who's that?" her mother-in-law said in a clear voice. Hae-sun did not know what to do.

"It's me, I'm going out to the privy," Hae-sun answered, wetting her lips with her tongue. And then she released the hair, opening the door noisily. Hae-sun could sleep no more that night because of her thumping heart.

She went to the sea again next day to gather kelp. In one corner of her mind she could not forget the memory of the night before, even in her breathless diving. On her way back, she collected sea-urchins and made soup for her mother-in-law.

"You'd better lock your door before you sleep," her

mother-in-law said, dipping the soup appreciatively.

Hae-sun could not raise her face. Instead of answering, she poured more hot soup into her mother-in-law's bowl.

Hae-sun was drying isinglass, spreading it on the rocks beside "Chamber Crag."

"Hae-sun, dear!" a masculine voice was heard.

Hae-sun, surprised, covered her breasts with her arms. It was Sang-su, an employee of the watch tower. Hae-sun acted as if she had heard nothing.

"Hae-sun, dear! Let's live together," Sang-su said, approaching her slowly.

Hae-sun, scantily clad in her diving suit, was dazzled by the feverishly shining eyes of Sang-su. She turned around without saying a word.

"Listen! Song-gu's gone. What are you torturing yourself for?"

She did not answer.

"Let's go back to my native village. Back in my home we have rice paddies and patches of farmland."

His father and mother lived comfortably in his village. Since his graduation from primary school he had been living happily, like other young fellows. His wife had died two years before, and since then he had been a roamer. His aunt was the owner of the watch tower, and since he had arrived at her house, he had been loafing there.

"How about it, Hae-sun dear?"

Sang-su put his hands on her shoulders. Hae-sun stood up, shaking them off. But he caught her arms instantly and he would not let them go. While they were struggling, a fishing boat was seen approaching them. Hae-sun stooped behind a rock. Meanwhile Sang-su succeeded in dragging her into the safety of Chamber Crag.

"Hae-sun, dear! Let's have a wedding ceremony, after selecting a good day."

"Oh! No! I hate you."

"Really?"

"Let me go! The sun is setting!"

"Well, then listen to me just once."

"Listen to what?"

Sang-su put his arms around her waist. Hae-sun twisted one of his fingers savagely, loosening herself from his hold.

"I'll spread the news if you don't listen to me."

"What news?"

"The news that you and I did something."

"When . . . ?"

"I mean on the night you grabbed my hair."

Hae-sun realized what he meant. It was her greatest secret, kept in a hidden corner of her mind. She lost herself in her anger and took her clam knife from her belt. Sang-su, alarmed, stepped back a few steps.

"I'll stab you, if you touch me again!" Hae-sun said coldly, raising the knife over her head.

"I won't touch you again! Please, dear! Listen to me once."

"You are spreading the news, aren't you?"

"No, I will not. So, please let me . . ."

"You are going to act familiar with me, aren't you?"

"No! No! Just listen to me once!"

Hae-sun, who was brandishing her knife wildly in her frenzy, was more lovely to him than she was terrifying. She could not shake off the memory of the night completely in spite of her threatening knife. Her upraised arm sank gradually below her cheek. Her eyelids were getting creamy and her eyes tenderer.

"Hae-sun, dear!" Sang-su said, drawing a step nearer to her.

Hae-sun backstepped with her knife raised again; as Sang-su came a step closer to her she began to wave her knife wildly in the air.

"Don't come any nearer! I'll stab you if you do!" Hae-sun warned.

"How I would like to be stabbed by you! If you stab me, I'll die holding you in my arms," he said, pointing at the lower end of his neck, "Just stab here, it's a vital point. Understand?"

Hae-sun shook herself once in revulsion. Sang-su came a step nearer once more.

"I won't stab you. So, please don't come!" she said in a trembling voice, leaning against a rock.

"My body longs to be stabbed by you. Stab me quick and let's die together," he said with burning eyes. Nevertheless his lips quivered as if he were inwardly smiling.

"What a wicked man you are," said she, peering into his eyes and throwing away her knife.

"Shall I sharpen it a little for you? This knife is too blunt to . . ." he said, picking up the knife and feeling the blade with his fingers.

"How can you be so wicked?"

"So you can slice my neck as you slice open a shell."

"What a cruel thing to say! You are just like a pirate."

"How I'd like to be one!"

"I'll go. . . ."

"Kill me first and then you can go!"

"Oh, my goodness! What do you want me to do?"

"Listen to me just once."

"Tell me quick then. . . ."

Sang-su threw his arms around her neck. But she shook him off. Crouching down, he began to strip the clothing from her shoulder.

That evening she made him promise several times not to spread the news. However, before two days were over, the women began to whisper that Sang-su and Hae-sun were in love.

It was the mackerel season again, but nothing had been heard of Ch'il-song's fishing boat. In the evenings, the wives gathered on the strand.

Old Man Pak, who was Ch'il-song's father, had been in bed since the catastrophe, because of some unknown disease. Ch'il-song's wife, announcing it as her father-in-law's order, told the wives to have a mourning ceremony in each home on the anniversary of the hurricane. All of the wives agreed to do so. It meant eight mourning ceremonies in one day in "H" village.

"You'd better marry again after the mourning," Hae-sun's mother-in-law said two days before the ceremony. "You are too young to be widowed."

Hae-sun was dizzy as if she had been struck a heavy blow on the head.

"There is a good man for you to marry. I have been asked several times already about your second marriage, but I am postponing it until the mourning is over. You may know whom I mean!"

Hae-sun could not help blushing. Of course, it was none other than Sang-su. Hae-sun's head sank gradually as if it were pressed down by a weight.

"A widow knows well how another widow feels. I can understand you because I was widowed in early life myself. I'm more sorry for you than for my son who died. Your brother-in-law is going to sea pretty soon. So don't worry about our food. . . . "

The next day, the rumor that Hae-sun was going to be married to Sang-su spread all over the village. The women were disheartened and sad at the news because they loved her so much. Some of them were tearful. Hae-sun was the idol of the whole village, particularly loved by the wives. She was lovely and she was gay and joyful. She never gossiped and she never told lies, and what would they do when the kelp season came? The wives could not help sighing.

But simple, innocent Hae-sun accepted the vague idea that everyone should marry a man after they had been together. While she was considering such things, she had to go to live, like the wife of the owner of the watch tower, with Sang-su to his home.

The village, deserted by Hae-sun, was lonely and sad. There was plenty of kelp on the sea bottom a fathom deep; however, nobody dared dive into the cold water to harvest it. From the end of spring to the beginning of summer was the hardest time for the villagers to live. They had consumed almost all of the grain that was harvested in the fall, and the summer grain was not yet ripe. Most of the villagers were living on seaweed.

It was mackerel season. The wives gathered on the sand three days before the second mourning ceremony.

"There'll be neither top shells nor earshells on the mourning table this year."

"They may understand why we can't arrange the table with a rice meal, but with the sea so near, I wonder how we can explain that . . ."

"The sea ghosts can't be consoled without top shells and earshells."

While they were saying such things someone rushed towards them with a joyful cry. It was Hae-sun.

"Isn't this the new bride?"

"New bride! What's the matter with you?"

"Did you come for the mourning?"

"How about your new groom?"

"Oh my dear," Suki's mother said, holding Hae-sun's cheeks gently in her palms as if she were welcoming her own daughter's homecoming from her husband's home.

"You've lost a little weight!"

"Sit down here so we can look at you," Ch'il-song's mother said.

"Are you all well, sisters?" Hae-sun managed to ask as the wives surrounded her.

"Have you seen your mother-in-law?"

Hae-sun nodded her head, without saying a word. As her mother-in-law looked at Hae-sun, she tried to say something, but her lips trembled and her eyes were full of tears. Nobody knew whether the tears were for her lost son or for her daughter-in-law who came back not forgetting her dead husband's mourning day. Hae-sun went into her room first and looked at her diving suit and tools. They were still there untouched in a basket on the shelf. Hae-sun was relieved to see them safe. Then she returned to the beach.

"I won't go back! I'll live here with you, sisters, from now on," she said.

She stood up suddenly and looked at the sea, breathing deeply. That was the salty smell which she had longed for so deeply. The wives, without uttering a word, looked into each other's eyes.

Hae-sun could not bear mountain life any longer after Sang-su was forced to go away, recruited as a. worker in a hard labor force. As she was working at the soy bean patch in early summer, she was choked by the stagnant atmosphere. After she had picked coarse weeds for a while, there was no more strength in her arms. On such occasions Hae-sun had visions of the wide spreading sea. If she could only dive into the cool water in her diving suit. . . . Hae-sun could not control her maddening desire to see the ocean.

It was the mackerel season again. One fine day Hae-sun threw away her weeding hoe and rushed up the hillside. But she could not behold the sea from there. She kept on climbing the mountain desperately, but there was no ocean to be seen. After this, there was a rumor among the villagers that she was haunted. Sang-su's people called a witch to their home and while they were busy preparing Shaman rites, she slipped out of the house, rolling down her sleeves. She ran the whole distance of thirty *ri* without a pause.

"You mean it, really?" Suki's mother asked eagerly. "Speak, please. Tell us so that we may understand what has happened to you."

"When I went to the broom corn strip, the broom corn looked like kelp, and when I went to the bean patch, the bean plants looked like the rippling waves of the sea. . . ." Hae-sun explained.

"So what?"

"I just kept on climbing the hillside in sheer hope of seeing the ocean, but there was no sea. . . . "

"And how about your new groom?"

"It's a long time since he left as a conscript laborer."

"What a pity!"

"Sang-su's people said that I was haunted."

The wives made little sounds of pity.

"I won't go back, even if I die for it! I'll just live here with you, sisters!"

At that moment the gong was heard pealing loudly from the watch tower.

"Ah! It's the dragnetting!"

"It means sand eels!"

"Won't you join us?"

"Why not?" Hae-sun said, cheerfully.

"Come out quickly. Just wear a skirt," Suki's mother said, directing her.

Hae-sun came out quickly in her working clothes. The wives marched to the watch tower proudly, Hae-sun walking in front of them. The half moon was hanging above the top of Mt. Tarum. The sand eels swam in the moon's patch in the water.

"Dehya, deya!"

It was a fine school of sand eels; they didn't often see so many.

—TRANS. BY KIM DAE-YUN

Shadow

[REPUBLIC OF KOREA]

by Hahn Moo-sook

IN THE END Son-hui never got to the funeral. She fluttered, picking up and putting down again the white handbag and gloves that now lay scattered over the little dressing table like white flower petals. She was unsettled and restless.

The hands of the cuckoo clock on the wall pointed to two o'clock and the cuckoo bird called twice. Son-hui had a fleeting illusion of all the weight going out of her body.

"It's too late now . . . too late."

She wanted to get out of going. But another voice inside her murmured:

"It probably hasn't started yet. It's not too late."

Suddenly she pulled herself together, stood up, and collected the handbag and gloves. A moment later she had slumped back into the chair, as though exhausted. The bag and gloves fell to the floor and the contents of the bag spilled out. She pressed her hands to her forehead as though she were trying to hide her eyes, which were already closed.

She had that feeling of weightless floating again. And the space where she seemed to float was echoing with one person's name. For her that name had meant everything to her in a previous world. For a long time past it had been her satisfaction and her sorrow. Whether together or apart, it had always been with her. In fact, it had been her life.

He was dead.

The sky had caved in.

He was dead. He was dead.

At first she had been angry. A senseless, impotent rage it had been. A meaningless anger that could be vented on no one.

Everything was over, but she could not accept the fact of his death. Everything seemed to be finished, and her mind was a confused and exasperated blank. It was difficult to know exactly why. It might have been because she had not seen him after he was dead, or it might have been an attempt to deceive herself because she did not want to believe that he was no longer alive.

The afternoon sunlight shone through the paper of the window screens and reached right through her closed eyelids, so that she was enclosed in a wine-colored twilight. Her sadness mounted slowly.

"Was I really the last page of his life, where he could not write his own existence?"

She grew more miserable as her tears flowed. She shook her head as though she were trying to free herself from her thoughts but did not realize what she was doing. What she saw against the wine-colored background was not his passionate expression of affection, but a wornout and exhausted man, seen from behind. He had looked like that from behind when they had parted.

There were stains on his back. She had averted her eyes so as not to see these marks on the clothes he had worn far too long and she had not been able to wash. It wrenched her heart. She could not see the back she had fondled and loved, but only the back of some distant, distant, unknown person. Maybe in her mind she was deliberately tormenting herself with the recurring memory of that parting, using it to deepen her distress.

She could not go on torturing herself indefinitely. If she could think of him only as some distant unknown person, then her life had been empty, and the last forty years had been time passed in vain.

She shook her head more determinedly. Every word he had said to her, every caress—she recalled them as precious gifts in a life of joy, but she had not been there when he died, not heard the last words of his lips, not been able to moisten those parched lips. Yet he had been the one who had given meaning to her life, and she had no regrets that she had devoted herself entirely to him. She had known that she could never be his wife in the proper sense, but she had opted for the second best and been prepared to spend her days as his "shadow wife." She had lived with a fleeting sense of sin that made her tremble in the midst of her delight with him. It had not happened often, but when his family had complained he said :

"Son-hui, I cannot go on with it any longer. I can't keep on like this. I shall have to pull myself together and get a divorce. This double life is too much."

When he said that, he had clasped her hand and looked deep into her eyes. Tears had welled up from under her eyelids, not so much like salt water as like long-buried crystals, translucently erupting.

She whispered as though she were terrified :

"How can you do that to a woman who has done nothing wrong? What about the children?"

That night after Yong-ho had gone she had not been able to sleep. He had said he would divorce his wife and marry her, but because he was scared of a row in his beastly family he had gone home without staying the night. Whatever sort of a woman was she to believe him?

She loved him quite sincerely, and because she was sincere she wanted to be faithful to him, but her unhappy mind kept returning to the idea of sin and guilt. Could it be wrong to be loyal to your own heart? She had not the courage to press her thoughts to their conclusion. She thought she could put up with anything rather than lose him.

She first met Yong-ho in the summer of her nineteenth birthday. It was in the south, at Pusan. Yong-ho had been enlisted in the student militia, but since he was assigned to the harbour guard at Pusan, he had not been sent overseas. Nevertheless he was very depressed with the worsening course that the war was taking, and had lapsed into self-pity about being a Korean in a Japanese army uniform.

Then he had seen the pretty young Son-hui on the wharf. He was struck by her shapely arms set off by the short sleeves of her dress, and the youthful perfection of her throat. He was a Seoul man, and it seemed to him that she was a rare woman from some distant land. She was buying odd-looking red seafruit.

He was a well-bred youth, and maybe it was only because he was wearing army uniform that he could bring himself to speak to a strange girl, but however it happened, he went up to her and said :

"What are they called?"

Son-hui was astonished to be spoken to in Korean by a soldier in a Japanese uniform—indeed, too surprised to answer. Yong-ho realized his rudeness and blushed. Barely conscious of what he was saying, he stammered :

"I . . . it's the first time I've seen them. What are they called?"

She answered him simply :

"In the dictionary it's *monggi,* but down here they say *unmonggaji."*

He was not yet used to the southern accent mixed with the standard language, and the girl's voice sounded like music in his ear.

"What do they taste like?"

Son-hui did not answer, but took the fish-seller's knife, split open one of the nipple-like buds on the monggi, and dug out the kernel-like center.

"At first it tastes a bit dry, but the aftertaste is good."

She offered it to Yong-ho. He had never seen such an uninhibited type of girl in Seoul, but he mastered his distaste at the appearance of the thing and ate it.

"You seem to be Korean. How come you're in the Japanese army? Are you a student militiaman?" she asked.

"Why do you treat me as though I was a fool on a string?"

Yong-ho's answer was more truculent than before. The southern girl, very sensitive to nuances of speech, was silent again. She opened her eyes wide, but she looked at the ground.

After a moment she looked him straight in the face and said :

"Since there's nothing to wait for, I'd better be going." And she closed her pretty lips tightly.

This was again something entirely fresh to him, something he had never seen in a Seoul girl. He hated to part from her.

After that they met frequently. They swore friendship. Sometimes when he was on guard duty at the military storehouse on the wharf she would come to buy fish and speak to him from a distance with sign language.

The truth was that they were both lonely people. Son-hui had grown up lonely as the only daughter of a widowed mother. They still retained some property and so life was not difficult, but when the girl wanted to go to Tokyo for more study her mother had fasted for three days to persuade her not to go. Yong-ho discovered that mother and daughter were living in constant tension.

The fact that Son-hui had such a life drew him even closer to her. He himself had lost both parents and had grown up in the care of his only brother, who was older than himself. He had been bright from childhood, but he had only just managed to get into college by earning his living as a family tutor. Then he had been drafted into the army. He had been used to laughing bitterly about it all, but "since I met Son-hui," as he would say to himself, getting called up had come to seem like the best thing that had ever happened to him.

The two passed their days as it were on the waves of a moonlit sea. They forgot the bad state of the war and his hated uniform : the Seoul lad in the enemy livery and the southern girl with her sweet accent had their eyes on far horizons, where they were sailing in a dream-laden white boat. The crying of the gulls was the only disturbance they recognized in life, and they were roused to a new zest for living.

So summer passed and winter was drawing on.

One day when Son-hui was out on the wharf Yong-ho came running up, grasped her by the hand and dragged her off towards the fish auction halls. In the mornings the place was crowded, but now in the afternoon the vast concrete space was simply an empty barracks.

Yong-ho looked around without moving his head, merely swivelling his eyes, and then started speaking in a whisper.

"Son-hui! Something terrible's happened. I'm not absolutely sure, but it seems pretty certain that our unit is moving to North China. The Americans have already landed on Okinawa and the Japs are preparing for a last stand."

Son-hui caught her breath in surprise.

"What can we do?"

He came closer to her and pressed her two hands in his :

"Son-hui, I've made up my mind. Help me. I've got to desert."

Her eyes and hands expressed her agreement with his determination. She looked straight into his eyes and pressed his hands to her side. She was waiting for him to say more.

"I'm not quite sure, but I think we'll leave the day after tomorrow, at dawn. I can't think of a good plan on the spur of the moment, so we'll have to see how things turn out. I might slip away in the confusion—but that's practically impossible. Even in wartime you can't expect so much confusion that I could pass unnoticed in daylight. Or I might jump out of the train. I could kill myself doing that. And you have to choose the spot for doing it. Or then . . ."

He thought of several things, but none were really practicable. Son-hui trembled with anxiety. She kept shaking her head.

"Here. First find out exactly when you are to leave. Then I will get hold of a suit of Korean clothes. Before you get on the train you'll be formed up in ranks. You must pretend to go to the lavatory or to buy a pencil or something. Anyway, get out of line and go to the station. I'll wait there with the clothes and then you can change. Your hair is cropped, but nowadays so many civilians have cropped hair that it won't matter."

"I don't know whether they will let a man go to the . . ."

"In that case you'll have to put on a bit of play-acting. You could look over there and shout out in surprise as though you saw somebody come to see you off, and then you would have to put a bold face on and speak to the sergeant."

But that did not seem a very good idea either. However, they decided to make a start and, in default of any definite plan, to prepare for something like Son-hui's idea by her going to see what the crowd at the station was like and then meeting again in the same place an hour later.

When she got to the station and took a look at things, she was sure that her idea was a sound one. In all that mess of people and baggage and dirt it would be a great deal easier to lose oneself than to find somebody else. But for certainty's sake she stopped a passing railway-man and asked him :

"Can I buy a ticket now for tomorrow morning's train?"

"Not in advance. They start selling them two hours

before they open the wicket, but it's a struggle to buy one. Look at all these people. They are all waiting to buy tickets."

Son-hui feigned ignorance :

"Oh, I say! Some of them must sleep in the waiting room."

"I should say so. It's full to the doors night and day. Trains go every hour, but the place is always so full of people it seems that nobody ever really gets away."

The man seemed to think he had been talking quite long enough, even to a pretty girl :

"You'd better get somebody to wait in the line for you," he said, and walked off. Son-hui's heart missed a beat as she watched him go.

She went straight back to the fish market. Yong-ho appeared. He was still not certain of the departure time, but it would be sometime between tomorrow morning early and the dawn of the day after. He was worried that he might have aroused suspicion by being with her for so long, so he returned quickly.

Son-hui went to see her aunt. With goods being in such short supply due to the war, she did not want to go to the market. She made up a story about a play at church and managed to borrow a suit of Korean clothes that belonged to her uncle.

That evening she told her mother that her best friend was about to get married and so she wanted to go and spend a few nights with her beforehand. Her mother complained about it but in the end gave in and allowed Son-hui to go for two nights.

Son-hui got out the old spectacles from the drawer of the desk her father had left when he died. Like an old-fashioned country gentleman, though his sight was neither long nor short, he had used spectacles for the sake of smartness. They were a bit big for Son-hui, and slipped on her ears, but they were plain glass, which was good. She said that the bundle in which she had wrapped her uncle's clothes was the change of dress she would be needing at her friend's house, and stuffed the spectacles inside it. Then she left the house.

As soon as she came out of the alley she started running. When she was away from her own neighborhood she got the glasses out of the bundle and put them on. Plain glasses worn for effect were suitable for both men and women, which was lucky for her.

That evening she started her wait, squatting near the smelly concrete urinal on the station. All the benches were so full of people that finding a seat was harder than catching flies by hand. She simply had to wait.

Night came on the crowded station that was already like a little hell. People were sleeping on their bundles all over the concrete and Son-hui had to pick her way among them as she walked to and fro between the lavatory and the railing, from which she could see the platform.

The crowds of passengers might succumb to sleep, but the station itself kept awake all night long. Train whistles sounded in the dark, and the trains themselves were shunted from one line to another, and having arrived at a new place let off hissing jets of steam.

Morning came, but no troop of soldiers had appeared. She would have to wait for another day.

It was another night with the same noises and confusion and filth. But still no soldiers. Nor the next day . . .

On the third morning, after three days without a wash, she went down to the wharf. She asked one of the men who worked at the fish auction halls, or the fruit market, or somewhere, whether the same troops were still looking after the military supply stores.

"Who knows anything about the army? But it looks as though they've changed the guard. They went out by launch to the battleship that was moored beyond the island."

Son-hui did not hear the end of his sentence. She had fallen in a dead faint on the concrete, among the fish scales and entrails and all the other filth.

In the autumn after the armistice of the Korean War, thirteen years later, the refugees were preparing to return. Many of them had grown very much attached to the Pusan people during their long stay, and many parties were being held before they returned.

Son-hui had a big beauty parlor on a very busy street, and perhaps it was owing to its favorable situation that she had so many customers. She was so young that they did not call her "Madam" but said "Miss So," which was very appropriate because she was still not married. But although she was so young, she ran a first-class establishment and she had many regular customers.

It was impossible to guess her age. Her complexion was fresh and her lips were fulsome, and she had the color of a girl of twenty, but there was a look in her eyes that suggested a lifetime of experience. She was cheerful and direct in her manner, and this seemed to attract the Seoul people, who sensed she had something that they lacked. As a result the local people tended not to patronize her, but Son-hui was rather pleased to have so many regulars from the refugee crowd. So it was only natural that when the Seoul ladies were preparing to return to the capital Son-hui should go along with them for an outing to the hot springs before they left.

They chose to go to a hotel that had been established in what had formerly been the holiday villa of some important Japanese official. It was not particularly well appointed, but it was said to be at the source of the warm springs and the garden was a famous one.

Son-hui was usually the center of the group, but for some reason or other she became detached and found herself walking in the garden alone. She had come out of the hot bath and had vague thoughts of cooling herself, so passing through the huge rhododendrons she stopped by a camellia, and stood watching a clear little stream that trickled out of a bamboo watercourse. As usual when she was alone, her face was clouded by a worried expression. Little birds twittered in the thick foliage of the quiet garden. Mingled in the sound of the trickling water she heard the sound of men laughing and of a stringed instrument being played.

She was standing in her usual abstracted state. Suddenly she started, as if her dream had been broken. She lost interest in the clear water droplets. She turned to move off in the direction of the voices, then stood as still as one of the trees around her.

A man with piercing eyes had appeared and was standing by a cedar tree, looking at her. He was of middle height, with a broad forehead and a straight nose and firmly closed lips. It must be Yong-ho, who had gone away to South China with no hope of return, but who had returned nevertheless.

Son-hui laughed a little bitterly, and shifted her stance. She had never been able to forget Yong-ho, but it would be silly to invite a repetition of her former experience.

The man still stood looking at her. Son-hui always prided herself that she could stare any man out. Trying to look friendly, she moved towards him as though to pass him, but he spoke to her :

"Are you by any chance So Son-hui, whose Japanese name was Shiroyama Yoshiko?"

That voice! Son-hui could not answer. The blood drained from her face. Her eyes burned like a blue flame, without expression. It was the look of a person who was about to fall. Yong-ho stepped forward and caught hold of her. Son-hui felt her whole body penetrate his breast.

Cuckoo! Cuckoo! Cuckoo!

The cuckoo clock struck four.

Son-hui opened her eyes and took her hand from her forehead. She looked in the mirror and saw herself sitting there in her white dress. Her cheeks were shiny and a few hairs straggled over her puffy face. She was more lonely than sad.

She looked dispassionately at the face, as though it belonged to someone else. She recognized the quality of the make-up. She had done it expertly. She had done her very best to get ready for the funeral.

His death was her death, his burial was the burial of her womanhood, and time had come to have no meaning for her. She had lived to the moment of truth, and now she was dumbfounded to find that she had so decked herself out for this day of all days. She saw herself tremble. New understanding began to dawn upon her.

If she had really been his wife she would have had her hair loose round her shoulders and rough hempen cords round her head and waist. She felt herself the most evil of women for having gone so far as to make her eyes sparkle when he was dead.

Misery took complete control of her and she slid to the floor in a paroxysm of weeping.

She had closed the shop from the day his death was announced. She seemed to think that the funeral was taking place in her own home, and so no normal activities could be carried on there. The employees had no idea why the place was being closed. Some of them were happy to get a holiday and others worried whether the closedown would last long or not. Life is like that. It is never plain and simple. She thought she might go to the funeral, but she could not show too much public grief. Superficially, at least, there should be no flaw on the last stage of the masquerade of her life. Her light make-up had not been so much an attempt of vanity to make herself pretty as a token of effort in the attempt to bear with her wretchedness.

She imagined the funeral house. As a southerner she did not know the Seoul customs. Since she did not know the details, the things she did know came even more vividly to her mind's eye. The screens would be set up. His corpse was at the end of the room and at the other the wife and children would be kneeling and wailing on the straw. The guests would come with tears and words of comfort for the bereaved.

"Such a fine man to die so young. . . ."

The widow's wailing rises in a crescendo and she begins to call his soul.

"There'll never by anyone else like him! Why did he have to go so soon? He was so different."

And more floods of tears.

Which was more pathetic, the noisy sorrow of the

funeral house or the empty tidiness of this room, would be hard to say. In both places the thought was the same : "How can we go on living?" They bewailed his death and his love. And their own fate.

Son-hui was not usually given to weeping. Since she had grown up she had only wept twice before : once when she had met Yong-ho again in the garden at the hot springs, and once when they had secretly visited a Buddhist temple together. Son-hui, who had been so honest in her days on the wharf, had earned her mother's anger by her lying. Her mother had not been able to believe that the two young people had not been kissing, so she was caught up in the scandal. Son-hui had not wept then. She had thought their love too precious.

She still had on the table in her room a temple bell made of sandalwood with a tassel that was fading with age. It was a souvenir of their visit to the temple. The temple was in Ch'ungch'ong province and they had taken advantage of the fact that Yong-ho had to travel in that area. They had started on the journey separately. He was going near to his family birthplace, and it was the first time in years that he had been able to visit the family graves. He pleaded that he did not need anyone to accompany him on a sad journey to a remote valley, so that he could set off alone.

In the temple, where no one knew them, they were accepted as husband and wife. Indeed they looked like a comfortable and well-established middle-aged couple.

Son-hui made a generous offering before the Buddha, because she wanted to express her happiness. It may have been due to a particular feature of the period of the temple furnishings, whatever that period may have been, but the many Buddhas were not the usual grotesque idol figures. They seemed rather to be portrait figures of individuals. Especially the Avalokiteshvara beside the principal image in the main hall of the temple seemed to have a body that throbbed with sensual life through the draperies of the robe, and in the picture hanging on the wall the uncovered belly of a cross-legged Buddha seemed to exude a warm body temperature.

Son-hui had no particular sense of sin at being before these images with her lover. She had not believed in Buddhism and so she could uninhibitedly accept the caresses of her friend in front of the statues.

The next morning after breakfasting on herbs and seaweed they came down from the temple and met a monk who saluted them, bowing with hands joined. He seemed to have guessed that they were due more than usual courtesy because of the unusually big offering. He showed them around and told them the history of the temple, including the fact that the place had once been forbidden to all women and how the principal statue and the cross-legged Buddha were famous for miracles and had many stories told about them. He went on to tell them one of the stories.

Once upon a time the widowed daughter-in-law of a great family, who was not able to sleep well, nevertheless had a brief dream. In the dream she became a flower blossom. But the flower was not blooming: it was burning and writhing in the heat. The fire could not be put out until a ray of light came from the west and extinguished the fire and left a smell of charring. She woke in the half light, feeling deeply ashamed. She interpreted the dream as expressing her uncontrollable physical desire. She eventually came to think that the direction from which the ray of light had come to put out the fire had been the direction of this temple with the miraculous cross-legged Buddha in it. To rid herself of her distress she came to the temple to bathe herself in the Buddha's compassion. Although she waited prostrate at the gate for three days like a penitent sinner, owing to the strict regulation forbidding women to enter the temple she could not go in. So she went across the valley and founded a little hermitage where she began to live as a nun. But there was no image of the Buddha there, because she was devoted to the Buddha she could not see.

"The hermitage is still here, just round the shoulder of the mountain."

The monk finished his long tale.

Tears started to course down Son-hui's face. Thinking of the old days when women were looked down on and could be considered unclean by Buddhism, she could not help herself. The young widow was unable to love anybody living, and could only quieten her desires by attaching her love to the Buddha. Son-hui knew she was confusing religion with physical feelings, but she could not help thinking that worshipping the unseen Buddha was rather like the way she loved Yong-ho.

Yong-ho was gentle and he may have understood her feeling, for he took her hand and stroked the back of it gently. The lines on his forehead stood out clearly in the morning sunlight, and his eyes seemed to well with tears.

Son-hui's feelings grew unhappier. Time passes like water flowing, but her heart told her that everything does not pass away with it. There is a truth that lasts. Here she had thrown herself before it.

When she had met Yong-ho in the garden at the hot

springs villa seven years earlier, he already had a wife. She no longer had the presumptuous hopes that she had seven years earlier, but she wept for pity.

It was not that the wife was in Son-hui's way with regard to Yong-ho; but his situation grieved her. She herself just wanted to have a man's love and enjoy it. She thought it would have been wrong to put away a wife who was the daughter of a benefactor, and so she herself had chosen to live in the shade.

She thought of how he was a prominent businessman with a happy family, like a man in a monthly magazine story.

"Life is only real when I am with you," he would say. "All the rest is empty, false deceit."

But in that "empty deceit" his children were born one by one, and Son-hui could find no real consolation for herself. If Yong-ho suggested making a settled arrangement, for some reason she could not understand she only felt even more wretched. Very few people knew what was between them. It was impossible to guess the secret of Son-hui's sorrow.

After her mother had died and she had cleared up the family affairs, she had sold the shop in Pusan and moved to Seoul, simply to be near to Yong-ho. She had a big beauty shop in the center of the city. She was pretty, cheerful, successful, and friendly. But at thirty-nine she remained unmarried. She had no men friends, but was very popular with all the women who came to the beauty parlor.

Thinking about it now, although Yong-ho's love had something to do with his health, other people would have seen him as a man with a double life, a sex devil in a gentleman's mask. He might not have seen himself like that, but the double life took its toll of him and his love.

That love was so precious to Son-hui. She had lit the fire in his breast, and had she not relied on it? However she looked at it she could not see that he was a hypocrite or an egoist. Perhaps she had just become an infatuated woman who had lost her critical faculties. Even in her dreams she was troubled by the change in his attitude.

This had been going on for more than six months. When they did meet, Yong-ho was not really affectionate. He even failed to turn up two or three times. He was forty-five, an age when a man is in his prime, so it was strange that he should be quiet when meeting a secret lover. Maybe married people begin to lose some of their sexual energy at that age, but Son-hui was not with him all the time. When she thought over the changeableness of men she grew giddy. Sometimes after they parted she felt she was no better than a prostitute. If a man's love is to be gauged simply in physical terms, then her choice of the shadow role had been a fearsome mistake.

Yong-ho's visits became less and less frequent. When they met he looked at her as though caressing her with his eyes, and she struggled inwardly. She read the misery in those eyes and it overflowed into her own soul.

The last few months had been a time of frigid whirling outrage for her. It had been a time of tyrannous passion, but she had given him her warmest love.

Cuckoo! Cuckoo!
The cuckoo clock on the wall sounded longer this time. It was six o'clock. The room faced south but the quick sunset of autumn meant that it was already

growing gloomy. Son-hui was motionless on the floor. She felt not only that the weight had all gone out of her body, but that the whole content of her life had slipped away with it. His wife might not have had his love, but she still had something of him left after his body was gone. A widow had a tombstone, and his children and his reputation and the rest of his achievement. Son-hui had nothing but the memory of his love, and even that was vain and empty.

There was a polite cough and the sliding door opened. The faithful maid, who had lived with her for a long time, came quietly into the room.

"It's getting dark. Shall I put the light on?"

Son-hui lay where she was and answered blankly.

"I don't want it."

The maid stood where she was for a moment and then moved over to the window as silently as a shadow.

"It's getting chilly," she said, and drew the warm curtains.

Inside the room it became even darker. The maid went out as quietly as she had come in, and Son-hui did not move. Her dim form soon became invisible in the complete darkness. The pretty little room might have been empty, save only for the ticking of the clock.

—TRANS. BY RICHARD RUTT

Poonek

[MALAYSIA]

by Lim Beng Hap

THE TELEGRAPH bell rang for slow as the launch was about to enter the river from the sea. The roar of the engine changed to a low hum, and the voice of a sailor throwing a lead-line from the bow of the boat could be heard chanting to the juragon on the bridge.

"Four feet above the mark."

"Four feet."

"Four feet below the mark."

"Three feet!"

The water gathered together and formed into rows of racing waves which pushed the boat, rolling and creaking, over the bar. The keel hit the sand several times with a hard bump. The breakers sprayed over the deck, splashing the passengers and adding to the miseries of those suffering from seasickness.

"Three feet and a half."

"Four feet above the mark."

"Five feet."

A triumphant "Six feet!" and the boat was over the bar. The telegraph bell clanged happily for full speed ahead in the calmer water. The seasickness disappeared as if by magic, and the launch glided into the brown river water leaving the pale green sea behind, far away.

A young man called Mahsen was one of the passengers and, being a Melanau, of a seafaring race, he was not affected by the sea throughout the voyage. He was going home after ten years at school; but home was still a further two hours upriver so he sat down on some boxes and looked at the scenery about him. Nothing had changed, he noted. Like the mouths of most of the rivers on that stretch of Sarawak coast, there was a belt of casuarina trees which extended on both shores, their needlelike leaves sighing in the salt winds. The river mouth was humming with activity, flashing a bright grin at the blue sky as the waves gambolled over the sandbar. Mahsen knew that the river mouth was not always peaceful like this; in rough weather it really showed its teeth, bellowing and snapping angrily at the lowering sky while rain pelted down onto the wind-swept sea and land.

The launch chased the lapping wavelets inland until the clear sand gave place to mud and mangrove trees lined both banks of the river. Fiddler crabs peeped shyly out of their mudholes at the passing launch whilst a solitary band of kera monkeys foraged among the twisted mangrove roots for shellfish. Occasionally on the branch of a tree a sea eagle stared at the water in deep concentration.

The salty tang of the air soon gave way to the sourish smell of rotting fronds as the graceful nipah palms began to appear in unending rows on the banks, their leaves rustling and clapping in the river breeze. Kingfishers in gay plumage darted in and out of the shadows. For several miles up the winding river these palms nodded and swayed, sometimes revealing a little hut or two, hidden behind their waving branches; at last their ranks began to thin out and the lush jungle behind managed to extend to the river's edge. There, in the bend of the river, was an untidy huddle of houses. Mahsen had come home to his village.

The launch tied up at a floating jetty in front of the small but inevitable Chinese bazaar. Mahsen elbowed his way out of the crowd of people who were jostling against the passengers and shouting to the crew to find out the whereabouts of their goods. Mahsen's mother was waiting for him with her two brothers. He took her hands in his and kissed them in greeting. He shook hands vigorously with his two uncles, forgetting that the custom of his people only requires a perfunctory handshake and the immediate covering of the heart with a hand. Allowing his uncles to carry his baggage he led his mother along the very short main street, at the end of which was the kampong road leading to his house which stood amongst a conglomeration of others on the river bank.

That night Mahsen was "at home" to his relations and friends. He sat in the middle of the bare living room, cross-legged on the floor, while his callers sat around him in a circle; a few talked, but most of them sat tongue-tied, in awe of the returned scholar. His sister, Boonsu, fussed around bringing out cups of coffee and platefuls of cakes for the visitors. The older women talked with his mother behind a portable screen. In the kitchen the young girls helped Boonsu to pour out the coffee and to bake sago cakes.

Mahsen's attention was caught by the twitter of voices and laughter coming from the kitchen. From the doorway an array of bewitching faces scrutinized him. Amongst them he could see Louisa, a cousin many times removed and a constant companion in the days when they both still wore very little clothing and played at make-believe below the house. Now she had grown into a beautiful maiden with sleek black hair reaching down to her waist. Her lips were colored red by the juice of the sireh and her beauty was further enhanced by a short nose and two bright eyes. Her skin was fair and had the delicate texture of porcelain. Her body was rounded but trim as a result of hard work in the sago outhouse which is a part of all Melanau houses. From the giggles and delighted shrieks of the other girls, Mahsen suspected that Louisa was being teased about him.

His surmise proved to be correct; when the excitement of homecoming had died down, his mother called him one afternoon to her own particular corner of the house. Here for years she had sat cutting and trimming the canes that she would later weave into a variety of baskets and handbags, and sell to the shops for the money which had kept Mahsen at school.

Mahsen sat before her, full of respect as he looked at her deft fingers weaving the colored strips of cane into an intricate pattern for a sewing basket. She came to the point at once, "Louisa's father wants you to marry her. He likes you and will only take a token dowry for her but you must become a Christian to marry her. I like Louisa and so does Boonsu."

Mahsen sat silent for a while, thinking. Then he said, "I like Louisa too, but I think of her as a sister, not wife. I don't want to marry yet. I want to improve the rubber garden and sago groves that Father left to us. There is no other reason; I am not thinking of any other girls in the town or here. I am not particular whether I become a Christian or a Mohammedan or remain a pagan as I am now. In this kampong we are a mixed community living happily together because we are all part of the Melanau race."

"But Louisa's father wants to give his daughter away to you. You know what that means. I have not much money in the house—only a few jars, and some porcelain that are our family heirlooms. I cannot afford a big dowry."

"But what does Louisa think about this?" asked Mahsen.

"She said she will do as her parents wish," chimed in Boonsu from the kitchen doorway.

"There you are," exclaimed Mahsen in triumph, "she does not love me enough to say so. How can I marry her?"

"You silly man," cried Boonsu, "she was saying yes in an old-fashioned way."

"But that does not mean she loves me. Old-fashioned, huh? Tell her father I won't marry her," said Mahsen with an air of finality, putting on a shirt so that he could go out and escape from the discussion.

"Now you are Poonek," said Boonsu gravely.

"What? Poonek? Rubbish! You people are full of false beliefs, like our neighbor next door calling in an exorcist to get the devils out of his body when he had only a cold from a night spent netting prawns in the river! The old crone who performed the ceremony was screeching nonsense and beating a drum the whole night long, disturbing everybody's sleep. If our neighbor continues like that he will surely die of exhaustion from lack of sleep, not from his illness which a few pills bought in the bazaar could cure."

"My son," said Mahsen's mother, "I do not believe in the babayoh ceremony like the man next door, but our ancestors taught us certain rules of behavior: if we are offered a good thing we must take it, or at least make a token acceptance, lest we offend the giver who wishes to share his property, food, or drinks with us. Thus we believe that refusal is bad behavior, and that it brings bad luck to the refuser."

"And so," Mahsen continued for his mother, "one becomes Poonek, liable to be stung by a scorpion, centipede, or perhaps a poisonous snake or, worse still, be struck dead by lightning. What a silly belief! I can't see why anybody should be in the wrong because he says 'No thank you' to the kind invitation of a friend to share his dinner."

"Saying thank you is not enough, son, there is still the act of refusal. You must touch the food or drink offered to you, first lightly with your finger, to be free from Poonek, especially if you are leaving in a hurry for the jungle, or to go on the river."

"Pooh!" scoffed Mahsen, "what do I have to do now after refusing to accept Louisa? Go and kiss her to be free from my Poonek?" Mahsen laughed at the idea.

"You are very rude to Mother," protested Boonsu.

Mahsen said he was only joking and walked out of the house to terminate the discussion. He was only a few yards from his house when he saw Louisa coming through the hibiscus hedge of a nearby house. She waited by the roadside when she saw Mahsen and plucked one of the red flowers to stick into her hair which she had tied into a bun at the back of her head. She was wearing a long blue baju over a black sarong. Another sarong of Javanese pattern was slung over one shoulder, always at hand to shield her from the curiosity of strangers or the hot sun.

"How proud you are these days," she said when Mahsen reached her side; "you did not even call at our house when you came back. My mother was talking about you this morning saying that you have forgotten all of us."

"Why, that's what I am just going to do; I am going to your house now," lied Mahsen gallantly. "This is one ant that is ever willing to die in the sweetness of your honey."

"You are always joking, Mahsen," she said, pleased by his flattery. "Come, let us walk side by side as we did many years ago."

Mahsen was surprised to find himself as happy as ever with her. He sang the songs he used to tease her with, and she laughed and joked back as if they were still in their fig-leaf days.

Thus they walked on completely absorbed in one another, but stopping now and then to acknowledge the greetings of friends from the windows and doors of houses. In a number of the sago outhouses by the riverside, the village maidens, their wet clothes clinging to them, stopped their work of washing sago to shout and wave at the pair. The smell of sago waste permeated the atmosphere; the wind which was strong enough to flap the lofty coconut trees could not blow it away. Fowls and ducks scratched in the mud below the outhouses.

When Louisa's house came into sight Mahsen suddenly realized that he was empty-handed, and it would be bad mannered to visit such old friends without a small gift; he looked around the kampong for signs of a shop. There was no shop but he noticed a long roofed-in boat lying in the mud, with the river lapping at its exposed propeller. It was a floating shop with a tin number-plate nailed to its side. Mahsen led Louisa to the little clearing which served as a public landing place; he told her to wait, and stepped over several small boats, going up to his ankles in mud at the water's edge.

On the bank Louisa was attracted by two ripe guavas on a nearby tree. The tree was not difficult to climb; the trunk was short and the branches gave easy footing. She climbed up until she reached the highest branch, stretched for the fruit, and leaned back then to rest, enjoying the slight swaying motion of the tree in the light breeze which heralded the returning tide, and watching Mahsen as he reached the floating shop.

The boat hawker was squatting on his haunches in the mud, armed with some tools and caulking his boat with oakum. He was looking for the small but troublesome cracks which let water in near the bottom of his boat.

"Ah Pek Ah Pong," called Mahsen, "have you got some chocolates?"

The man peered at him. He was old and had plied his trade up and down the river for more years than Mahsen could remember.

"Aiya!" exclaimed the old man, "Mahsen big fellow now, huh! Come, help Ah Pek find the little holes."

Mahsen squatted down, feeling for slight cracks with his fingers in the well-painted side of the boat. He wiped some of the mud away.

"Watch out, Mahsen, watch out!" Mahsen turned to

look at Louisa. She was still sitting on the branch of the tree, but now she was pointing towards the water.

"Buaya!" she screamed. "A crocodile!" Mahsen looked at the river. The water was still. There was scarcely a ripple. The tide was about to turn. The boat's propeller glistened in the sunshine.

Ah Pek Ah Pong started to move towards the front of the boat. This is a poor joke on the part of Louisa, Mahsen thought. How could she know that his family considered him Poonek?

"No, no," shouted Louisa, "don't move that way. The crocodile is on the other side of the boat. It is coming up the mud bank!"

Mahsen took in the situation in a flash. This particularly wily crocodile was coming round the fore part of the boat to charge them into the river! A bit of the snout appeared round the corner. Louisa screamed again.

"Aiya! Aiya! Mati-lah, mati! Tua Pek Kong, tolong, tolong!" howled Ah Pek Ah Pong, looking at the now much longer black snout.

Mahsen grabbed the old man and pushed him towards the stern, then he lifted him and heaved and pushed until Ah Pek Ah Pong disappeared over the side, into the boat, accompanied by a crash of broken crockery as he landed in the kitchen of his floating shop.

Mahsen looked up again. The beast was already facing him with its mouth wide enough to swallow him whole!

The animal was ready for a charge. In an instant it came, as fast as an arrow, as big as a log, plunging along, ploughing a sheet of black mud into the air.

But Mahsen was also fast. He whipped round the

stern of the boat and ran up the mud bank feeling as though his heart would burst. He could hear the crocodile slap into the water like a cannon shot. He reached the top of the bank exhausted.

Louisa was waiting for him, white-faced. He felt he would like to fall down before her and kiss her foot! Hundreds of faces now appeared, the afternoon's indolence broken by the noise. Men came out with spears and guns. Ah Pek Ah Pong let off crackers and waved joss-sticks to the heavens in thanksgiving to Tua Pek Kong.

Three months later Mahsen and Louisa were on their way to Kuching for a belated honeymoon. A kindly sailor had cleared a space in the fore-part of the launch for them to spread their bedding. The river mouth was before them, grinning as amiably as ever in a long white line of breakers. Louisa was going to cross the bar for the first time. Her eyes were wide and sparkling as she listened to the chanting voice.

"Three feet above the mark."

"Three feet and a half below the mark."

"Three feet."

"Four feet above the mark."

"Five feet."

Then the triumphant "Six feet!"

They were over the sand bar. The ship lurched and rolled and a thousand banging noises joined the discordant coughing of the engine. Louisa moaned; she was experiencing the first twinges of seasickness! She looked pale, but she was still beautiful. Mahsen kissed her.

"Stop it," she said, "people may be looking."

"I don't want to be Poonek on the high seas," whispered Mahsen happily.

The Jade Bracelet

[MALAYSIA]

by Mary Frances Chong

SIEW MAY had been playing "masak-masak" with the twins. Everything had been fine until she refused to eat the rice they had cooked over a real fire. It was a horrid day. She pattered into the cool of the house. As she crossed the hall, the clock struck three. It was almost time for the hawker to be coming along. She thought of his bucket of gluey sweet. At times when he felt generous, he would dip into his pail and scoop up a sizeable amount to wind round the ten-cent stick. It would be brown, golden brown, very sticky, very sweet. You could suck it, or nibble the edges, or, best of all, by gripping a bit between the teeth, pull fine plastic strips from the whole and pile or loop them into all sorts of shapes. And it would last for at least a quarter of an hour or more if you happened to get an especially large blob. At the thought, she made her way swiftly to her grandmother's room. She saw her mother and uncle together. They were whispering urgently. She was just able to catch her uncle's last words, ". . . send her to Sam Poh Tong at once."

"Mama! Uncle!"

"Shh! Not so loud.... Run along now, Uncle and I are very busy.... No, don't go in—Grandmother is very ill."

"Why?"

But her mother was already pushing her away.

As she watched her daughter scampering off, Mrs. Wong heaved a sigh of relief. Really, Siew May's interminable questions often tried her patience. Only the Lord Buddha knew the trials she had undergone. For years she had been nursing her bedridden mother. Why, even the neighbors were perpetually surprised at the extent of her filial devotion. It was indeed fortunate that one of these good people had happened to visit her that morning. Earlier, Mrs. Wong had brought her mother the breakfast broth which she had carefully prepared with her own hands. But not a mouthful was taken. So Mrs. Wong gave in to what she thought was the old woman's peevish whim. Never would she permit any word of complaint to pass through her lips—not a single word. But Mrs. Lee had been so concerned that she allowed herself the luxury of the faintest sigh, expressing regretfully her own anxiety over her mother's growing fretfulness and the waste of the fine broth. Mrs. Lee was all sympathy and wished to pay the invalid a call. Mrs. Wong remembered gazing at her mother as she led the visitor into the room. She had never failed to be amazed, even irritated, that her mother contrived to look such a gaunt derelict despite all the solicitous care. The only flabbiness about her was the heavy folds of flesh under her eyes. Her hands were lined with cordlike purple veins. The jade bracelet appeared to be more like a manacle encumbering the bony length.

Meanwhile, the caller had stooped over the still form and recoiled. She was obviously in a state of agitation. In less than a second she was at the threshold beside Mrs. Wong.

"Aiiya! Your mother is dying . . . !"

The grandmother lay inert and quiet. The jade bracelet rested on her wrist—green, hard, smooth, placid. It was the one thing that could really be called her own. The rest, her earrings, chain, and rings, were safely tucked away. Her son-in-law who had been so liberal was often amused by her "hoarding." But the bracelet was part of her, it breathed with her. She could feel its coolness and calming smoothness; Siew May had loved swivelling it round her arm. Siew May would have it once she was gone. At least she could bequeath to her young one not an heirloom but something of her, that had been part of her. . . .

Puzzled and bewildered, Siew May wandered into the kitchen. Ah Ching was there peeling potatoes. Glum, sullen most times, she was not exactly cheerful company. Just a week ago, Siew May had to admit with an uncomfortable feeling akin to shame that her mother did not cook for the family. She was the odd one out, since all her three friends' mothers were the most domesticated creatures on earth. Ah Ching did all the housework. She was speaking to her now. Without removing her eyes from the potatoes nor pausing in her work, Ah Ching announced flatly, "Your grandmother is about to die. You know?"

"You lie. . . . Mama said she was ill and . . ."

This time the servant put down her knife and said with extreme deliberation, "She is so ill that she is dying."

Sitting in the car, Siew May wanted her grandmother to assure her that what Ah Ching had said was all nonsense. But something held her back, awed her into unusual silence, even frightened her. Her grandmother, bundled in a blanket, was propped up in the back seat. Her mouth opened and worked, making funny motions, but no word could be heard. It gaped grotesquely, speechlessly, and she was gasping as if she wanted to swallow the air. Grandmother did not speak. Nobody spoke.

The car swept up the drive of the cave temple, Sam Poh Tong, circumventing in a wide arc the lotus ponds glimmering in the late afternoon sun before grinding to a halt near a small assembly of nuns and monks. With a minimum of fuss, the grandmother was borne off to a specially arranged chamber. Two nuns came forward to direct the newcomers. Mounting the steps into the temple, they entered the main hall of worship from which branched a number of tunnels whose dark openings could be seen. The altar, massive, glittering with gold paint and vermilion lacquer, stood squarely in the centre of the hall. Gigantic effigies loomed on either side. The smoke of scented incense hung thick, slumberous, and acrid. It spread everywhere, choking the labyrinth of caves.

The passage they had to go through was a natural tunnel lit only by candles which flickered on innumerable statues almost concealed in the gloom of niches, either natural or man-hewn. Further on, with a rattle of beads, a nun rose from the shadows in which she had sat meditating or dreaming. She joined them. As they shuffled along, the tunnel echoed hollowly with the drip-drop of trickling water and the distant tock-tock beaten out rhythmically by the monks at prayers. They emerged upon an open courtyard, their eyes blinking in the light after the semi-darkness behind them.

Crossing the courtyard, Siew May spied a moss-encrusted pond partly protected by a crumbling stone balustrade. Queer black shapes bobbed to the surface of the murky green waters. Tortoises! But the little group was moving on rapidly. Perhaps later she could find an opportunity to feed them. As she caught up with the rest, it struck her that the nuns themselves looked very much like the tortoises they kept—hunched in their black robes with clean-shaven pates and long, pale, thin necks. She giggled; no one else saw the resemblance or found it funny.

Finally they arrived at the living quarters of the religious community. The rooms where they had to put up for the night were drearily uniform—yellowing mosquito nets, kerosene lamps on tables otherwise bare, and a few chairs. A mustiness pervaded and festered in the rooms, not unlike that of the incense—probably it was the mosquito nets this time.

Mrs. Lee and her brother made the necessary arrangements with the abbot. They were to stay in the temple until the grandmother "departed" and the funeral rites and cremation were duly carried out. The abbot coughed in the mustiness, and, just hesitating to recover his breath before resuming the thread of the discussion, delicately ventured a practical consideration. The coffin? Certainly the best wood possible—solid and spacious for repose. Yes, varnished without question! Such filial care! Mrs. Wong's generosity overwhelmed him. It drew from the venerable head the smallest involuntary protest . . . but who was he, a mere agent of the divine, to stifle such pious zeal? The donation would be put to needy use, the extension of an eastern wing perhaps.

Mrs. Wong, in a high state of pious fervor, burned two dozen joss sticks at one of the branch altars. This would be the last time that she had to shoulder the burden of her Duty. It seemed to her as if she was both daughter and son; Ah Kow was exasperatingly irresponsible. He had never been able to keep his interest and his job for long. He was lucky to have a brother-in-law who could resolve his financial difficulties. At the moment her husband was away in Hong Kong. So she had to make the decisions. Even had he been home he would not have been too pleased over being actively involved. It was rather fortunate that he was abroad. The last time he had followed a cortege, he was stricken down with fever for weeks and his business suffered. He had this allergy to deaths and funerals. Certainly superstitions were not to be scoffed at. She could manage quite well alone really.

All through the night she kept solitary watch as the dying woman lay with eyes open and staring, her breath coming in jerky rasps. Her vigil was at last relieved by a firmly insistent nun. Wearied to the bone, she sought the comfort of her bed. It seemed to her that she had barely slept for ten minutes when she awoke. It was cold but not chilly; yet she was suddenly seized by a spasm of quivering as if her very flesh was being loosed from her body. When the tremors had ceased, she was filled with uneasiness, foreboding, and an indefinable wretchedness. She threw a wrap around her shoulders and hurried out into the raw thin air of the morning. She was not aware of what she herself intended to do; but, before she had walked halfway across the court, she distinguished, with a sense of numbed shock, a billowing figure bearing down upon her. Mrs. Wong stood where she was until the nun, her robe flapping at her ankles, drew near.

"Your mother has passed away. ..."

She caught the words as they floated to her in the stillness. She had known, even before being told. Flesh had been sundered from flesh. All the mooring ropes were untied, the ship was cast adrift, its sails billowing in the dawn breeze.... A wave of acute loneliness and finality engulfed her; then the ship was caught and sucked by the churning waters; how it struggled to surface!

The nun stood hunched against the whipping cold wind—like a tortoise, Mrs. Wong thought. Did anyone notice the likeness, she wondered. Possibly not.

"I know. I shall be ready," she told the nun.

It was only as they hurried along in the gloom that Mrs. Wong realized that she was crying. The tears were wet and warm on her cool cheeks. All at once she felt hatred surging uncontrollably through her. She hated her husband, hated him!

At the cremation, the fire roared about the passive mother; the flames leaped and gyrated frenziedly like things alive, their tongues licked the coffin, charring the beautiful varnished surface—outside the closed furnace, the monks sat in straight-backed chairs chanting and keeping time to the wail of their instruments. A small group of nuns wept noisily with admirable efficiency; but even veterans' eyes and throats suffered dryness after a lengthy session. The abbot, resplendent in a bright, gaudy ceremonial gown, had offered incense, prayers, invocations, food, and wine. For Siew May the

spectacle and elaborate proceedings were a feast for
eyes and ears. However, as the night wore on, the novelty
wore off. She was tired, but she did not relish the alterna-
tive of the temple's hard bed and frowsy room. The
monks and nuns were perspiring under the hot red
glare of naked bulbs which shone on their bare heads
glistening with sweat and light. She longed for the clean,
cool sheets and well-plumped mattress of the bed at
home and the bedtime chats with Grandmother.
Suddenly, the nausea of homesickness was too much.
Why were they here at all?

"I want to go home. . . . Grandmother will be waiting
alone!"

Querulously loud and imperative, her voice startled
the lull in the lamenting and mourning. There was not
another sound to be heard. Then someone laughed.
Then everybody laughed. Everyone was uproariously
amused. Such naiveté in the child! The elderly members
of the temple, the "ancient," grinned, showing their
cavernous mouths. Her grandmother's mouth had
gaped too; then she remembered why they had to be
in the temple—because Grandmother was not at home
but burning in the furnace over there. Nevertheless, the
whole concourse was pleased with her. She must have
said something which they considered clever. Happy in
the applause she had received, Siew May fell asleep on
her mother's lap.

On the following morning, the aunt and cousins
managed to arrive in time for the collection of the bones
of the deceased. Each relative was given a pair of
chopsticks with which to pick from the ashes the bones
that could conveniently be stored in a porcelain urn.
Mrs. Wong chose to discard the chopsticks because the

remains of her own mother, she declared, appeared perfectly clean to her. The rest followed her example. During the sorting, the jade bracelet was discovered; it was amazingly whole—not a single crack flawed its surface; it was no longer clear green but semi-white, like concrete ash. All admired and wondered at its intact wholeness. The daughter held it gingerly in the palm of her hand. Her mother had given express instructions that the bracelet should be for Siew May. It was really an absurd fancy on the old woman's part. Mrs. Wong was a rather sentimental person. She had not been able to bring herself to remove the object before the cremation. Even the monks and nuns would have been horrified at her depriving her mother of such a treasured and familiar possession in the "other world." But now it seemed that the dead had taken a hand in safeguarding her perverse wish. Her musings were interrupted by Siew May.

"Can I have it? Can I—?"

"Absurd! Ridiculous!" said Mrs. Wong, as if she was voicing aloud her own thoughts, "Uncle will have it—Ah, Fook Kee, since you are the only son in our family you ought to take it."

"But Mama, grandmother said—"

But Siew May's mother, with extreme deliberation, handed over the heirloom to the dubious male successor.

Along Rideout Road
That Summer

[NEW ZEALAND]

by Maurice Duggan

I'D WALKED the length of Rideout Road the night
before, following the noise of the river in the darkness,
tumbling over ruts and stones, my progress, if you'd
call it that, challenged by farmers' dogs and observed
by the faintly luminous eyes of wandering stock, steers,
cows, stud-bulls, or milk-white unicorns or, better, a full
quartet of apocalyptic horses browsing the marge. In
time and darkness I found Puti Hohepa's farmhouse and
lugged my fiber suitcase up to the verandah, after
nearly breaking my leg in a cattlestop. A journey
fruitful of one decision—to flog a torch from somewhere.
And of course I didn't. And now my feet hurt; but it
was daylight and, from memory, I'd say I was almost
happy. Almost. Fortunately I am endowed both by
nature and later conditioning with a highly developed
sense of the absurd; knowing that, you can imagine the
pleasure I took in this abrupt translation from shop-
counter to tractor seat, from town pavements to back-
country farm, with all those miles of river-bottom
darkness to mark the transition. In fact, and unfor-

tunately there have to be some facts, even fictional ones,
I'd removed myself a mere dozen miles from the parental
home. In darkness, as I've said, and with a certain
stealth. I didn't consult dad about it, and, needless to
say, I didn't tell mum. The moment wasn't propitious;
dad was asleep with the *Financial Gazette* threatening to
suffocate him and mum was off somewhere moving,
as she so often did, that this meeting make public its
whole-hearted support for the introduction of flogging
and public castration for all sex offenders and hanging,
drawing, and quartering, for almost everyone else, and
as for delinquents (my boy!) ... Well, put yourself in
my shoes, there's no need to go on. Yes, almost happy,
though my feet were so tender I winced every time I
tripped the clutch.

Almost happy, shouting Kubla Khan, a bookish lad,
from the seat of the clattering old Ferguson tractor,
doing a steady five miles an hour in a cloud of seagulls,
getting to the bit about the damsel with the dulcimer and
looking up to see the reputedly wild Hohepa girl perched
on the gate, feet hooked in the bars, ribbons fluttering
from her ukulele. A perfect moment of recognition,
daring rider, in spite of the belch of carbon monoxide
from the tin-can exhaust up front on the bonnet. Don't,
however, misunderstand me : I'd not have you think
we are here embarked on the trashy clamor of boy
meeting girl. No, the problem, you are to understand,
was one of connection. How connect the dulcimer with
the ukulele, if you follow. For a boy of my bents this
problem of how to cope with the shock of the recognition
of a certain discrepancy between the real and the written
was rather like watching mum with a shoehorn wedging
nines into sevens and suffering merry hell. I'm not

blaming old STC for everything, of course. After all, some other imports went wild too; and I've spent too long at the handle of a mattock, a critical function, not to know that. The stench of the exhaust, that's to say, held no redolence of that old hophead's pipe. Let us then be clear and don't for a moment, gentlemen, imagine that I venture the gross unfairness, the patent absurdity, the rank injustice (your turn) of blaming him for spoiling the pasture or fouling the native air. It's just that there was this problem in my mind, this profound cultural problem affecting dramatically the very nature of my inheritance, nines into sevens in this lovely smiling land. His was the genius as his was the expression which the vast educational brouhaha invited me to praise and emulate, tranquilizers ingested in maturity, the voice of the ring-dove, look up though your feet be in the clay. And read on.

Of course I understood immediately that these were not matters I was destined to debate with Fanny Hohepa. Frankly, I could see that she didn't give a damn; it was part of her attraction. She thought I was singing. She smiled and waved. I waved and smiled, turned, ploughed back through the gull-white and coffee loam and fell into a train of thought not entirely free of Fanny and her instrument, pausing to wonder, now and then, what might be the symptoms, the early symptoms, of carbon monoxide poisoning. Drowsiness? Check. Dilation of the pupils? Can't check. Extracutaneous sensation? My feet. Trembling hands? Vibrato. Down and back, down and back, turning again, Dick and his Ferguson, Fanny from her perch seeming to gather about her the background of green paternal acres, fold on fold. I bore down upon her in all the eager erubescence of youth, with my hair slicked back. She trembled, wavered, fragmented and re-formed in the pungent vapor through which I viewed her. (Oh for an open-air job, eh mate?) She plucked, very picture in jeans and summer shirt of youth and suspicion, and seemed to sing. I couldn't of course hear a note. Behind me the dog-leg furrows and the bright ploughshares. Certainly she looked at her ease and, even through the gassed-up atmosphere between us, too deliciously substantial to be creature down on a visit from Mount Abora. I was glad I'd combed my hair. Back, down and back. Considering the size of the paddock this could have gone on for a week. I promptly admitted to myself that her present position, disposition, or posture, involving as it did some provocative tautness of cloth, suited me right down to the ground. I mean to hell with the idea of having her stand knee-deep in the thistle thwanging her dulcimer and plaintively chirruping about a pipedream mountain. In fact she was natively engaged in expressing the most profound distillations of her local experience, the gleanings of a life lived in rich contact with a richly understood and native environment : A Slow Boat to China, if memory serves. While I, racked and shaken, composed words for the plaque which would one day stand here to commemorate our deep rapport : *Here played the black lady her dulcimer. Here wept she full miseries. Here rode the knight Fergus' son to her deliverance. Here put he about her ebon and naked shoulders his courtly garment of leather, black, full curiously emblazoned—Hell's Angel.*

When she looked as though my looking were about to make her leave I stopped the machine and pulled out the old tobacco and rolled a smoke, holding the

steering wheel in my teeth, though on a good day I
could roll with one hand, twist and lick, draw, shoot the
head off a pin at a mile and a half, spin, blow down the
barrel before you could say:

Gooday. How are yuh?

All right.

I'm Buster O'Leary.

I'm Fanny Hohepa.

Yair, I know.

It's hot.

It's hot right enough.

You can have a swim when you're through.

Mightn't be a bad idea at that.

Over there by the trees.

Yair, I seen it. Like, why don't you join me, eh?

I might.

Go on, you'd love it.

I might.

Goodoh, then, see yuh.

A genuine crumpy conversation if ever I heard one,
darkly reflective of the Socratic method, rich with
echoes of the Kantian imperative, its universal mate,
summoning sharply to the minds of each the history of
the first trystings of all immortal lovers, the tragic and
tangled tale, indeed, of all star-crossed moonings, mum
and dad, mister and missus unotoo and all. Enough?
I should bloody well hope so.

Of course nothing came of it. Romantic love was surely
the invention of a wedded onanist with seven kids. And
I don't mean dad. Nothing? Really and truly nothing?
Well, I treasure the understatement; though why I
should take such pleasure in maligning the ploughing
summer white on loam, river flats, the frivolous ribbons,

and all the strumming, why I don't know. Xanadu and jazzy furrows, the wall-eyed bitch packing the cows through the yardgate, the smell of river water. .... Why go on? So few variations to an old, old story. No. But on the jolting tractor I received that extra jolt I mentioned and am actually now making rather too much of, gentlemen: relate Fanny Hohepa and her uke to that mountain thrush singing her black mountain blues.

But of course now, in our decent years, we know such clay questions long broken open or we wouldn't be here, old and somewhat sour, wading up to our battered thighs (forgive me, madam) at the confluence of the great waters, paddling in perfect confidence in the double debouchement of universal river and regional stream, the shallow fast fan of water spreading over the delta, Abyssinia come to Egypt in the rain ... ah, my country! I speak of cultural problems, in riddles and literary puddles, perform this act of divination with my own entrails: Fanny's dark delta; the nubile and Nubian sheila with her portable piano anticipating the transistor-set; all gathered into single, demesne, O'Leary's orchard. Even this wooden bowl, plucked from the flood, lost from the hood of some anonymous herdsman as he stopped to cup a drink at the river's source. Ah, Buster. Ah, Buster. Buster. Ah, darling. Darling! Love. You recognize it? Could you strum to that? Suppose you gag a little at the sugar coating, it's the same old fundamental toffee, underneath.

No more cheap cyn ... sm intended. She took me down to her darkling avid as any college girl for the fruits and sweets of my flowering talents, taking me as I wasn't but might hope one day to be, honest, simple, and broke to the wide. The half-baked verbosity and the conceit she must have ignored, or how else could she have born me? It pains me, gentlemen, to confess that she was too good for me by far. Far. Anything so spontaneous and natural could be guaranteed to be beyond me: granted, I mean, my impeccable upbringing under the white-hot lash of respectability, take that, security, take that, hypocrisy, take that, cant, take that where, does it seem curious?, mum did all the beating flushed pink in ecstasy and righteousness, and that and that and THAT. Darling! How then could I deem Fanny's conduct proper when I carried such weals and scars, top-marks in the lesson on the wickedness of following the heart. Fortunately such a question would not have occurred to Fanny: she was remarkably free from queries of any kind. She would walk past the Home Furnishing Emporium without a glance.

She is too good for you.

It was said clearly enough, offered without threat and as just comment, while I was bent double stripping old Daisy or Pride of the Plains or Rose of Sharon after the cups came off. I stopped what I was doing, looked sideways until I could see the tops of his gumboots, gazed on *Marathon*, and then turned back, dried off all four tits and let the cow out into the race where, taking the legrope with her, she squittered off wild in the eyes.

She is too good for you.

So I looked at him and he looked back, I lost that game of stare-you-down, too. He walked off. Not a warning, not even a reproach, just something it was as well I should know if I was to have the responsibility of acting in full knowledge—and who the hell wants that? And two stalls down Fanny spanked a cow out through the flaps and looked at me, and giggled. The summer sun thickened and blazed.

The first response on the part of my parents was silence: which can only be thought of as response in a very general sense. I could say, indeed I will say, stony silence; after all they were my parents. But I knew the silence wouldn't last long. I was an only child (darling, you never guessed?) and that load of wood-chopping, lawnmowing, hedgeclipping, dishwashing, carwashing, errandrunning, gardenchoring, and the rest of it was going to hit them like a folding mortgage pretty soon. I'd like to have been there, to have seen the lank grass grown beyond window height and the uncut hedges shutting out the sun: perpetual night and perpetual mold on Rose Street West. After a few weeks the notes and letters began. The whole gamut, gentlemen, from sweet and sickly to downright abusive. Mostly in mum's masculine hand. A unique set of documents reeking of blood and tripes. I treasured every word, reading between the lines the record of an undying, all-sacrificing love, weeping tears for the idyllic childhood they could not in grief venture to touch upon, the care lavished, the love squandered upon me. The darlings. Of course I didn't reply. I didn't even wave when they drove past Fanny and me as we were breasting out of the scrub back on to the main road, dishevelled and, yes, almost happy in the daze of summer and Sunday afternoon. I didn't wave. I grinned as brazenly as I could manage with a jaw full of hard boiled egg and took

Fanny's arm, brazen, her shirt only casually resumed, while they went by like burnished doom.

Fanny's reaction to all this? An expression of indifference, a downcurving of that bright and wilful mouth, a flirt of her head. So much fuss over so many fossilized ideas, if I may so translate her expression which was, in fact, gentlemen, somewhat more direct and not in any sense exhibiting what mum would have called a due respect for elders and betters. Pouf! Not contempt, no; not disagreement; simply an impatience with what she, Fanny, deemed the irrelevance of so many words for so light and tumbling a matter. And, for the season at least, I shared the mood, her demon lover in glossy brilliantine.

But as the days ran down, the showdown came nearer and finally the stage was set. Low-keyed and somber notes in the sunlight, the four of us variously disposed on the unpainted Hohepa verandah, Hohepa and O'Leary, the male seniors, and Hohepa and O'Leary, junior representatives, male seventeen, female ready to swear, you understand, that she was sixteen, turning.

Upon the statement that Fanny was too good for me my pappy didn't comment. No one asked him to: no one faced him with the opinion. Wise reticence, mere oversight, or a sense of the shrieking irrelevance of such a statement, I don't know. Maori girls, Maori farms, Maori housing: you'd only to hear my father put tongue to any or all of that to know where he stood, solid for intolerance, mac, but solid. Of course, gentlemen, it was phrased differently on his lips, gradual absorption, hmm, perhaps, after, say, a phase of disinfecting. A pillar of our decent, law-abiding community,

masonic in his methodism, brother, total abstainer,
rotarian, and non-smoker, addicted to long volleys of
handball, I mean pocket billiards cue and all. Mere
nervousness, of course, a subconscious habit. Mum
would cough and glance down and dad would spring
to attention hands behind his back. Such moments of
tender rapport are sweet to return to, memories any
child might treasure. Then he'd forget again, straight,
mate, there were days, especially Sundays, when mum
would be hacking away like an advanced case of t.b.
Well, you can picture it, there on the verandah. With
the finely turned Fanny under his morose eye, you know
how it is, hemline hiked and this and that visible from
odd angles, he made a straight break of two hundred
without one miscue. Daddy! I came in for a couple of
remand home stares myself, bread and water and solitary
and take that writ on his eyeballs in backhand black
while his mouth served out its lying old hohums and
there's no reason why matters shouldn't be resolved
amicably, etc., black hanging-cap snug over his tonsure
and tongue moistening his droopy lip, ready, set, drop.
And Puti Hohepa leaving him to it. A dignified dark
prince on his ruined acres, old man Hohepa, gravely
attending to dad's mumbled slush, winning hands down
just by being there and saying nothing, nothing, while
Fanny with her fatal incapacity for standing upright un-
supported for more than fifteen seconds, we all had a
disease of the spine that year, pouted at me as though it
were all my fault over the back of the chair (sic). All my
fault being just the pater's monologue, the remarkably
imprecise grip of his subject with consequent prolifera-
tion of the bromides so typical of all his ilk of elk, all
the diversely identical representatives of decency,

caution, and the color bar. Of course daddy didn't there and then refer to race, color, creed, or uno who. Indeed he firmly believed he believed, if I may recapitulate, gentlemen, that this blessed land was free from such taint, a unique social experiment, two races living side by side, respecting each others etc. As a banker he knew the value of discretion, though what was home if not a place to hang up your reticence along with your hat and get stuck into all the hate that was inside you, in the name of justice? Daddy Hohepa said nothing, expressed nothing, may even have been unconscious of the great destinies being played out on his sunlit verandah, or of what fundamental principles of democracy and the freedom of the individual were being here so brilliantly exercised; may have been, in fact, indifferent to daddy's free granting tautologies now, of the need for circumspection in all matters of national moment, all such questions as what shall be done for our dark brothers and sisters, outside the jails? I hope so. After a few minutes Hohepa rangatira trod the boards thoughtfully and with the slowness of a winter bather lowered himself into a pool of sunlight on the wide steps, there to lift his face broad and grave in full dominion of his inheritance and even, perhaps, so little did his expression reveal of his inward reflection, full consciousness of his dispossessions.

What, you may ask, was my daddy saying? Somewhere among the circumlocutions, these habits are catching, among the words and sentiments designed to express his grave ponderings on the state of the nation and so elicit from his auditors (not me, I wasn't listening) admission, tacit though it may be, of his tutored opinion, there was centered the suggestion that old man Hohepa and his daughter were holding me against my will, ensnaring me with flesh and farm. He had difficulty in getting it out in plain words; some lingering coward-ice, perhaps. Which was why daddy Hohepa missed it, perhaps. Or did the view command all his attention?

Rideout Mountain far and purple in the afternoon sun; the jersey cows beginning to move, intermittent and indirect, towards the shed; the dog jangling its chain as it scratched; Fanny falling in slow motion across the end of the old cane lounge chair to lie, an interesting composition of curves and angles, with the air of a junior and rural odalisque. Me? I stood straight, of course, rigid, thumbs along the seams of my jeans, hair at the regulation distance two inches above the right eye, heels together, and bare feet at ten to two, or ten past ten, belly flat, and chest inflated, chin in, heart out. I mean, can you see me, mac? Dad's gravesuit so richly absorbed the sun that he was forced to retreat into the shadows where his crafty jailer's look was decently camouflaged, blending white with purple blotched with silver wall. Not a bad heart, surely?

As his audience we each displayed differing emotions. Fanny, boredom that visibly bordered on sleep; Puti Hohepa, an inattention expressed in his long examina-tion of the natural scene; Buster O'Leary, a sense of complete bewilderment over what it was the old man thought he could achieve by his harangue and, further, a failure to grasp the relevance of it all for the Hohepas. My reaction, let me say, was mixed with irritation at certain of father's habits. (Described.) With his pockets filled with small change he sounded like the original gypsy orchestra, cymbals and all. I actually tried mum's old trick of the glance and the cough. No luck. And he went on talking, at me now, going so wide of the mark, for example, as to mention some inconceivable, undocumented, and undemonstrated condition, some truly monstrous condition, called your-mother's-love. Plain evidence of his distress, I took it to be, this obscenity uttered in mixed company. I turned my head the better to hear, when it came, the squelchy explosion of his heart. And I rolled a smoke and threw Fanny the packet. It landed neatly on her stomach. She sat up and made herself a smoke and then crossed to her old man and, perching beside him in the brilliant pool of light, fire of skin and gleam of hair bronze and blue-black, extracted from his pocket his battered flint lighter. She snorted smoke and passed the leaf to her old man.

Some things, gentlemen, still amaze. To my dying day I have treasured that scene and all its rich implications. In a situation so pregnant of difficulties, in the midst of a debate so fraught with undertones, an exchange (quiet there, at the back) so bitterly fulsome on the one hand and so reserved on the other, I ask you to take special note of this observance of the ritual of the makings, remembering, for the fullest savoring of the nuance, my father's abstention. As those brown fingers moved on the white cylinder, or cone, I was moved almost, to tears, almost, by this companionable and wordless recognition of our common human frailty, father and dark child in silent communion and I too, in some manner not to be explained because inexplicable, sharing their hearts. I mean the insanity, pal. Puti Hohepa and his lass in sunlight on the steps, smoking together, untroubled, natural, and patient; and me and daddy glaring at each other in the shades like a couple of evangelists at cross pitch. Love, thy silver coatings and castings. And thy neighbors! So I went and sat by Fanny and put an arm through hers.

The sun gathered me up, warmed and consoled; the bitter view assumed deeper purples and darker rose; a long way off a shield flashed, the sun striking silver from a water trough. At that moment I didn't care what mad armies marched in my father's voice nor what the clarion was he was trying so strenuously to sound. I didn't care that the fire in his heart was fed by such rank fuel, skeezing envy, malice, revenge, hate, and parental power. I sat and smoked and was warm; and the girl's calm flank was against me, her arm through mine. Nothing was so natural as to turn through the little distance between us and kiss her smoky mouth. Ah yes, I could feel, I confess, through my shoulder blades as it were and the back of my head, the crazed rapacity and outrage of my daddy's Irish stare, the blackness and the cold glitter of knives. (Father!) While Puti Hohepa sat on as though turned to glowing stone by the golden light, faced outward to the violet mystery of the natural hour, monumentally content and still.

You will have seen it, known it, guessed that there was between this wild, loamy daughter and me, sunburnt scion of an ignorant, insensitive, puritan, and therefore prurient Irishman (I can't stop) no more than a summer's dalliance, a season's thoughtless sweetness, a boy and a girl and the makings.

In your wisdom, gentlemen, you will doubtless have sensed that something is lacking in this lullaby, some element missing for the articulation of this ranting tale. Right. The key to daddy's impassioned outbrust, no less. Not lost in this verbose review, but so far unstated.

Point is he'd come to seek his little son (someone must have been dying because he'd never have come for the opposite reason) and, not being one to balk at closed doors and drawn shades, wait for it, he'd walked straight in on what he'd always somewhat feverishly imagined and hoped he feared. Fanny took it calmly; I was, naturally, more agitated. Both of us ballocky in the umber light, of course. Still, even though he stayed only long enough to let his eyes adjust and his straining mind take in this historic disposition of flesh, those mantis angles in which for all our horror we must posit our conceivings, it wasn't the greeting he'd expected. It wasn't quite the same, either, between Fanny and me, after he'd backed out, somewhat huffily, on to the verandah. Ah, filthy beasts! He must have been roaring some such expression as that inside his head because his eyeballs were rattling, the very picture of a broken doll, and his face was liver-colored. I felt sorry for him, for a second, easing backward from the love-starred couch and the moving lovers with his heel hooked through the loop of Fanny's bra, kicking it free like a football hero punting for touch, his dream of reconciliation in ruins.

It wasn't the same. Some rhythms are slow to reform. And once the old man actually made the sanctuary of the verandah he just had to bawl his loudest for old man Hohepa, Mr. Ho-he-pa, Mr. Ho-he-pa. It got us into our clothes anyway, Fanny giggling and getting a sneezing fit at the same time, bending forward into the hoof-marked brassiere and blasting off every ten seconds like a burst air hose until I quite lost count on the one-for-sorrow two-for-joy scale and crammed myself sulkily into my jocks.

Meantime dad's laboring to explain certain natural facts and common occurrences to Puti Hohepa, just as though he'd made an original discovery; as perhaps he had considering what he probably thought of as natural. Puti Hohepa listened, I thought that ominous, then silently deprecated, in a single slow movement of his hand, the wholly inappropriate expression of shock and rage, all the sizzle of my daddy's oratory.

Thus the tableau. We did the only possible thing, ignored him and let him run down, get it off his chest, come to his five battered senses, if he had so many, and get his breath. Brother, how he spilled darkness and sin upon that floor, wilting collar and boiling eyes, the sweat running from his face and Fanny, shameless, langorous, and drowsy, provoking him to further flights. She was young, gentlemen: I have not concealed it. She was too young to have had time to accumulate the history he ascribed to her. She was too tender to endure for long the muscular lash of his tongue and the rake of his eyes. She went over to her dad, as heretofore described, and when my sweet sire, orator general to the dying afternoon, had made his pitch about matters observed and inferences drawn, I went to join her. I sat with my back to him. All our backs were to him, including his own. He emptied himself of wrath and for a moment, a wild and wonderful moment, I thought he was going to join us, bathers in the pool of sun. But no.

Silence. Light lovely and fannygold over the pasture; shreds of mist by the river deepening to rose. My father's hard leather soles rattled harshly on the bare boards like rim-shots. The mad figure of him went black as bug out over the lawn, out over the loamy furrows where the tongue of ploughed field invaded the home paddock, all my doing, spurning in his violence anything less than this direct and abrupt charge towards the waiting car. Fanny's hand touched my arm again and for a moment I was caught in a passion of sympathy for him, something as solid as grief and love, an impossible pairing of devotion and despair. The landscape flooded with sadness as I watched the scuttling, black, ignominious figure hurdling the fresh earth, the waving arms seemingly scattering broadcast the white and shying gulls, his head bobbing on his shoulders as he narrowed into distance.

I wished, gentlemen, with a fervor foreign to my young life, that it had been in company other than that of Puti Hohepa and his brat that we had made our necessary parting. I wished we had been alone. I did not want to see him diminished, made ridiculous and pathetic among strangers, while I also brashly joined the mockers. (Were they mocking?) Impossible notions; for what was there to offer and how could he receive? Nothing. I stroked Fanny's arm. Old man Hohepa got up and unchained the dog and went off to get the cows in. He didn't speak : maybe the chocolate old bastard was dumb, eh? In a minute I would have to go down and start the engine and put the separator together. I stayed to stare at Fanny, thinking of undone things in a naughty world. She giggled, thinking, for all I know, of the same, or of nothing. Love, thy sunny trystings and nocturnal daggers. For the first time I admitted my irritation at that girlish, hic-coughing, tenor giggle. But we touched, held, got up, and with our arms linked went down the long paddock through the infestation of buttercup, our feet bruising stalk and flower. Suddenly all I wanted and at whatever price was to be able, sometime, somewhere, to make it up to my primitive, violent, ignorant, and crazy old man. And I knew I never would. Ah, what a bloody fool. And then the next thing I wanted, a thing far more feasible, was to be back in that room with its shade and smell of hay-dust and warm flesh, taking up the classic story just where we'd been so rudely forced to discontinue it. Old man Hohepa was bellowing at the dog; the cows rocked up through the paddock gate and into the yard; the air smelled of night. I stopped; and holding Fanny's arm suggested we might run back. Her eyes went wide: she giggled and broke away and I stood there and watched her flying down the paddock, bare feet and a flouncing skirt, her hair shaken loose.

Next afternoon I finished ploughing the river paddock, the nature of Puti Hohepa's husbandry as much a mystery as ever, and ran the old Ferguson into the lean-to shelter behind the cow shed. It was far too late for ploughing: the upper paddocks were hard and dry. But Puti hoped to get a crop of late lettuce off the river flat : just in time, no doubt, for a glutted market, brown rot, wilt, and total failure of the heart. He'd have to harrow it first, too; and on his own. Anyway, none of my worry. I walked into the shed. Fanny and her daddy were deep in conversation. She was leaning against the flank of a cow, a picture of rustic grace, a rural study of charmed solemnity. Christ knows what they were saying to each other. For one thing they were speaking in their own language : for another I couldn't hear anything, even that, above the blather and splatter of the bloody cows and the racket of the single cylinder diesel, brand-name Onon out of Edinburgh so help me.

They looked up. I grabbed a stool and got on with it, head down to the bore of it all. I'd have preferred to be up on the tractor, poisoning myself straight out, bellowing this and that and the other looney thing to the cynical gulls. Ah, my mountain princess of the golden chords, something was changing. I stripped on sullenly: I hoped it was me.

We were silent through dinner: We were always silent, through all meals. It made a change from home where all hell lay between soup and sweet, everyone taking advantage of the twenty minutes of enforced attendance to shoot the bile, bicker and accuse, rant and wrangle through the gray disgusting mutton and the two veg. Fanny never chattered much and less than ever in the presence of her pappy: giggled maybe but never said much. Then out of the blue father Hohepa opened up. Buster, you should make peace with your father. I considered it. I tried to touch Fanny's foot under the table and I considered it. A boy shouldn't hate his father: a boy should respect his father. I thought about that too. Then I asked should fathers hate their sons; but I knew the answer. Puti Hohepa didn't say anything, just sat blowing into his tea, looking at his reputedly wild daughter who might have been a beauty for all I could tell, content to be delivered of the truth and so fulfilled. You should do this: a boy shouldn't do that—tune into that, mac. And me thinking proscription and prescription differently ordered in this farm world of crummy acres. I mean I thought I'd left all that crap behind the night I stumbled along Rideout Road following, maybe, the river Alph. I thought old man Hohepa, having been silent for so long, would

know better than to pull, of a sudden, all those general-
izations with which for seventeen years I'd been beaten
dizzy—but not so dizzy as not to be able to look back
of the billboard and see the stack of rotting bibles.
Gentlemen, I was, even noticeably, subdued. Puti
Hohepa clearly didn't intend to add anything more
just then. I was too tired to make him an answer. I
think I was too tired even for hate; and what better
indication of the extent of my exhaustion than that?
It had been a long summer; how long I was only beginning to discover. It was cold in the kitchen. Puti Hohepa
got up. From the doorway, huge and merging into the
night, he spoke again : You must make up your own
mind. He went away, leaving behind him the vibration
of a gentle sagacity, tolerance, a sense of duty (mine,
as usual) pondered over and pronounced upon. The
bastard. You must make up your own mind. And for
the first time you did that mum had hysterics and dad
popped his gut. About what? Made up my mind about
what? My black daddy? Fanny? Myself? Life? A
country career and agricultural hell? Death? Money?
Fornication? (I'd always liked that.) What the héll was
he trying to say? What doing but abdicating the soiled
throne at the first challenge? Did he think fathers
shouldn't hate their sons, or could help it, or would if
they could? Am I clear? No matter. He didn't have one
of the four he'd sired at home so what the hell sort of
story was he trying to peddle? Father with the soft
center. You should, you shouldn't, make up your own
mind. Mac, my head was going round. But it was
brilliant, I conceded, when I'd given it a bit of thought.
My livid daddy himself would have applauded the
perfect ambiguity. What a bunch : they keep a dog on

a chain for years and years and then let it free on some purely personal impulse and when it goes wild and chases its tail round and round, pissing here and sniffing there in an ecstasy of liberty, a freedom for which it has been denied all training, they shoot it down because it won't come running when they hold up the leash and whistle. (I didn't think you'd go that way, son.) Well, my own green liberty didn't look like so much at that moment; for the first time I got an inkling that life was going to be simply a matter of out of one jail and into another. Oh, they had a lot in common, her dad and mine. I sat there, mildly stupefied, drinking my tea. Then I looked up at Fanny; or, rather, down on Fanny. I've never known such a collapsible sheila in my life. She was stretched out on the kitchen couch, every vertebra having turned to juice in the last minute and a half. I thought maybe she'd have the answer, some comment to offer on the state of disunion. Hell. I was the very last person to let my brew go cold while I pondered the nuance of the incomprehensible, picked at the dubious unsubtlety of thought of a man thirty years my senior who had never, until then, said more than ten words to me. She is too good for you : only six words after all and soon forgotten. Better, yes, if he'd stayed mum, leaving me to deduce from his silence whatever I could, Abora Mountain and the milk of paradise, consent in things natural, and a willingness to let simple matters take their simple course.

I was wrong : Fanny offered no interpretation of her father's thought. Exegesis to his cryptic utterance was the one thing she couldn't supply. She lay with her feet up on the end of the couch, brown thighs charmingly bared, mouth open, and eyes closed in balmy sleep, displaying in this posture various things but mainly her large unconcern not only for this tragedy of filial responsibility and the parental role but, too, for the diurnal problem of the numerous kitchen articles, pots, pans, plates, the lot. I gazed on her, frowning on her bloom of sleep, the slow inhalation and exhalation accompanied by a gentle flare of nostril, and considered the strength and weakness of our attachment. Helpmeet she was not, thus to leave her lover to his dark ponderings and the chores.

Puti Hohepa sat on the verandah in the dark, hacking over his bowl of shag. One by one, over my second cup of tea, I assessed my feelings, balanced all my futures in the palm of my hand. I crossed to Fanny, crouched beside her, kissed her. I felt embarrassed and, gentlemen, foolish. Her eyes opened wide; then they shut and she turned over.

The dishes engaged my attention not at all, except to remind me, here we go, of my father in apron and rubber gloves at the sink, pearl-diving while mum was off somewhere at a lynching. Poor bastard. Mum had the natural squeeze for the world; they should have changed places. (It's for your own good! Ah, the joyous peal of that as the razor strop came whistling down like tartar's blade.) I joined daddy Hohepa on the verandah. For a moment we shared the crescent moon and the smell of earth damp under dew, Rideout Mountain massed to the west.

I've finished the river paddock.

Yes.

The tractor's going to need a de-coke before long.

Yes.

I guess that about cuts it out.

Yes.

I may as well shoot through.

Buster, is Fanny pregnant?

I don't know. She hasn't said anything to me so I suppose she can't be.

You are going home?

No. Not home. There's work down south. I'd like to have a look down there.

There's work going here if you want it. But you have made up your mind?

I suppose I may as well shoot through.

Yes.

After milking tomorrow if that's okay with you.

Yes.

He hacked on over his pipe. Yes, yes, yes, yes, yes is Fanny pregnant? What if I'd said yes? I didn't know one way or the other. I only hoped, and left the rest to her. Maybe he'd ask her; and what if she said yes? What then, eh Buster? Maybe I should have said why don't you ask her. A demonstrative, volatile, loquacious old person : a tangible symbol of impartiality, reason unclouded by emotion, his eyes frank in the murk of night and his pipe going bright, dim, bright as he calmly considered the lovely flank of the moon. I was hoping she wasn't, after all. Hoping; it gets to be a habit, a bad habit that does you no good, stunts your growth, sends you insane, and makes you, demonstrably, blind. Hope, for Fanny Hohepa.

Later, along the riverbank, Fanny and I groped, gentlemen, for the lost rapport and the parking sign. We were separated by just a little more than an arm's reach. I made note then of the natural scene. Dark water, certainly; dark lush grass underfoot; dark girl;

the drifting smell of loam in the night : grant me again as much. Then, by one of those fortuitous accidents not infrequent in our national prosings, our hands met, held, fell away. Darkness. My feet stumbling by the river and my blood going like a tango. Blood pulsed upon blood, undenied and unyoked, as we busied ourselves tenderly at our ancient greetings and farewells. And in the end, beginning my sentence with a happy conjunction, I held her indistinct, dark head. We stayed so for a minute, together and parting as always, with me tumbling down upon her the mute dilemma my mind then pretended to resolve and she offering no restraint, no argument better than the dark oblivion of her face.

Unrecorded the words between us : there can't have been more than six, anyway, it was our fated number. None referred to my departure or to the future or to maculate conceptions. Yet her last touch spoke volumes. (Unsubsidized, gentlemen, without dedication or preamble.) River-damp softened her hair : her skin smelled of soap : Pan pricking forward to drink at the stream, crushing fennel, exquisitely stooping, bending . . .

And, later again, silent, groping, we ascended in sequence to the paternal porch.

Buster?

Yair?

Goodnight, Buster.

'Night, Fanny. Be seein' yuh.

. . .

Fourteen minute specks of radioactive phosphorous brightened by weak starlight pricked out the hour : one.

In the end I left old STC in the tractor tool box along with the spanner that wouldn't fit any nut I'd ever tried it on and the grease gun without grease and the last letter from mum, hot as radium. I didn't wait for milking. I was packed and gone at the first trembling of light. It was cold along the river-bottom, cold and still. Eels rose to feed: the water was like pewter; old pewter. I felt sick, abandoned, full of self-pity. Everything washed through me, the light, the cold, a sense of what lay behind me and might not lie before, a feeling of exhaustion when I thought of home, a feeling of despair when I thought of Fanny still curled in sleep. Dark. She hadn't giggled: so what? I changed my fiber suitcase to the other hand and trudged along Rideout Road. The light increased; quail with tufted crests crossed the road; I began to feel better. I sat on the suitcase and rolled a smoke. Then the sun caught a high scarp of Rideout Mountain and began to finger down slow and gold. I was so full of relief, suddenly, that I grabbed my bag and ran. Impetuous. I was lucky not to break my ankle. White gulls, loam flesh, dark water, damsel, and dome; where would it take you? Where was there to go, anyway? It just didn't matter; that was the point. I stopped worrying that minute and sat by the cream stand out on the main road. After a while a truck stopped to my thumb and I got in. If I'd waited for the cream truck I'd have had to face old brownstone Hohepa, and I wasn't very eager for that. I'd had a fill of piety, of various brands. And I was paid up to date.

I looked back. Rideout Mountain and the peak of ochre red roof, Maori red. That's all it was. I wondered what Fanny and her pappy might be saying at this moment, across the clothes-hanger rumps of cows. The

relief went through me again. I looked at the gloomy
bastard driving : he had a cigarette stuck to his lip like
a growth. I felt almost happy. Almost. I might have
hugged him as he drove his hearse through the tail-end
of summer.

The Bulls

[NEW ZEALAND]

by Roderick Finlayson

THE NEW young bull arrived on the farm that morning. He was a handsome two-year-old Jersey, sleek and quiet-eyed. Steve, the drover from Matapoi, brought him along and turned him into the yard. The old man and the boy came out and looked him over. The boy could tell the old man was pleased with the bull by the way he shuffled slowly around the yard with his hands behind his back looking at the animal while he whistled a little through his rangy moustache. The boy thought the bull looked good too.

"Well, you can take the old fella, Steve," the old man said.

The drover didn't bother to reply. He was a thickset florid man with a red-veined nose, hard, unfriendly blue eyes, and close-cropped sandy hair. His dog was a lean yellow cur, unfriendly too, slinking and showing his teeth when the boy spoke to him. The drover rode a gaunt chestnut mare so long-legged the man looked too tall in the saddle. He sat staring hard down on the boy.

"Wouldn't want to tag along with that man—not

at any price," the boy thought, edging away from the unfriendly gaze.

"Come along in, Steve, the missus has dinner on the table," the old man said. He looked at the boy. "Come on, boy, don't keep us waiting, looking like you're dumb."

The drover dismounted and led his horse to the water trough. "Gotta be getting on the road," he grumbled as if ungrateful for the offer of a meal. "You never know when it comes to getting an old bull away from his home paddocks."

Nevertheless, once he was in the farm kitchen, he ate a real good fill, gobbling great mouthfuls of beef and potato without any sign of enjoyment and without speaking a word. But when he had had enough and was handed his second cup of tea, he sat back and smirked at the old man's wife. "Meal like this here, missus, reminds me of when I rode champion steeplechasers and was feasted and feted by the girls all up and down the country." Having made this statement he drank the tea in long sucking gulps and became as morose as before.

When the men left the house the drover went straight to his horse and mounted. "Come on, Thomson, where's old devil?" he shouted.

The old man with the boy went on foot to the back paddock, opened the gate, and called to the big red bull. "Hey-aah, bully! Hey-aah!" The red bull lumbered out with a slow toss of his horns. They followed him up the drive past the cow-paddock gate where he eyed the grazing herd.

"Run ahead and open the road gate, boy," the old man said.

The old bull, sensing what they meant to do, balked at the gate. But the drover spurred his horse forward and cracked his whip angrily. The yellow cur snapped at the bull's heels and swung on his tail. And with the horseman lashing at his hind-quarters, the old bull was rushed through the gate and out onto the open road. It was a back country road of sandy yellow clay now dry and dusty, and it twisted aimlessly among clumps of manuka scrub and native heather. Gorse grew thick along the barbwire boundary fences.

"Keep him at the bloody gallop," yelled the drover. "He won't get no chance to be no bloody trouble."

But the old bull braked with his four legs bunched and turned quick as a cat turning to double back toward the gate that led to home and the herd. The drover swore freely and let out half-choked yells. His horse seemed to the boy to be far too long-legged for this kind of a job, and the man was too heavy and too high in the saddle.

The yellow dog leaped beside the bull. The old man and the boy tried to head the animal, but he charged past and jumped the fence. He was in his home paddock again. Slowly he stalked toward the cows, indignantly shaking his head.

"Do you think I have time to waste?" the drover shouted. "Get him out of there, Thomson."

Again the boy opened the road gate. Steve cantered in with his whip cracking and the yellow dog made straight for the bull, but neither man nor dog could get the bull near the gate.

"I'll turn some of the herd out with him," the old man said. "Run them up the road a ways and then let them drop behind when we've got the old fella on the move."

The drover cantered round the herd, and they got half a dozen cows and the old bull on the run. They stampeded them up the road, the cows moo-ing and blaa-ing at such unusual treatment, the bull tossing his head in agitation as he ran with the foremost cows. But Steve impatiently galloped among the mob and tried to rush the bull out ahead and up the road. The old fellow was too knowing. He swerved sharply into the gorse and leapt the neighbor's fence. There he stood in the strange paddock pawing the ground until the sod flew. Then he drove his horns into the broken ground and tossed the dirt high over his head.

The neighbor, a man named Jackson, had been watching from up by his shed. His herd in the next paddock was becoming restive and his bull was trotting excitedly up the dividing fence, so he put his two dogs on the intruder at the same time that the drover, who had swung open the road gate, now charged across the paddock with his dog. Steve slashed the bull's flanks with his stock-whip and the three dogs snapped and slavered at his heels, forcing him over to the fence, forcing him to a short standing jump that brought him down on the wires with the barbs ripping his legs.

The old man called out to the boy, "Boy, we gotta get him on his way ourselves. That damn man's no good. He's only maddening the beast. Now be ready to head him away from home. You're young and nimble on your feet. I've got to keep at his heels."

The big red bull was free of the twanging wires and was crashing through the manuka scrub. I'd like to stay handy to duck under that fence, the boy thought, but look out or you'll get pinned against that barbwire. Better keep to the open.

He was on his toes, tensed in the middle of the dusty yellow road. Suddenly he saw the bull coming, head low, neck arched. The little eyes were bloodshot and threads of saliva were trailing from the bull's lolling tongue. His flanks were streaked with blood and sweat and dust, and the places where the barbs had ripped were growing redder. The old fella's taking it hard, the boy thought. But he's dangerous like that, he reminded himself. He spread his arms and jumped up and down on his toes until the bull was almost up to him. Then he spun around and jumped aside into the manuka as the bull, made to change his course slightly, lumbered past, his great neck muscles bulging.

Boy, the boy said to himself, when it comes to leaving, you are as bad as that old bull.

The old man had the dog on to him turning him before the drover could catch up. They got the bull on the run up the road again, but again he skidded in the dust, swung around, and charged back.

"Shake your coat at him, boy," the old man shouted. "Boss the bull, boss him!"

The boy peeled off his jacket and shook it at the bull, jumped up and down shaking it in front of the bull. The bull changed course somewhat. The dog harried him, giving the boy a chance to jump clear of his path into the manuka. The bull crashed through the scrub, flattening the bushes in his way.

I must watch my step, thought the boy. Better not slip on a stone or trip in the scrub.

Again the old man and the dog turned the bull, again the boy danced and pirouetted in front of him and kept his eyes away from home. These actions of the boy with his flapping coat, the old man with his prodding stick, his whoops and cries, were not without a plan. If they did not drive the bull up the road, at least they kept him from home. It was a game of chase, a game between dancing toes and pounding hoofs around the scattered manuka clumps by the dusty yellow road. No one, neither the bull nor the men, would admit defeat.

"We cannot drive him, boy," the old man gasped when he found a chance to be near the boy. "We must wear him down. It isn't hard to wear him down when you are young and nimble on your feet. Keep in front of him."

The old bull was no longer so nimble 'n his feet. Gradually they were wearying him. He panted, and his tongue lolled. The unconcerned drover left him to the man and the boy on foot. Sour faced, he sat on his tall horse at the roadside, while he rolled a cigarette.

The old man and the boy were tiring too. With his cigarette unlit the drover quickly uncoiled his stockwhip and gave a mighty crack. "Leave him to me," he yelled. Spurring his horse forward, whistling his eager yellow dog, he made a final charge that carried the stumbling bull before him up the road, with no chance of turning back.

"That's goodbye to him," the old man said. "That's goodbye."

A cloud covered the sun, and the boy, standing still on the road watching the distant lumbering bull, felt the chill of the evening breeze. He shrugged into his old brown coat.

Next day after breakfast, the old man said, "Well, now we must ring the young one." He and the boy went out to the stock-yard where the young bull was. He looked at them with great wondering eyes. His coat was sleek and the muscles rippled when he moved.

The old man walked as he often walked, with his hands loosely clasped behind his back, but now in his right hand he carried a length of rope. He walked with a shambling sideways gait, and he did not look at the bull. But the bull kept his eyes on the man. Not looking at the bull but slowly shambling as though to go past him, all the time drawing nearer the animal, the old man slowly and casually backed the bull into the corner where the bail post was.

The bull constantly shifted ground to keep his eyes on the old man. Then the old man flipped a noose of rope over the bull's horns, over his head, and threw his weight on the rope as the bull backed, and took a turn around the strong post. As the bull kept backing round and round, the shortening rope pulled his head down to the post.

"Now we've got him where we want him," the old man said. "Have you got the things?"

The boy had the necessary things—the bright new copper ring and the steel spike and the old tin can and "dopper" black with cattle tar. He put these down on the dry hard ground near the post. The bull was rolling his eyes till the whites showed; his curling tongue licked at his nostrils and he panted a little.

"Hold the rope, boy." As the boy kept the rope taut, the old man took hold of the bull by the horns as though to wrestle with him and slowly he forced the bull to his knees and then right off his feet so that he rolled over and lay on his side in the dust.

"Now hold him by his horns," said the old man.

The boy grasped the strong young horns.

"Now sit on his back—up there by his neck. That's right. Hold him down while I do the job."

"How can I hold him down if he goes to get up?" asked the boy.

"Don't you worry boy. It's just sitting there that does the trick," the old man said.

So the boy sat on the bull's back. He could feel the muscles quivering, the nerves twitching, beneath the sleek hide. On his bare legs where his jeans had slipped up, he could feel the animal warmth and the silky smoothness. He looked at the nervous rolling eye, the clean sharp young hoofs. He slipped his hand from one curved polished horn and fondled the thick curls below it. Some of the bull's great strength seemed to fill the boy's slender body. Soon he would be leaving the farm. He, and the old bull, would be gone—and this young bull and the old man left.

Yesterday and today I've bossed two bulls, the old one and the young, he thought, and I feel fine. Going out into the world, leaving this farm, don't worry me any more.

The young bull trembled all over and gave a low moaning "blah." With the steel spike the old man was piercing the flesh between the nostrils. It was tough going. Sweat dripped from the old man's brow and his hands were trembling before the steel came through. Then he pulled the spike out and reached for the cattle tar and put a daub of that on the wound. The bull sniffed the stinging fumes and bowed his head, his whole body relaxing.

"Now hand me the ring—and the screw and screwdriver," the old man said. But now he was shaky and nervous and the old blunt fingers fumbled with the little screw after he had forced the open ring through the bull's nose. "Here boy, you do it," he cried at last. "Your fingers are still young and nimble."

So the boy slid from the bull's back and fixed the ring in the bull's nose and the job was done. The old man undid the rope and the young one, after lying inert for a few minutes, felt that he was free and slowly got to his feet. He gave another low "blah" and shook his head and ambled off. Then he broke into a trot and then into a gallop, cavorting a little as he went, so very young and nimble on his feet.

The old man watched him go. Slowly he gathered up his things and shambled toward the house. The boy followed him with just a bit of a swagger in his walk.

The Sea Beyond

[PHILIPPINES]

by N.V.M. Gonzalez

THE ADELA, the reconverted minesweeper that had become the mainstay of commerce and progress in Sipolog Oriental, was on her way to San Roque. As Horacio Arenas, our new assistant, wanted to put it, the *Adela* was "expected" at San Roque, which was the provincial capital, "in seven hours." He spoke at some length of this particular voyage, looking worn-out instead of refreshed after the two-week vacation we had hoped he would enjoy.

There he was, he said, one of the hundred-odd impatient passengers that shivered under the low canvas awning of the upper deck. A choppy sea met the ship as she approached Punta Dumadáli, and the rise and fall of the deck suggested the labored breathing of an already much-abused beast of burden. Her hatches were in fact quite full, Arenas said. Hundreds of sacks of copra had filled her hold at Dias. Piled all over the lower deck were thousands of pieces of lauan boards from the mills of San Tomé. The passageways alongside the engine room were blocked by enormous baskets of cassava and bananas. A dozen wild-eyed Simara cows, shoulder to shoulder in their makeshift corral at stern, mooed intermittently as though the moon-drenched sea were their pasture.

For the moon had risen over the Maniwala Ranges three miles to the starboard. As more and more the *Adela* rounded the Punta Dumadáli, the wind sent the ship buckling wildly. An hour before, all this would have been understandable; it was puzzling, if not thoroughly incomprehensible, now. This kind of sea was unusual for the reason that the Dumadáli headland was known to mariners to throw off, especially this time of the year if at no other, the full force of the *noroeste*. If some explanation were to be sought, it would be in some circumstance peculiar only to this voyage. This was the consensus, which made possible the next thought: that some presence was about, some evil force perhaps— so the talk went on board—which, until propitiated, might yet bring the ship to some foul end. The cows, so insistent in their lowing before, were markedly quiet now. The ship continued to pitch about; whenever the wind managed to tear at the awnings and cause loose ends of the canvas to beat savagely at the wire-mesh that covered the railings, small unreal patches of sea glimmered outside in the moonlight.

It was no secret that there was a dying man on board. He was out there in the third-class section. Whatever relation his presence had to the unpleasantness in the weather no one could explain, but the captain did do something. He had the man moved over to the first-class section, where there were fewer passengers and possibly more comfort.

The transfer was accomplished by two members of the

crew. They carried the cot in which the man lay, and two women, the man's wife and her mother, followed them. Ample space was cleared for the cot; the two women helped push the heavy canvas beds and chairs out of the way. Finally the two men brought the canvas cot down. The ship listed to the starboard suddenly; and it seemed that from all quarters of the deck the hundred-odd passengers of the *Adela* let out a wild scream.

Then the ship steadied somehow. For a moment it seemed as if her engines had stopped. Then there was a gentle splashing sound as though the bow had clipped neatly through the last of those treacherous waves. Either superior seamanship or luck held sway, but the ship might have entered then an estuary, perhaps the very mouth of a river.

The excitement had roused the passengers and, in the first-class section at least, everyone had sat up to talk, to make real all over again the danger they had just been through. The steaming-hot coffee which the steward began serving in thick blue-rimmed cups encouraged conversation. The presence of the two women and the man in the extra cot in their midst was hardly to be overlooked. A thick gray woolen blanket covered the man all over, except about the face. His groans, underscored by the faint tapping of the wind on the canvas awnings, were becoming all too familiar. The mother attracted some notice, although for a different reason; she had a particularly sharp-edged face—brow and nose and chin had a honed look to them. The wife, who had more pleasing features, evoked respect and compassion. It was touching to see her sit on the edge of the empty cot beside her husband's and tuck in the hem of her skirt under her knees. She could not have been more than twenty, and already she wore the sadness of her widowhood. The glare of the naked electric bulb that hung from the ridgepole of the deck's canvas roof accentuated it, revealed that she was about six months gone with child, and called attention to her already full breasts, under a rust-colored *camisa*, that soon would be nourishing yet another life.

It was four hours before, at Dias, where the accident had occurred. Although Dias was a rich port, no wharf had been constructed either by the government or the local association of copra and rice merchants. The old method of ferrying cargo in small outriggered *paráos* was less costly perhaps, it was even picturesque. But it was only possible in good weather. And already the *noroeste* had come. The same waves that pounded at the side of the *Adela* at anchor lashed at the frail *paráos* that were rowed over toward the ship and were brought into position for hauling up the copra. The man, one of the *cargadores*, had fallen off the ship's side.

He would have gone to the bottom had he not let go of the copra sack that he had held aloft, and more so had he not been caught across the hips by the outriggers of his *paráo*. Nevertheless, the next wave that had lifted the ship and gathered strength from under her keel it seemed flung him headlong toward the prow of the boat. The blunt end of this dugout pressed his body against the black, tar-coated side of the *Adela*. The crew pulled him out with difficulty, for the sea kept rising and falling and caused the prow's head to scrape continuously against the ship's side. The crew had expected to find a mass of broken flesh and bones, but in actuality the man came through quite intact. He did not start moaning and writhing until his wet undershirt and shorts had been changed and he had been laid out on the cot. There was nothing that could be done further except to keep him on board. Something after all had broken or had burst open somewhere inside him.

His family was sent for. The wife, accompanied by her mother, clambered up the ship's side thirty minutes later, to the jocose shouts of "Now you can see San Roque!" from innocent well-wishers in the *paráos*. The shippers, the Dias Development Co., had sent a telegram to the provincial doctor at San Roque, and an agent of the company had come on board and personally commended the *cargador* to the captain. When at last the fifty-ton copra shipment was on board, the *Adela* weighed anchor.

Now, for having transferred the man from the third-class to the first-class section, the captain earned some praise, and the connection between this act and the pleasant change in the weather elicited much speculation. If only the man did not groan so pitifully, if only he kept his misery to himself; if only the two women were less preoccupied too by some bitter and long-unresolved conflict between them. "Don't you think he is hungry?" the mother once asked; to which the wife answered, "He does not like food. You know that." And then the mother asked, "How about water? He will be thirsty perhaps." To which the wife's reply was, "I shall go down and fetch some water." The matter could have stopped there, but the mother wanted to have the last word. "That's better than just standing or sitting around."

The wife got up and walked away, only to return about ten minutes later with a pitcher and a drinking cup from the mess room below. The mother had the pitcher and drinking cup placed at the foot of the sick man's bed, for, as she explained, "He will ask for water any time and you won't be near enough to help me." The mother waited to see what her daughter would make of this; and the latter did have her say: "I'll be right here, Mother, if that's all you're worried about."

The man grew restless. His wife's assurance (she said again and again, "You will be all right!") drew nothing but interminable sighs ("O, God of mine!"). Between the man and his wife, some inexplicable source of irritation had begun to fester. "It is in your trying to move about that the pain comes," the wife chided him gently. "We are getting there soon. It will not be long now." Whereupon the man tried to raise his knee and twist his hips under the blanket. The blanket made a hump like one of the Maniwala mountains in the distance, and he let out a wail, followed by "But this boat is so very slow, God of mine! Why can't we go faster? Let the captain make the boat go faster. Tell him. Will someone go and tell him?"

Almost breathless after this exertion, he lay still. The mother, this time as if her son-in-law were an ally, took it upon herself to comfort him. "Better keep quiet and don't tire yourself. The captain will make the boat go faster, surely." And by putting down his knee carefully, the hump that the blanket had made before leveled off now into foothills instead of those high ranges of the Maniwala.

The business of the telegram came after this lull. It was preceded by a prolonged groan, and then the question was there before them: "And did they send the telegram?" "They" meant the Company of course, in whose service the man had enlisted as a *cargador*. If the answer to this was in the affirmative, then there was reason to say that the doctor would attend to him and put him together again and return him to his work. His wife assured him that the telegram had been dispatched. "So be quiet," she added. "The other people here would not want to be disturbed now. They want to sleep, no doubt," she said, looking about her, as if to solicit the approval of the twenty or twenty-five passengers around—which included merchants, students, and at least three public school teachers on some Christmas holiday jaunt.

The mother asked about food—a proper question, although under the circumstances perhaps a tactless. one. "I am not hungry, Mother," was what the daughter said, firmly. "I'll sit here," the mother offered, in a less authoritative tone than she had been accustomed to use. "I'll do that myself if you are hungry," countered the daughter. "I don't care for food," the mother assured her. "And did I tell you I wanted to eat?" Whereupon the daughter declared that she was not hungry—"let me tell you that, Mother." The mother alleged that her most loving daughter was no doubt "too choosy" about food, "that's why." She ought to "go down below and ask for anything to eat." "Eat whatever you can find," was her solemn injunction, as if to overwhelm her daughter's claim that she was not hungry at all. "Don't worry about me, Mother," the wife added, pointedly. "I don't get hungry that easily." And then to round off this phase of their quarrel, the mother said, loud enough for anyone who cared to hear: "Maybe it's sitting at the captain's table that you've been waiting for all this time."

The daughter said nothing in reply and the mother did not press her advantage either. It was clear, though, that the meaning of the remark, its insinuation, was not to be easily dismissed. What the mother had so expressed was a little out of the ordinary; the air, as Arenas put it, was rife with conjectures. It was not difficult to remember, he said, that ship officers, or sailors in general, had never been known to endow women their highest value. What remained to be understood was why the mother thought of her daughter in some such awful connection as this.

Five hours later, Arenas said, after the *Adela* had docked at the San Roque pier and the discharging of some of her cargo had begun, the subject came up again. Perhaps the first person to disembark had been the captain himself, to infer from the fact that somebody, possibly one of the mates, had shouted to someone standing on the wharf : "Duty before pleasure, captain!" A jeep of the Southern Star Navigation Co. had rolled up the ramp and then hurried off the mile-long seaside road toward the town, into San Roque *población* itself. The town was brightly lighted, particularly the section along the seaside.

"Now he's gone and we have not even thanked him," said the mother. "And the doctor has not come. How can we leave this ship? Answer that," she demanded. "You are too proud, that's what. All that you needed to say was a word or two, a word of thanks, surely." The wife remained silent through all this. "And he could have taken you in the jeep, to fetch the doctor; if there was that telegram, and it has been received—" She did not go further. The wife assured her calmly that the telegram was sent. "So what harm could it have done to have spoken to the captain, to have reminded him, since he would be riding into town anyway?" the mother said; and to this the daughter's reply was the kind of serenity, Arenas said, that can come only from knowledge: "All men know is to take advantage of us, Mother," she said.

Taken aback by these words, the mother searched the faces of people round her for help. She got nothing and she said nothing. The passengers had crowded at the railing to watch the lumber being unloaded. A gang of *cargadores* tossed pieces of lumber from over the ship's side to the wharf ten feet away while someone chanted: "A hundred and fifty-three—and fifty-four—and fifty-five ..." and the wood cluttered askew on the fast-mounting pile. The cows lowed again from their corral at the stern of the ship. This blended afresh with the man's groans and with the chant and the clatter of the boards. Meanwhile, the wife talked on softly: "We have arrived, and it's the doctor's jeep we're waiting for and nothing more," wiping her husband's brow with a handkerchief. "Two hundred and three—and four—and five ..." chanted the counter, over down below. "This is San Roque now," the wife continued. "A big town it is, with many lights. And with many people." Her husband's brow sweated profusely and it was all she could do with her handkerchief. "And the lights are bright, and so many. Rest now and tomorrow we can see the town," she said softly, folding her handkerchief this way and that so as not to get any section of it too damp with sweat.

It was at this point, Arenas said, that a motor sounded from down the road, followed by the blare of a jeep's horn and the swing of its headlights. The lights caught the man who was chanting his count of the lumber being unloaded, and they held him transfixed. He shouted out the numbers louder. The jeep stopped in the middle of the now cluttered up wharf, for what with the stacked rows of copra and the lauan boards from San Tomé there was no space for the jeep to move in. The driver, having gone no farther than possible, turned off his engine and slid off his seat awkwardly, and then approaching the man who was doing the counting, he demanded: "How much longer?" And the other replied, "Possibly until two o'clock—what with the men we have. You know how it is, sir." To which the other said, sternly: "Stop calling me 'sir.' And to think that the captain just told me he'll pull out in two hours, not a second later."

Words, Arenas said, which, although intended for somebody else did make the wife say to her husband: "They'll first move you over there, to the wharf—that will be solid ground at least—and there we shall wait for the doctor." She had dropped her voice to a whisper.

Across the ten feet of water to the edge of the wharf, lights fell harshly on the piles, on the heads and arms of the *cargadors* who slid up and down the gangplank with the copra sacks on their shoulders, looking like so many over-sized ants. To the right was the driver in his jeep; he had not turned off his lights and it flooded the first-class section with a garish glare. "What shamelessness," cried the wife. The jeep's lights singled her out. The driver had got stuck between the wall of copra to his left and a new pile of lumber to his right. He was trying to turn the jeep about but did not have the room. The man who had addressed him "sir" had stopped his work, and the clatter of the boards had ceased. Up on the deck, Arenas said, the wife shouted:

"What does he want of me? What does he want me to do now?" The mother pulled her away. "She's overwrought. Forgive her," she begged. "And as you've observed, I've been hard on her myself. I don't know why. Why must God punish us so?"

Once more the driver tried to maneuver his jeep and all the time his lights seemed to fix themselves forever on the wife, who, to meet this challenge, sprang away from the ship's railing and rushed down to the lower deck, shouting: "Here, here I am. Take me. What can you want of me?"

It was that way, Arenas said. Two hours later, the man was moved to the wharf, and there behind a pile of copra and another pile of lauan lumber the wife and the mother waited. Word was abroad that the captain, who had returned from town, had said that he had contacted the doctor. Contacted, Arenas said, was the very word. And wasn't that so revealing?

We didn't know at first what he meant, we told him. Did he want to remind us about the war, the same one during which the *Adela* had swept the mine-strewn sea in behalf of progress and civilization? The word Arenas had used belonged to that time, and he seemed to say, All this because it had been that way at that time. You must understand, you might forgive, even.

But we didn't want him to be apologetic like the mother-in-law he had described; and so, afterward, when he talked again about the subject, wearing that worried look on his face with which we had become familiar, we had to urge him: "Better not think about it any more."

The Day the Dancers Came

[PHILIPPINES]

by Bienvenido N. Santos

AS SOON as Fil woke up, he noticed a whiteness outside, quite unusual for the November mornings they had been having. That fall, Chicago was sandman's town, sleepy valley, drowsy gray, slumbrous mistiness from sunup till noon when the clouds drifted away in cauliflower clusters and suddenly it was evening. The lights shone on the avenues like soiled lamps centuries old and the skyscrapers became monsters with a thousand sore eyes. Now there was a brightness in the air and Fil knew what it was and he shouted, "Snow! It's snowing!"

Tony, who slept in the adjoining room, was awakened. "What's that?" he asked.

"It's snowing," Fil said, smiling to himself as if he had ordered this and was satisfied with the prompt delivery. "Oh, they'll love this, they'll love this."

"Who'll love that?" Tony asked, his voice raised in annoyance.

"The dancers, of course," Fil answered. "They're arriving today. Maybe they've already arrived. They'll walk in the snow and love it. Their first snow, I'm sure."

"How do you know it wasn't snowing in New York while they were there?" Tony asked.

"Snow in New York in early November?" Fil said. "Are you crazy?"

"Who's crazy?" Tony replied. "Ever since you heard of those dancers from the Philippines, you've been acting nuts. Loco. As if they're coming here just for you."

Tony chuckled. Hearing him, Fil blushed, realizing that he had, indeed, been acting too eager, but Tony had said it. It felt that way—as if the dancers were coming here only for him.

Filemon Acayan, Filipino, was fifty, a U.S. citizen. He was a corporal in the U.S. Army, training at San Luis Obispo, on the day he was discharged honorably, in 1945. A few months later, he got his citizenship papers. Thousands of them, smart and small in their uniforms, stood at attention in drill formation, in the scalding sun, and pledged allegiance to the flag and the republic for which it stands. Soon after he got back to work. To a new citizen, work meant many places and many ways: factories and hotels, waiter and cook. A timeless drifting: once he tended a rose garden and took care of a hundred-year-old veteran of a border war. As a menial in a hospital in Cook County, all day he handled filth and gore. He came home smelling of surgical soap and disinfectant. In the hospital, he took charge of a row of bottles on a shelf, each bottle containing a stage of the human embryo in preservatives, from the lizard-like foetus of a few days, through the newly born infant, with its position unchanged, cold and cowering and afraid. He had nightmares through the years of himself inside a bottle. That was long ago. Now he had a more pleasant job as special policeman in the post office.

He was a few years younger than Tony—Antonio
Bataller, a retired Pullman porter—but he looked older
in spite of the fact that Tony had been bedridden most of
the time for the last two years, suffering from a kind of
wasting disease that had frustrated doctors. All over
Tony's body, a gradual peeling was taking place. At
first, he thought it was merely *tinia flava,* a skin disease
common among adolescents in the Philippines. It had
started around the neck and had spread to his extremities.
His face looked as if it was healing from severe burns.
Nevertheless, it was a young face, much younger than
Fil's, which had never looked young.

"I'm becoming a white man," Tony said once,
chuckling softly.

It was the same chuckle Fil seemed to have heard
now, only this time it sounded derisive, insulting.

Fil said, "I know who's nuts. It's the sick guy with
the sick thoughts. You don't care for nothing but your
pain, your imaginary pain."

"You're the imagining fellow. I got the real thing,"
Tony shouted from the room. He believed he had
something worse than the whiteness spreading on his
skin. There was a pain in his insides, like dull scissors
scraping his intestines. Angrily, he added, "What for
I got retired?"

"You're old, man, old, that's what, and sick, yes, but
not cancer," Fil said, turning towards the snow-filled
sky. He pressed his face against the glass window.
There's about an inch now on the ground, he thought,
maybe more.

Tony came out of his room looking as if he had not
slept all night. "I know what I got," he said, as if it
were an honor and a privilege to die of cancer and Fil

was trying to deprive him of it. "Never a pain like this. One day, I'm just gonna die."

"Naturally. Who says you won't?" Fil argued, thinking how wonderful it would be if he could join the company of dancers from the Philippines, show them around, walk with them in the snow, watch their eyes as they stared about them, answer their questions, tell them everything they wanted to know about the changing seasons in this strange land. They would pick up fistfuls of snow, crunch it in their fingers or shove it into their mouths. He had done just that the first time, long, long ago, and it had reminded him of the grated ice the Chinese sold near the town plaza where he had played *tatching* with an older brother who later drowned in a squall. How his mother had grieved over that death, she who had not cried too much when his father died, a broken man. Now they were all gone, quick death after a storm, or lingeringly, in a season of drought, all, all of them he had loved.

He continued, "All of us will die. One day. A medium bomb marked Chicago and this whole dump is *tapus,* finished. Who'll escape then?"

"Maybe your dancers will," Tony answered, now watching the snow himself.

"Of course, they will," Fil retorted, his voice sounding like a big assurance that all the dancers would be safe in his care. "The bombs won't be falling on this night. And when the dancers are back in the Philippines . . ."

He paused, as if he was no longer sure of what he was going to say. "But maybe, even in the Philippines the bombs gonna fall, no?" he said, gazing sadly at the falling snow.

"What's that to you?" Tony replied. "You got no

more folks ove'der, right? I know it's nothing to me. I'll be dead before that."

"Let's talk about something nice," Fil said, the sadness spreading on his face as he tried to smile. "Tell me, how will I talk, how am I gonna introduce myself?"

He would go ahead with his plans, introduce himself to the dancers, and volunteer to take them sightseeing. His car was clean and ready for his guests. He had soaped the ashtrays, dusted off the floor boards, and thrown away the old mats, replacing them with new plastic throw rugs. He had got himself soaking wet while spraying the car, humming, as he worked, faintly-remembered tunes from the old country.

Fil shook his head as he waited for Tony to say something. "Gosh, I wish I had your looks, even with those white spots, then I could face every one of them," he said, "but this mug . . ."

"That's the important thing, your mug. It's your calling card. It says, Filipino. Countryman," Tony said.

"You're not fooling me, friend," Fil said. "This mug says, Ugly Filipino. It says, old-timer, *muchacho*. It says *Pinoy, bejo.*"

For Fil, time was the villain. In the beginning, the words he often heard were: too young, too young; but all of a sudden, too young became too old, too late. What had happened in between? A weariness, a mist covering all things. You don't have to look at your face in a mirror to know that you are old, suddenly old, grown useless for a lot of things and too late for all the dreams you had wrapped up well against a day of need.

"It also says sucker," Tony said. "What for you want to invite them? Here? Aren't you ashamed of this hole?"

"It's not a palace, I know," Fil answered, "but who

wants a palace when they can have the most delicious *adobo* here and the best stuffed chicken ... yum ... yum...."

Tony was angry. "Yum, yum, you're nuts," he said, "plain and simple loco. What for you want to spend? You've been living on loose change all your life and now on a treasury warrant so small and full of holes, still you want to spend for these dancing kids who don't know you and won't even send you a card afterwards."

"Never mind the cards," Fil answered. "Who wants cards? But don't you see, they'll be happy; and then, you know what? I'm going to keep their voices, their words and their singing and their laughter in my magic sound mirror."

He had a portable tape recorder and a stack of recordings, patiently labelled, songs and speeches. The songs were in English, but most of the speeches were in the dialect, debates between him and Tony. It was evident Tony was the better speaker of the two in English, but in the dialect, Fil showed greater mastery. His style, however, was florid, sentimental, poetic.

Without telling Tony, he had experimented on recording sounds, like the way a bed creaked, doors opening and closing, rain or sleet tapping on the window panes, footsteps through the corridor. He played all the sounds back and tried to recall how it was on the day or night the sounds had been recorded. Did they bring back the moment? He was beginning to think that they did. He was learning to identify each of the sounds with a particular mood or fact. Sometimes, like today, he wished that there was a way of keeping a record of silence because it was to him the richest sound, like snow falling. He wondered as he watched the snow blowing in the wind, what took care of that moment if memory didn't. Like time, memory was often a villain, a betrayer.

"Fall, snow, fall," he murmured and, turning to Tony, said, "As soon as they accept my invitation, I'll call you up. No, you don't have to do anything, but I'd want you to be here to meet them."

"I'm going out myself," Tony said. "And I don't know what time I'll be back." Then he added, "You're not working today. Are you on leave?"

"For two days. While the dancers are here," Fil said.

"It still don't make sense to me," Tony said. "But good luck, anyway."

"Aren't you going to see them tonight? Our reserved seats are right out in front, you know."

"I know. But I'm not sure I can come."

"What? You're not sure?"

Fil could not believe it. Tony was indifferent. Something must be wrong with him. He looked at him closely, saying nothing.

"I want to, but I'm sick, Fil. I tell you, I'm not feeling so good. My doctor will know today. He'll tell me," Tony said.

"What will he tell you?"

"How do I know?"

"I mean, what's he trying to find out?"

"If it's cancer," Tony said. Without saying another word, he went straight back to his room.

Fil remembered those times, at night, when Tony kept him awake with his moaning. When he called out to him, asking, "Tony, what's the matter?" his sighs ceased for a while, but afterwards, Tony screamed, deadening his cries with a pillow against his mouth.

When Fil rushed to his side, Tony drove him away. Or he curled up in the bedsheets like a big infant suddenly hushed in its crying. The next day, he would look all right. When Fil asked him about the previous night, he would reply, "I was dying," but it sounded more like disgust over a nameless annoyance.

Fil had misgivings, too, about the whiteness spreading on Tony's skin. He had heard of leprosy. Every time he thought of that dreaded disease, he felt tears in his eyes. In all the years he had been in America, he had not had a friend until he met Tony, whom he liked immediately and, in a way, worshipped, for all the things the man had which Fil knew he himself lacked.

They had shared a lot together. They made merry on Christmas, sometimes got drunk and became loud. Fil recited poems in the dialect and praised himself. Tony fell to giggling and cursed all the railroad companies of America. But last Christmas, they hadn't gotten drunk. They hadn't even talked to each other on Christmas day. Soon, it would be Christmas again.

The snow was still falling.

"Well, I'll be seeing you," Fil said, getting ready to leave. "Try to be home on time. I shall invite the dancers for luncheon or dinner maybe, tomorrow. But tonight, let's go to the theater together, ha?"

"I'll try," Tony answered, adding after a pause, "Oh, Fil, I can't find my boots. May I wear yours?" His voice sounded strong and healthy.

"Sure, sure!" Fil answered. He didn't need boots. He loved to walk in the snow.

The air outside felt good. Fil lifted his face to the sky and closed his eyes as the snow and a wet wind drenched his face. He stood that way for some time, crying, more,

more! to himself, drunk with snow and coolness. His car was parked a block away. As he walked towards it, he plowed into the snow with one foot and studied the scar he made, a hideous shape among perfect footmarks. He felt strong as his lungs filled with the cold air, as if just now it did not matter too much that he was the way he looked and his English was the way it was. But perhaps he could talk to the dancers in his dialect. Why not?

A heavy frosting of snow covered his car and as he wiped it off with his bare hands, he felt light and young, like a child at play, and once again, he raised his face to the sky and licked the flakes, cold and tasteless on his tongue.

When Fil arrived at the Hamilton, it seemed to him the Philippine dancers had taken over the hotel. They were all over the lobby on the mezzanine, talking in groups animatedly, their teeth sparkling as they laughed, their eyes disappearing in mere slits of light. Some of the girls wore their black hair long. For a moment, the sight seemed too much for him who had but all forgotten how beautiful Philippine girls were. He wanted to look away, but their loveliness held him. He must do something, close his eyes perhaps. As he did so, their laughter came to him like a breeze murmurous with sounds native to his land.

Later, he tried to relax, to appear inconspicuous. True, they were all very young, but there were a few elderly men and women who must have been their chaperones or well-wishers like him. He would smile at everyone who happened to look his way. Most of them smiled back, or rather, seemed to smile, but it was quick, without recognition, and might not have been for him but for someone else near or behind him.

His lips formed the words he was trying to phrase in his mind : *Ilocano ka? Bicol? Ano na, paisano? Comusta?* Or should he introduce himself? How? For what he wanted to say, the words didn't come too easily, they were unfamiliar, they stumbled and broke on his lips into a jumble of incoherence.

Suddenly, he felt as if he was in the center of a group where he was not welcome. All the things he had been trying to hide now showed : the age in his face, his horny hands. He knew it the instant he wanted to shake hands with the first boy who had drawn close to him, smiling and friendly. Fil put his hands in his pocket.

Now he wished Tony had been with him. Tony would know what to do. He would charm these young people with his smile and his learned words. Fil wanted to leave, but he seemed caught up in the tangle of moving bodies that merged and broke in a fluid strange hold. Everybody was talking, mostly in English. Once in a while he heard exclamations in the dialect right out of the past, conjuring up playtime, long shadows of evening on the plaza, *barrio* fiestas, *misa de gallo.*

Time was passing and he had yet to talk to someone. Suppose he stood on a chair and addressed them in the manner of his flamboyant speeches recorded in his magic sound mirror?

"Beloved countrymen, lovely children of the Pearl of the Orient Seas, listen to me. I'm Fil Acayan. I've come to volunteer my services. I'm yours to command. Your servant. Tell me where you wish to go, what you want to see in Chicago. I know every foot of the lakeshore drive, all the gardens and the parks, the museums, the huge department stores, the planetarium. Let me be your guide. That's what I'm offering you, a free tour of Chicago, finally, dinner at my apartment on West Sheridan Road—pork *adobo* and chicken *relleno,* name your dish. How about it, *paisanos?"*

No. That would be a foolish thing to do. They would laugh at him. He felt a dryness in his throat. He was sweating. As he wiped his face with a handkerchief, he bumped against a slim, short girl who quite gracefully stepped aside, and for a moment he thought he would swoon in the perfume that enveloped him. It was fragrance long forgotten, essence of *camia,* of *ilang-ilang,* and *dama de noche.*

Two boys with sleek, pomaded hair were sitting near an empty chair. He sat down and said in the dialect, "May I invite you to my apartment?" The boys stood up, saying, "Excuse us, please," and walked away. He mopped his brow, but instead of getting discouraged, he grew bolder as though he had moved one step beyond shame. Approaching another group, he repeated his invitation, and a girl with a mole on her upper lip, said, "Thank you, but we have no time." As he turned towards another group, he felt their eyes on his back. Another boy drifted towards him, but as soon as he began to speak, the boy said, "Pardon, please," and moved away.

They were always moving away. As if by common consent, they had decided to avoid him, ignore his presence. Perhaps it was not their fault. They must have been instructed to do so. Or was it his looks that kept them away? The thought was a sharpness inside him.

After a while, as he wandered about the mezzanine, among the dancers, but alone, he noticed that they had begun to leave. Some had crowded noisily into the two elevators. He followed the others going down the stairs. Through the glass doors, he saw them getting into a bus parked beside the subway entrance on Dearborn.

The snow had stopped falling; it was melting fast in the sun and turning into slush.

As he moved about aimlessly, he felt someone touch him on the sleeve. It was one of the dancers, a mere boy, tall and thin, who was saying, "Excuse, please." Fil realized he was in the way between another boy with a camera and a group posing in front of the hotel.

"Sorry," Fil said, jumping away awkwardly.

The crowd burst out laughing.

Then everything became a blur in his eyes, a moving picture out of focus, but gradually, the figures cleared, there was mud on the pavement on which the dancers stood posing, and the sun threw shadows at their feet.

Let them have fun, he said to himself, they're young and away from home. I have no business messing up their schedule, forcing my company on them.

He watched the dancers till the last of them was on the bus. The voices came to him, above the traffic sounds. They waved their hands and smiled towards him as the bus started. Fil raised his hand to wave back, but stopped quickly, aborting the gesture. He turned to look behind him at whomever the dancers were waving their hands to. There was no one there except his own reflection in the glass door, a double exposure of himself and a giant plant with its thorny branches around him like arms in a loving embrace.

Even before he opened the door to their apartment,

Fil knew that Tony had not yet arrived. There were no boots outside on the landing. Somehow he felt relieved, for until then he did not know how he was going to explain his failure.

From the hotel, he had driven around, cruised by the lakeshore drive, hoping he would see the dancers somewhere, in a park perhaps, taking pictures of the mist over the lake and the last gold on the trees now wet with melted snow, or on some picnic grounds, near a bubbling fountain. Still taking pictures of themselves against a background of Chicago's gray and dirty skyscrapers. He slowed down every time he saw a crowd, but the dancers were nowhere along his way. Perhaps they had gone to the theater to rehearse. He turned back before reaching Evanston.

He felt weak, not hungry. Just the same, he ate, warming up some left-over food. The rice was cold, but the soup was hot and tasty. While he ate, he listened for footfalls.

Afterwards, he lay down on the sofa and a weariness came over him, but he tried hard not to sleep. As he stared at the ceiling, he felt like floating away, but he kept his eyes open, willing himself hard to remain awake. He wanted to explain everything to Tony when he arrived. But soon his eyes closed against a weary will too tired and weak to fight back sleep—and then there were voices. Tony was in the room, eager to tell his own bit of news.

"I've discovered a new way of keeping afloat," he was saying.

"Who wants to keep afloat?" Fil asked.

"Just in case. In a shipwreck, for example," Tony said.

"Never mind shipwrecks. I must tell you about the dancers," Fil said.

"But this is important," Tony insisted. "This way, you can keep floating indefinitely."

"What for indefinitely?" Fil asked.

"Say in a ship. . . . I mean, in an emergency, you're stranded without help in the middle of the Pacific or the Atlantic, you must keep floating till help comes. . . ." Tony explained.

"More better," Fil said, "find a way to reach shore before the sharks smell you. You discover that."

"I will," Tony said, without eagerness, as though certain that there was no such way, that, after all, his discovery was worthless.

"Now you listen to me." Fil said, sitting up abruptly. As he talked in the dialect, Tony listened with increasing apathy.

"There they were." Fil began, his tone taking on the orator's pitch, "Who could have been my children if I had not left home—or yours, Tony. They gazed around them with wonder, smiling at me, answering my questions, but grudgingly, edging away as if to be near me were wrong, a violation in their rule book. But it could be that every time I opened my mouth, I gave myself away. I talked in the dialect, Ilocano, Tagalog, Bicol, but no one listened. They avoided me. They had been briefed too well: Do not talk to strangers. Ignore their invitations. Be extra careful in the big cities like New York and Chicago, beware of the old-timers, the *Pinoys*. Most of them are bums. Keep away from them. Be on the safe side—stick together, entertain only those who have been introduced to you properly.

"I'm sure they had such instructions, safety measures,

they must have called them. What then could I have done, scream out my good intentions, prove my harmlessness and my love for them by beating my breast? Oh, but I love them. You see I was like them once. I, too, was nimble with my feet, graceful with my hands; and I had the tongue of a poet. Ask the village girls and the envious boys from the city—but first you have to find them. After these many years, it won't be easy. You'll have to search every suffering face in the village gloom for a hint of youth and beauty or go where the graveyards are and the tombs under the lime trees. One such face . . . oh, God, what am I saying?

"All I wanted was to talk to them, guide them around Chicago, spend money on them so that they would have something special to remember about us here when they return to our country. They would tell their folks: We met a kind, old man, who took us to his apartment. It was not much of a place. It was old—like him. When we sat on the sofa in the living room, the bottom sank heavily, the broken springs touching the floor. But what a cook that man was! And how kind! We never thought that rice and *adobo* could be that delicious. And the chicken *relleno*! When someone asked what the stuffing was—we had never tasted anything like it—he smiled saying, 'From heaven's supermarket,' touching his head and pressing his heart like a clown as if heaven were there. He had his tape recorder which he called a magic sound mirror, and he had all of us record our voices. Say anything in the dialect, sing, if you please, our *kundiman,* please, he said, his eyes pleading, too. Oh, we had fun listening to the playback. When you're gone, the old man said, I shall listen to your voices with my eyes closed and you'll be here again and

I won't ever be alone, no, not anymore, after this. We wanted to cry, but he looked very funny, so we laughed and he laughed with us.

"But Tony, they would not come. They thanked me, but they said they had no time. Others said nothing. They looked through me. I didn't exist. Or worse, I was unclean. *Basura*. Garbage. They were ashamed of me. How could I be Filipino?"

The memory, distinctly recalled, was a rock on his breast. He gasped for breath.

"Now, let me teach you how to keep afloat," Tony said, but it was not Tony's voice.

Fil was alone and gasping for air. His eyes opened slowly till he began to breathe more easily. The sky outside was gray. He looked at his watch—a quarter past five. The show would begin at eight. There was time. Perhaps Tony would be home soon.

The apartment was warming up. The radiators sounded full of scampering rats. He had a recording of that in his sound mirror.

Fil smiled. He had an idea. He would take the sound mirror to the theater, take his seat close to the stage, and make tape recordings of the singing and the dances.

Now he was wide awake and somehow pleased with himself. The more he thought of the idea, the better he felt. If Tony showed up now. ... He sat up, listening. The radiators were quiet. There were no footfalls, no sound of a key turning.

Late that night, back from the theater, Fil knew at once that Tony was back. The boots were outside the door. He, too, must be tired, and should not be disturbed.

He was careful not to make any noise. As he turned

on the floor lamp, he thought that perhaps Tony was awake and waiting for him. They would listen together to a playback of the dances and the songs Tony had missed. Then he would tell Tony what happened that day, repeating part of the dream.

From Tony's bedroom came the regular breathing of a man sound asleep. To be sure, he looked into the room and in the half-darkness, Tony's head showed darkly, deep in a pillow, on its side, his knees bent, almost touching the clasped hands under his chin, an oversized foetus in the last bottle. Fil shut the door between them and went over to the portable. Now. He turned it on to low. At first nothing but static and odd sounds came through, but soon after there was the patter of feet to the rhythm of a familiar melody.

All the beautiful boys and girls were in the room now, dancing and singing. A boy and a girl sat on the floor holding two bamboo poles by their ends flat on the floor, clapping them together, then apart, and pounding them on the boards, while dancers swayed and balanced their lithe forms, dipping their bare brown legs in and out of the clapping bamboos, the pace gradually increasing into a fury of wood on wood in a counterpoint of panic among the dancers and in a harmonious flurry of toes and ankles escaping certain pain—crushed bones, and bruised flesh, and humiliation. Other dances followed, accompanied by songs and live with the sounds of life and death in the old country; Igorot natives in G-strings walking down a mountainside; peasants climbing up a hill on a rainy day; neighbors moving a house, their sturdy legs showing under a moving roof; lovers at Lent hiding their passion among wild hedges, far from the crowded chapel; a distant gong sounding

off a summons either to a feast or a wake. And finally,
prolonged ovation, thunderous, wave upon wave ...

"Turn that thing off!" Tony's voice was sharp above
the echoes of the gongs and the applause settling into
silence.

Fil switched off the dial and in the sudden stillness, the
voices turned into faces, familiar and near, like gesture
and touch that stayed on even as the memory withdrew,
bowing out, as it were, in a graceful exit, saying, thank
you, thank you, before a ghostly audience that clapped
hands in silence and stomped their feet in a sucking
emptiness. He wanted to join the finale, such as it was,
pretend that the curtain call included him, and attempt
a shamefaced imitation of a graceful adieu, but he was
stiff and old, incapable of grace; but he said, thank you,
thank you, his voice sincere and contrite, grateful for the
other voices and the sound of singing and the memory.

"Oh, my God..." the man in the other room cried,
followed by a moan of such anguish that Fil fell on his
knees, covering the sound mirror with his hands to
muffle the sounds that had started again, it seemed to
him, even after he had turned it off.

Then be remembered.

"Tony what did the doctor say? What did he say?"
he shouted and listened, holding his breath, no longer
able to tell at the moment who had truly waited all day
for the final sentence.

There was no answer. Meanwhile, under his hands,
there was a flutter of wings, a shudder of gongs. What
was Tony saying? That was his voice, no? Fil wanted to
hear, he must know. He switched dials on and off, again
and again, pressing buttons. Suddenly, he didn't know
what to do. The spools were live, they kept turning.

His arms went around the machine, his chest pressing down on the spools. In the quick silence, Tony's voice came clear.

"So they didn't come after all?"

"Tony, what did the doctor say?" Fil asked, straining hard to hear.

"I knew they wouldn't come. But that's okay. The apartment is old anyhow. And it smells of death."

"How you talk. In this country, there's a cure for everything."

"I guess we can't complain. We had it good here all the time. Most of the time, anyway."

"I wish, though, they had come. I could . . ."

"Yes, they could have. They didn't have to see me, but I could have seen them. I have seen their pictures, but what do they really look like?"

"Tony, they're beautiful, all of them, but especially the girls. Their complexion, their grace, their eyes, they were what we call talking eyes, they say things to you. And the scent of them!"

There was a sigh from the room, soft, hardly like a sigh. A louder, grating sound, almost under his hands that had relaxed their hold, called his attention. The sound mirror had kept going, the tape was fast unravelling.

"Oh, no!" he screamed, noticing that somehow, he had pushed the eraser.

Frantically, he tried to rewind and play back the sounds and the music, but there was nothing now but the full creaking of the tape on the spool and meaningless sounds that somehow had not been erased, the thud of dancing feet, a quick clapping of hands, alien voices and words: *in this country . . . everything . . . all of them ... talking eyes ... and the scent ...* a fading away into nothingness, till about the end when there was a screaming, senseless kind of finale detached from the body of a song in the background, drums and sticks and the tolling of a bell.

"Tony! Tony!" Fil cried, looking towards the sick man's room, "I've lost them all."

Biting his lips, Fil turned towards the window, startled by the first light of dawn. He hadn't realized till then the long night was over.

The Grandmother

[THAILAND]

by K. Surangkhanang

WATCHED OVER with care, with new kindling sticks
placed carefully one by one, picked up from the woman's
side as she sat there and put them on top of the old
sticks which were almost burnt out, the fire did not take
long to burn up again, licking at the new tinder until
its flames gradually came back to life in the half-light of
dawn.

By the blaze, now burning bright under the three-
legged iron stove on which sat a big steaming-pan,
always standing there at this same spot in the space
under the flooring of this woman wholesaler's house,
built high up on piles, a close cropped head of hair could
be seen, the color of white weedflowers, bobbing up
and down five or six paces away to the right of the stove.
The head was bent down below the level of a flat, smooth
bamboo pole, polished to a shade of shining yellow at
the middle. The two ends of the pole were small and
slightly bent up just at the right places where scoring
marks had been made on both sides by four old rattan
strings, plaited at the top and hanging down to form a

kind of sling for two old crumbling baskets, black with age, one at each end. The baskets themselves each held a flat plaited bamboo tray, on which were placed, one on top of another, a few white enameled bowls with cracks and black chipped spots on them. There were also an old cigarette tin containing bamboo pins and a small piece of rag serving as a cloth for wiping the hands.

What else could all these represent but a *mai-khan* and *saraek?** The *mai-khan* itself, so long in service on human shoulders, shone in the middle a beautiful color of gold.

The sound of water boiling came from under the two-tier steamer. Steam was pushing its way through the seam where the cone-shaped cover met the steamer. Sitting by the side of the stove was a middle-aged woman. She was wearing an old creased *pha-lai†* with several patches and a long-sleeved, gray-flannel blouse open in front. When the woman stretched out her hand to pour some water into the pan, the sound of boiling subsided while a heavy cloud of steam billowed out for the last time before it gradually disappeared. The woman then got up and took off the cover of the steamer, laid it on its back on the ground, lifted the steamer up and put it on a wooden stand where a girl was sitting adroitly rolling dough into dumplings and putting them into another empty steamer. The soft and well-kneaded tiny tapioca grains were flattened in her palm by the tips of

* In Thailand, peddlers, especially women, carry their loads in two baskets which hang from the two twisted-up ends of a pole (*mai-khan*). The *saraek* are the strings of rattan which form the slings for those baskets.

†A kind of printed cloth popularly used by Thai women as a version of *sarong*.

her fingers, then wrapped around a stickly filling, which had been well fried and seasoned with both salty and sweet tastes. The white dough was then rounded off and pinched tight over dark brown pork-stuffing. When her hand was dry, the girl dipped it into a small bowl of water, then moulded more dumplings into a round and smooth shape before placing them in the steamer, ready-lined with banana leaves oiled with fat to prevent the tapioca paste from sticking to the iron of the steamer. The uncooked dumplings looked white and quite different from those already steamed. When she heard the noise made by the steamer being put there by her side, she took a quick look towards one of the thick posts forming the piles for the house above. There she saw the bending form of an old woman, huddled up against the cold. A pitiful sight indeed!

But this was only a daily scene, too familiar for any other feeling to be aroused in the girl but the usual sympathy. She lifted the steamer filled with dumplings which she had arranged in neat rows with her own hands and passed it on to her mother to set on the pan, before calling out to the old woman: "Oh, grandma. Bring your bowl over here. I'll count the dumplings for you."

Her whole body starting up from slumber, the old woman lifted up her wrinkled face marked with old age, to look at whoever had called. "Yes ... what did you say, my dear girl? My hearing isn't good any more."

"I said ... bring your bowl over here, grandma. I'll put the tapioca dumplings in it for you."

Once she had heard clearly, the old woman got up awkwardly, then clumsily poked about for the bowl in her basket. With her back bent she walked over, bringing it to the young girl. Fixing her gaze on the cooked and shining dumplings, still steaming hot, she opened her mouth, with the chew of betel still in it, to say : "Only fifty today, my dear. I want to come home early today, so I can have time to look around for something to offer to the monks. Tomorrow is a holy day."

The daughter of the wholesale dumpling dealer did not answer. She had her work to do, and apparently it called for quite a lot of attention and patience. She dipped her hand into a bowl with chipped rim; the lard inside was hard because it was cold. She spread it on the dumplings to prevent the tapioca from sticking to her hand. Then, separating the dumplings from each other, she arranged them neatly in the bowl. When the heat was too much for her hand, she would blow hard on it. ... But why worry about a little thing like that? She was not the one who was going to eat those dumplings. The bowl was soon filled. She patted the dumplings with her hand to make them look smooth and even, topped them with some golden fried garlic and red and green hot peppers, then handed the lot to the old woman.

Watching her all the time, the old one reached out for the bowl the minute it was handed to her, taking care that her grasp was firm enough so that the bowl would not slip from it. But before walking back to her baskets, she could not help turning around to ask in a voice tremulous because the teeth were not there any more to bar the way of the breath coming out : "Have you put in the three extra dumplings as usual, my child?"

"You needn't worry about being cheated, grandma. If you don't trust me, you can count them yourself!" The young girl was sensitive and a bit snappy. The tone of her voice showed that she was not in a very good mood.

"I didn't mean that, bless you, dear. I'm just afraid that you might forget." Her voice dragged on, while betel-juice trickled out from the wrinkled corners of her sagging lips. "If you haven't forgotten, then it's all right, bless you. Then they're there all right."

She shuffled back to her baskets, put the bowl of tapioca dumplings on the bamboo tray, mumbling something to herself the way old folks do, touched this and that for a moment, then lifted the pole on to her shoulder where patches could be seen on the creased old flannel jacket, stained all over with spots from the betel juice. Tottering a little, she trudged off from the house.

Lights of gold and silver were gleaming on the horizon, but mist was still covering the whole area. The cold penetrated into her very bones. Those bare feet, which had never worn shoes, stepped rather gingerly on the gravel road. Everything seemed to hurt in the cold season; even this fine gravel cut into the soles. The old woman took a short cut across a patch of grass growing under a row of trees by the roadside. A car's horn sounded just behind and she faltered in her steps. Only when she felt the sensation of a car speeding past her in a commotion of noise did she feel relieved. She stopped then at another house to get more dumplings, put them in another basket, so that the weight of the two baskets would balance, then hastened on towards the village market, so as to get there in good time.

Once there, she put down her load next to a roadside grocery store, arranged the two baskets so that they would not be in the way, then sat down. Her knees stuck up over her drooping head and she kept lifting up her face, that face with signs of approaching death written all over it, to cry her wares to get the customers to buy from her.

"Sakoo-sai-moo* ... *miang-lao*†! Buy hot *sakoo-sai-moo,* my ladies!"

The people came early to market. They bought vegetables and they bought fish and pork, until their baskets were all full, but not a soul bent down to ask for her hot tapioca dumplings or her newly wrapped *miang-lao.*

Some passed so close that their skirts even brushed against the rattan strings which supported the baskets. Instead of feeling sorry when they turned around and saw her, they would abruptly turn their faces away as if they had brushed against a log and not a human being. The old woman could only follow them with her eyes. Her mouth, which was just opening to cry her wares, slowly closed. She remained sitting there until the sun was high and the market stalls had nearly all packed up. Still she could not sell anything. Already, she had chewed three or four mouthfuls of pounded betel. With no more patience left, she was just getting up when a woman's voice right in front of her said:

"Grandma, give me three *satangs'* worth of *sakoo.*"

The hands trembled that were wrapping the dumplings in banana leaves. She was fastening the package with a bamboo pin when the buyer stopped her.

---

* A kind of dumpling made of tapioca paste with stuffing made of pork and peanuts. They are eaten with parsley or lettuce.

†Another kind of dumpling with nearly the same kind of stuffing wrapped in pickled cabbage-leaves, to be eaten with fried popped rice.

"Where's the parsley, grandma?"

She looked around, but could not find any. She searched everywhere, even to the bottom of the baskets, but in vain. She must have forgotten to bring it along. Her lips trembling, she pleaded, "I forgot to bring it along. Please wait a moment, my good lady. I'll buy some for you".

"I can't wait." The customer was a woman of a little over twenty. On her waist was a small skinny child with a snotty nose that often ran down to his mouth. "Have you ever seen anything like it. Selling *sakoo-sai-moo,* and forgetting to bring any parsley along? If there's no parsley, then I don't want any!" She fairly croaked with displeasure.

"Well then, so you don't want any, my dear." The old hawk looked up downheartedly at the buyer. She was blaming herself for being so forgetful. She could have earned three *satangs,* but now ... nothing!

The young mother had not moved more than three steps away when the child on her waist began to struggle and cry for the dumplings in a mixture of greed and temper. The mother had to turn back to the old peddler, who was putting the dumplings back into the bowl.

"All right, grandma, give 'em to me. Curse this greedy boy!" she said, "Don't bother to wrap them up. I'll give them to him right now." She threw a five-*satang* piece on to the bamboo tray, took the dumplings, smelled them, bit and chewed half of the dumpling herself, and stuffed the other half into the mouth of the child.

The old woman lifted the tray up, put her band into the basket, and pulled out a piece of cloth which was once red, but which had now turned nearly black, untied the

knot and counted the one-*satang* coins in it: one ...
two ... not this one, it's still new. Let me give her an
old black one instead. Before giving the change, she
looked at the coins well once more to make sure whether
there were two or three. Once assured that they were only
two, she handed them to the woman. Then she picked
up the five-*satang* piece and dropped it on the cement
floor. It sounded all right, not a counterfeit one, so she
put it back into the old cloth and tied a new knot very
tight and put it back into the bottom of the basket. As
she was lifting the pole onto her shoulder, she stopped
as if remembering something, and set it down again.
Once more she lifted the tray up, pulled out the cloth,
untied the knot, and took out a few copper coins;* they
could be used to buy some parsley!

Leaving the market, she then edged along in front of
row-house shops and then dwelling-houses, stopping
here and there to hawk her wares. She had been walking
since early morning, when the air was still quite chilly,
until it was noon, and then through the afternoon in
the hot sun, all the time painfully making her way on hot
gravel and asphalt roads. She kept looking at the
dumplings still left in her bowls while she walked on.
Little by little she sold them. Every time she stopped to
rest, and to grind herself a mouthful of betel, she would
untie the knot to count and recount the money, and
repeat the performance again to make sure. In this knot
was the money to be invested in *sakoo-sai-moo*, in the
other that for *miang-lao*. Today's profit would be put
together with those of the previous days in a separate
knot.

---

* In Thailand the one-*satang* coins are copper, the five-*satang*
nickel, the tens and twenty-fives silver. One *baht* has 100 *satangs*.

Once she had regained her strength, she put the load back on her shoulders, and continued hawking:

"Come buy my *sakoo-sai-moo* and *miang-lao*!"

"Master, would you like some *saskoo-sai-moo?* Here's your hawker."

"Where? Oh, no ... better not. The hawker is an old woman. She's dirty!"

"Mammy, I want to eat *chakoo-chai-moo*!" pleaded a child.

"Wait till I give you a good slap! Asking for this, asking for that when the evening meal is so near. You didn't bring along any bags of gold or silver at your birth, you know! Old woman, go and hawk your goods somewhere else, or you'll be making me spend my money."

"Come buy my *sakoo-sai-moo* and *miang-lao*," the hawking sounded more feeble now.

"Buy my *sakoo-sai-moo*! I've got *miang-lao* too!"

"Grandma, give me five *satangs'* worth of *sakoo*. What? They're all gone? Then why were you still hawking it?"

"Forgetful, master. Old folks are, you know."

Putting the load (which was by then much lighter than in the morning) back onto her shoulder, she continued her painful steps. The sun had already gone down behind a row of trees. Only ten or more *miang-lao* were left. It would not matter even if they were not all sold since they would not spoil. She could keep them until tomorrow. Passing through the market, she stopped there to buy two salted eggs, one salted *pla-too** and five well-ripened freckled bananas, put them all in the

---

* A fish of the same family as mackerel, one of the cheapest in Thailand.

empty basket and headed for home, which she could already glimpse a good way off ahead. But why ... why was it that her legs felt so tired and without any strength?

As for those who were left behind at home, when the evening approached they would be waiting and expecting her return ... not to welcome home this poor old soul as you would wait for a person who had brought you up, and for whom it is now your turn to care. As soon as the mother saw old grandma, tottering along in the distance, she hurried to tell her daughter and her three sons:

"Look, children, your grandmother is back. Go and ask her for some sweets."

And the children would run out to surround their grandmother from all sides. The quick ones would snatch whatever was left in the baskets and put them into their mouths. Those who were slower would cry and fight for some. So, the minute the old woman reached home, with the load scarcely taken off her shoulder, the eldest boy, in one jump, driven by hunger and greed, reached for the bowl of left-over *miang-lao*. He was a boy of eight, wearing a shred of a pair of shorts with no shirt on, grubby from head to toe. His eyes were quick and cunning. When his sister and brothers protested, they fought noisily until the mother had to tell them sharply to share the food; the noise then subsided.

The old woman could only look forlornly at the disappearing *miang-lao*, but would not dare to interfere or stop the children from eating them. What a pity ... what a great pity! After all, she had been hoping all the way home that she could keep them for tomorrow. Of course, she should not have forgotten that these grandchildren would come around and snatch whatever was left over from today's sale, just the way they had been doing every day. She could only look at them putting the *miang-lao* into their mouths, chewing and swallowing them. Nothing was overlooked, not even the popped rice in the tin box.

She hurried to put the load away in its usual place, because only then did she remember the salted eggs and the freckled bananas that she had put in the basket. If one of the children happened to find them, they would also be gone. She did not mean to keep these two things for herself to eat; they were meant as offerings to the monks. It would not matter much if she would have to eat only one meal out of two. It would be like this only in this life. With all her good deeds and the offerings she had made, she might be born again a great king's daughter in her next life.

The mother looked as if she could hardly wait for the old grandmother to get home. She pretended to scold the children: "What children, snatching grandma's things? Leave them alone so she can sell them tomorrow. Get away, get away from here, go and eat them somewhere else."

The old one could understand only too well that her daughter was scolding the children in the "mouth-scolding, eye-winking" fashion. She often pitied herself for all the troubles and all the hardships that she had to endure, for having a grown-up daughter who had married and had children of her own, on whom she could not depend for anything, not mentioning the fact that she had to strive and labor so hard to earn her own living, even at her ripe old age.

The old woman did not utter a word, for she felt too hungry to bother about anything. Furtively she reached for the red rag holding the money and put it in the pocket of her one-sleeve tunic, then tiptoed into the kitchen, opened the earthen rice pot with a broken edge, only to see some burnt rice left over at the bottom of it. The few dishes of food scattered around the rice-bin bore the look of something waiting to be taken away and washed up more than something that could be eaten. Anyway, taking out a wide bowl, filling it with rice, she sat down and reached over for the dish with a few legs of salted crab left in it. She mixed together whatever left-overs there were; it would be enough for subsistence.

As she was lifting the mouthful of it to her mouth with her hand, the daughter came into the kitchen.

"Mother, have you got some money? Lend me about thirty, will you? There's no more kerosene for the lamp." Those were her words.

The hand that was lifting the rice to her mouth was weakly lowered. In order to avoid looking at her daughter's face, she looked down at the grains of rice in the bowl instead, and remained silent for quite a while. With whatever small profit she had made today she had bought food that was intended as an offering to the monks. What was left was only the money she would have to hand over to the dealer as the cost of the dumplings, so that she could get a new lot for tomorrow's sale. It was a long while before she was able to utter a halting answer: "No, I haven't got any. I only have enough for the cost of the dumplings."

"Why, didn't you make anything at all selling things today?" asked the daughter, the tone in her voice showing displeasure.

"I did not sell them all. Didn't you see the ten left-over

miang-lao that your kids have eaten up?'' This was the only answer the old woman could make, feeling hurt to the point of tears by her daughter's words.

Already put in a bad mood by the thought of not being able to screw any money out of her mother, the daughter was now touched on the raw by her mother's mentioning the *miang-lao* that her own children had eaten. Taking it as reproof for ingratitude that her old mother was directing at the children, she raised her voice and retorted :

"If I had known it, I would not have let them eat them!'' Then abruptly she left the kitchen, went straight to one of the girls who was enjoying herself playing a game, slapped her once on the cheek and spat out : "Here, you wicked brat. Why did you have to eat your grandmother's things? There ... there ... for being so greedy, not knowing what you should eat and what you shouldn't. Didn't you know that they were not for you, you little devil?''

The little girl howled because she was quite hurt and unprepared for the punishment. She was absorbed in her game and did not know what it was all about when her mother rained blows on her.

"I did not eat them. Phi Choi* did,'' she cried and struggled. "Please mother, don't hurt me.''

"You're all alike. Come here, Ai Choi!† Come here, you villain, or I'll have your blood, I will!''

With her hands on the hips she yelled at the boy,

* *Phi* means "elder brother or sister.'' A Thai uses this word to address someone who is older and deserves respect—in this case, "elder brother Choi.''

†*Ai*, the opposite of *phi*, is used when addressing a person one holds in contempt.

pointing her finger at him. A few bamboo sticks were stuck between the slats of the wall. The sight of Choi, trying to hide in fear behind the water jar, made her temper still worse. She ran for a stick and rained blows on him without mercy. She called him names while beating him: a child who was born to ruin his parents, born to waste all the money, born to make her bankrupt, etc. But Choi, though the blows hurt, was not the only one to howl. His other two small sisters also joined in this chorus of caterwauling.

The grandmother saw everything and heard every sarcastic word directed at her by the daughter whom she had borne and brought up with all due care until she should get married and raise a few children of her own, and who, even then, still had to depend on her old mother. Old as she was, instead of being cared for by her children like other mothers, she had to go out to peddle in order to earn a bit here and there to support herself. She could not hold back her tears thinking of this. She bent down to dry her eyes on the lap of her skirt.

The rice she was trying to swallow seemed to get stuck there in her throat. Every word that passed through her ears hurt her so. She would not blame her daughter, but thought instead that all this must be the result of the bad deeds she had committed in a former life. Joining her two hands and putting them above her head, she murmured : "I'm doing only good deeds in this life. Do not let me come across such a heartless child in my next life . . . please!"

What was left over was all eaten up, but the poor woman still had not eaten her fill. Only a lump of rice remained at the bottom of the pot, yellow because it was burnt. She poured some fish sauce on it, then mixed it up and ate it the way poor people did in times of hardship. She could not help thinking back to the time when she was still raising her own children: never would she let any of her little ones eat plain rice with fish sauce. There had to be at least rice mashed with bananas or with soup. In better days they would have rice with meat-curry, or sweet-and-salted pork stew. But now that the time had come for her to ask the children to take care of her, all she got in return for the kindness she had bestowed upon them was some rice left at the bottom of a pot mixed with fish sauce, which tasted more like salt water than something that was supposed to be made of small shrimps and fishes.

Well ... at least with this daughter she could still find a roof to sleep under and something to eat. From the other four daughters and sons she had got nothing except signs of disdain. Her eldest son was now the abbot of a monastery in the country. Since he was a monk and not an ordinary person, if she went to visit him often, the temple boys would insinuate that old grandma went there to be fed with whatever food was left over in the begging bowl, which by rights should belong to the serving boys. So now she had to force herself to feel that her eldest boy had no more place in her life.

As for her second daughter, she was married to an orchard owner with two big wooden houses. The old mother once dragged herself over to stay with them, but found it impossible to remain after a few days, because that daughter, Piam, would keep nagging at her: "Do help Phi Boon to cut down those weeds in the ditches of the orchards, mother, or he will say that

I brought you into this house only to treat you like a princess. Near the bamboo clump over there. The hired men have done it so many times already, but they just don't seem to get rid of them fast enough."

So, not long afterwards, she had to bring her old frail self back across the river from the orchards in Klong Mon, to come and stay with her third child. Nearly every night she did not get to sleep; this son would come home nearly every evening drunk and start beating his wife and children. If she intervened, he would push her so hard that she would be sent reeling.

The fourth child was the most wretched of them all. When the mother went to her asking to stay with her for a certain length of time, she burst out crying and complained: "How can you stay with me, mother, when I myself can't stand the harsh treatment of my mother-in-law yet? They are all people of blue blood. I'm so afraid that you'll come here and do something awkward and funny, then I'll have to be ashamed of you. Please don't stay here; go and stay with Nang Phew!"

Phew was her fifth child and the youngest, the one she was now staying with. She was poorer than the others, because she was married to a lazy man who did not like to work. He could never stay long at one job, giving as reason that the work was too hard, or that he was not strong enough for the work. Things being like this, the old woman could not sit still; she had to get herself a pole and a pair of baskets, and go out peddling whatever she could.

When the son-in-law and her own daughter were able to make some money, they would quietly spend it themselves without letting her in on it. But if she ever earned any, the daughter would always be there pressing her for a share. This she did not mind so much; she realized that she was living with them, so it was only natural for her to help out. But showing their displeasure toward her by beating their own children! Often she cried, pitying her poor own self and wishing for death to come soon as a means of escape from all this misery.

Phew kept it up for a long time, scolding her children with the intention of directing her spite at her mother, until she was so tired that she had to stop. Dusk came, but she pretended not to notice and let the whole house remain in darkness. There was no light; her small children stumbled over uneven planks in the floor and cried.

The old grandmother could not stand it any longer. In the dark she had to look for the bottle and then went down the steps to go out and buy some kerosene for the lamp.

Around half past seven her son-in-law came home with a few packages of sweets for his wife and children. They got around together to enjoy the sweets, but who would expect them to have enough heart to hand some over to the poor old soul? The good smell of the food came wafting past her nose and she could only swallow betel-juice and choke over her hurt feelings.

That night, before the poor creature could fall asleep, she had to get up several times to get a drink of water to quiet the pangs of hunger and to quench the thirst caused by eating salted food that evening. She thought of the freckled bananas which she had hidden in the basket ... but they were intended as offerings to the monks. It would not matter if she had to starve herself, but let the holy ones have them, so she could have merit in the next life. Little did she realize it, but the one monk who came around to receive the offerings, the minute he saw her coming down those rickety steps, would say to himself words that would have shocked her : "Here comes this old wretched woman again! Hasn't she got anything else except salted eggs and freckled bananas? I'm so sick of the stuff!"

What would she get in return, this poor creature who so deprived herself in order to give to another? Heaven!

It is nature's law that ripe fruits will finally fall off the branch, and this old creature was thus like a ripe fruit . . . so old, so ripe! How many more days could she last? Every night before going to sleep she would repeat in her prayers her wish for the god of death to come soon to take her, and she prayed she would go in such a way that it would cause neither grief nor trouble to anyone. Little did she know that these wishes were soon to come true, on this very day, without her being the least conscious of their fulfilment.

That morning, she woke up before her daughter. In the kitchen she cooked rice and then went to make merit with her offerings of a salted egg and a package of cake wrapped in dried banana leaves. After breakfast, she went as usual to get the dumplings for her daily round of peddling. She still felt strong, both in body and mind. Then came midday when she felt faint; she had been walking in the heat of the sun without any rest. But she forced herself to keep on hawking along the street. She took a different route today. On the left side of the street there was a small canal with water about one meter deep. She intended to turn and cross over to the left bank of the canal by a little bridge made of a single plank with a rail of bamboo to hold on to. A small lane led from this bridge to the house of a man who was a good customer for her dumplings.

The minute she stepped on to the bridge, her sense of hearing became dull and thousands of little lights danced before her eyes. Her heart felt funny, but she thought it was nothing serious, for she could still see her way. With her hand she grasped tightly the bamboo rail and thus supporting herself, continued until reaching the middle of the bridge. Then everything suddenly became dark; her step missed the plank and she tumbled down on one side. Her hand let go of the rail and she fell down into the water below.

Five minutes later, only the banana leaves, which were used to wrap the parsley, could be seen floating in the water. Bubbles came up all around the spot and gradually disappeared. The flow of water carried away the banana leaves and other light objects which came up from under the water later. Some of them floated along and then got stuck in the bushes of tall grass or the Java weeds with pale purple flowers growing on the side of the canal. None of the people who crossed the bridge would ever suspect that deep down below them was the deathbed of a poor old woman!

The people in the neighborhood of Samsen Nai, Bangsue, will no more hear her voice. The familiar hawking of *"Sakoo-sai-moo ... miang-lao"* will no more reach their ears. Those she left behind will feel sad, will miss her or mourn her death only when they begin to miss her helping hand and the good deeds she once rendered them. But what good would mourning do, when the person herself has gone and never will return ... never!

—TRANS. BY THAILAND P.E.N. CLUB

Champoon

[THAILAND]

by Dhep Maha-Paoraya

BEFORE WE went to the building and to the special ward, the director of the hospital stopped and warned me.

"This patient comes from a good family and the story which I have pieced together from relatives and friends of his is connected with people who are still living, wealthy, and ... and influential. And his symptoms and signs are such that, well, we, the doctors of this hospital ... we cannot come to any definite conclusion. You see, we hesitate to call him insane, especially from the legal sense.

"Officially, I can only state this patient received a violent shock. It's five months now, and yet he cannot get free of it. The whole world is shut off from his consciousness. Only what led up to the event causing shock is remembered. His brain cannot accept any other impressions. This is the whole trouble. We have tried everything we can to bring him back to normal consciousness, to make him react the normal way. If we can do it, he will be a normal person, we think, but if we can't, then ..."

The doctor shrugged, spread out both his hands in front of him in a rather hopeless gesture, then went on :

"I have told yo⹁ something of the background of the main actor in this drama. It is up to you to decide if it is to be staged before an audience."

The patient was a young man of about twenty-seven or twenty-eight. He was well built, and his illness had in no way affected his looks. He was not pale or emaciated as one might be led to suppose. In fact, he did not look like a patient of that hospital at all. He was good-looking and had an intelligent face, and his clothes were good. He got up to greet us with dignity, like a well-brought-up person who had moved in good society. He also revealed by his manner the personality of a leader and not of a follower.

But after the usual introductions performed by the doctor, he gazed vaguely at me and maintained a disturbing silence until I remembered the doctor's observations and began :

"You must have lived some time in Bhuket?"

"No, not for any long time. It was at Taimuang, in Pa-nga, that I stayed many years."

"Taimuang is the meeting point of many mining districts, isn't it? It must have been great fun."

"It was hell."

I was alarmed. "What? Did it have anything that other places didn't have? Like Haadyai, for example?"

"Haadyai and other such places had women, drinking, and gambling. But Taimuang had champoons, crocodiles, and iron chains."

"I don't understand. What had champoons, crocodiles, and iron chains to do with the three vices you mentioned?"

"I will tell you," he said.

From thence on, the current flowed. I had succeeded in breaking the dam and the flood poured forth. What follows is the story I got from him, except here and there, where I have helped with the sequence of the narration. In some places, there were gaps which I have had to fill from information gathered elsewhere. The names, of course, of all the persons and places are fictitious.

"My father was governor of Pa-nga. I was educated in a boarding school, said to be one of the best educational institutions in Bangkok at the time. However, when I was sixteen I began to run a little wild. My father wired for me to go back to Pa-nga, then he sent me to school in Penang. I was there five years until I finished my schooling. It was about the same time that my father retired.

"My father was one of those rare persons who realized long ago that we Thai should do something towards freeing ourselves from foreign economic domination. He had always tried to encourage me towards going into business rather than to work with the government, and I fell in with his view quite easily. It suited my character better. When my father went back home to Bangkok after he was retired, I separated from him and took a clerical job with an Australian mining company in Pa-nga. My rather irregular life and education had equipped me for this job, because I spoke Malay, Hokkien, and Hainam. The firm was ready to pay any price for someone who knew these languages in addition to a knowledge of English and Thai. I was paid two hundred baht, a salary I couldn't dream of getting if I went to live with my father in Bangkok.

"However, I worked only two years with the Australians. An American company, the Yukon Gold Mining Company, opened a mine near Taimuang and wanted someone who could supervise all its Asiatic laborers and also act as liaison with the government officials for it. I applied at once and, out of more than ten applicants, the company chose me, the youngest man of all. I was paid a salary of one hundred and fifty American dollars, which was about four hundred baht. Besides this, the manager allowed me to handle all its buildings and other contracts, so that in a very short time I came to earn, on the average, about eight hundred baht a month.

"For a young man of twenty-four to earn eight hundred baht a month, though it was not unusual for Bhuket, the way lay open leading to a significant change in my outlook on life. When I earned two hundred baht, I had always had enough money left to put into the savings bank at the end of the month. I led a quiet life, I read, and listened to the radio after work.

"But when I began to earn eight hundred, my money rarely lasted through the month. It was not at all anything to wonder about. Nai Amnuey made a reputation for himself, a reputation for all the vices there were in the region. Yes, I was always in the forefront where women, drinking, and gambling were concerned.

"I was also in the forefront in other things. I never allowed anybody to be superior to me. I was always a leader, never a follower, in any society. And I carried it off well too, because, I believe, it was my social background that helped. I felt at home in any company, either Thai or foreign. And what is more, there was my money which opened all doors to me.

"The places I loved best to spend my time in were the many clubs in Taimuang. The town was the center of land communication of the region, from which roads went in all directions. From there one could go to many places by land, and my company's headquarters were only a short distance away. All the most interesting dens were to be found here, too.

"I would like you to pay great attention here, because it's important to what follows.

"There were two ways of travelling between Taimuang and the mouth of the river where the company's headquarters were situated. From here you could go upstream in a boat until you found the Takuapa-Tungmaprao Road on the other bank. You waited until you could catch a bus and then you went again downstream to Taimuang, and towards the mouth of the river. This took a lot of time. It meant sitting stiff in the boat for five or six hours, and then you could never be sure whether you could catch a bus or how long you would have to wait for one.

"The other way was to get a boat that would take you across the river right to the area near the mouth. Then you trekked on foot across the jungle to Taimuang. This would take about three hours before you reached your destination. There were serious disadvantages travelling this way. You could easily lose your way in the jungle unless you knew the paths very well. And oh, there were crocodiles in that part of the river, in the greatest number and the fiercest that I have ever seen. When my father was governor of Nakorn Sritammaraj, I accompanied him on crocodile hunting trips in the Pak Payur district, which was said to be the worst infested area. But it could not really compare with this river near our mines. Here, in this river the crocodiles would jump right on men in a boat. It was no wonder that part of the country was deserted with only a few habitations on the banks of the river; and very few people would venture to cross it, especially in a small boat. This district was notorious all over the province of Bhuket. Taimuang people who wanted to visit our mines would refuse to cross that river even at the narrowest part, unless the boat was strong enough with good close sides.

"I, of course, used the company's boat, which was sufficiently big, and so I was able to cross even at places where the river was at widest, and from the bank I would cut across the jungle. I got to know the paths very well and used them as often as I wished. But even so, I would time it so that I would get out of the jungle before dark, because tigers' footprints were not a rare sight in the district.

"You see how attractive vice is. Even tigers and crocodiles could not keep us away.

"I don't want to boast, but I have to say that I was very popular at Taimuang. I was in fact quite a distinguished person. Quite a guy, perhaps, as some might say? And this led me into a clash with an important person of Taimuang, in fact, of Bhuket. The man was Taokae Soon.

"Taokae Soon was known also as Big Brother Soon. Now if this man had prospered in Bangkok, his name would have been pronounced in a way so the Chinese meaning would be always kept. But in the Southern dialect, it was made to sound local or foreign, as suitable to the occasion. Taokae Soon was a friend and acquaintance to every man in the region round Bhuket, big men and small men without exception. But the areas where his influence was felt most were Takuatung, Takuapa,

Pa-nga, Koakloy, and Tungmaprao. It could be said that every case, legal and illegal, was tried by some means by Big Brother before it was tried in court, or was settled outside of court. All high government officials were entertained by him. All VIP's travelled over what roads there were in that area in Big Brother's cars, and stopped at places where he thought he could best provide them comfort.

"All the luxuries obtainable in the region would then be put at the VIP's disposal. If a VIP made a wish known, it was fulfilled at once. Big Brother had the reputation of being the most lavish entertainer. Young government officials easily succumbed to him and were soon turned into useful instruments.

"It was this kind of success Big Brother won that brought me into conflict with him. Big Brother was strongly nationalist, for his own fatherland, of course. This was in no way blameworthy. But what made me grind my teeth was when he would insult Thai young manhood in general, when any young man made a slip and misbehaved himself in any way. I, too, was violently nationalist. Taokae Soon, of course, was never openly insulting. He was always sarcastic and subtle. I thought I could match his subtlety, and was never openly hostile. He was a veteran gambler, while I was young and new in gambling circles, but I managed 'to erase the tiger's stripes several times with some original tactics. People began to talk about it and laughed. And this was something Soon could not forgive.

"Even though we did not get into open conflict, it soon became known all over the area, and it was always incomprehensible to me how everyone, both Chinese and Thai, could manage to give us opportunities for a clash. It seemed to be some kind of a game for them to see me, a greenhorn, at war with an old tiger like Soon. I began to worry that one day they might force us into open battle. Soon had been the king of the jungle so long that it was impossible for him to tolerate the situation. How could the lion allow a strange animal to invade his territory without doing anything about it? I warned myself that something would happen to me, if not in daylight, then at dark of night. I walked more and more warily. Until...

"Do you know the champoon?"

I was startled out of my train of thought while following his narration. I felt afraid. "Goodness! The doctor has left me alone with this patient. Am I safe?" I quickly replied. "I have heard of it, but have never really seen one."

"It's a rare flower in Bangkok, but in the southern provinces it is quite common, especially in the area around Taimuang. I will describe it to you.

"It's of the family of champa. It looks something like a champee, but with a velvety calyx which at first wraps up the petals inside while the flower is a bud. Then this velvety part opens out first and later the petals. The fragrance is then released. The petals are waxlike, thick and stiff. They don't fade like those of a champee. After it opens, the champoon lasts several days. The scent dominates that of all other flowers around it. The scent is overpowering, compelling, and unyielding.

"Isn't it strange that Soon with all his nationalism should name his only daughter after this flower? Champoon. He probably knew how it suited her. At nineteen, Champoon was a bright and attractive girl. She did not attract at first sight, just like the flower she was named after. But once you took a careful look, her beauty was revealed to you. Her emotions were exactly what you would expect from a girl with that name. They changed frequently, and they had the same power as the scent of that flower. They made Champoon an overpowering, compelling, and unyielding personality. Champoon was a girl who, once her mind was made up, would let nothing in the world change or stop her from carrying out what she was determined to do.

"Champoon went to school in Bhuket until she was twelve years old. Her father thought it was now time she should stay at home like a good Chinese girl. But Champoon was at that time in Matayom IV, and had tasted enough of the freedom of a Thai girl to rebel at the idea of spending her life the way her father had planned for her. Soon was a strong-minded person, but he somehow realized and appreciated the fact that Champoon had inherited her strong mind from him. He compromised by allowing her to go and continue her education at a convent in Penang. This shows that it was not education for girls in itself that he objected to; what he wanted was to prevent Champoon from becoming absorbed into Thai life. It means, of course, that he did not wish his daughter to marry a Thai.

"It was not long after Champoon's return home from school that her father's will clashed with hers. Taokae Soon could not get rid of the idea of keeping his daughter caged up. And Champoon would not accept that sort of treatment. There was some kind of a cold war waged between father and daughter. Champoon would yield in some ways to a certain degree, such as refraining from going out by herself and not appearing in the front part of the house, which is against the custom of the

Chinese. This would appease her father somewhat, but should Champoon decide that she had to go anywhere, or her presence was required at any place, she would not let her father's conservative ideas stand in her way. And her father would pretend he knew nothing about it, because his courage failed when faced with her stubbornness, and he would not press for obedience whenever it was more convenient to seem amenable.

"I must describe to you the way houses are built in the south, so that you will understand what I mean when I say Champoon agreed not to appear in the front part of the house.

"Lodgings in the southern provinces are built so that they look more or less like rows of tenement houses in Bangkok, one built next to another, along the side of the street. The houses seem of the same depth from the street as tenement houses in Bangkok, but they usually stretch much longer along it. Each house may be thirty or forty *wah* in length [*wah* = nearly one meter]. To obtain sufficient light, the roof is open in certain places. The openings are covered either with glass or tin, depending on the wealth of the owner. The glass or tin sheets are movable so that the openings can be closed when it rains. The wealthiest Chinese in the region live in this kind of house, because Chinese businessmen build beautiful mansions only for show, but they prefer to live in the places they have prospered in.

"Taokae Soon's home was built in the way that I have just described. But the house was outside the town and did not face a busy street, while the back of the house was on the fringe of the jungle. In Chinese homes, girls were rarely seen in the front part, and though Champoon did not approve of the custom of keeping women secluded, she did not care to show herself there and be conspicuously different from her neighbors. She really enjoyed keeping busy with all kinds of housework and homecrafts. She read a great deal, having books sent to her from Penang and Bangkok, and she enjoyed going on excursions into the jungle.

"We met by accident, and fell in love, as if it had been planned by long-ago Brahma. Our love was sudden, strong, and deep. The fact that we had to keep it secret, and that it seemed hopeless, served only to intensify it. We knew very well that Taokae Soon would rather see Champoon laid out in a coffin than to see her married to the man whom he hated and regarded as his worst enemy on earth.

"I want you to take note of this. Champoon was a very determined girl. She loved with a strong and deep love. It was like life itself to her. But try how she might, she saw no ray of hope of our love ever being fulfilled in the customary way. Still she refused to elope with me. Her education and upbringing prevented her. As for me, I can swear by all the gods that I loved her truly and deeply. And I, too, could not take advantage of her. Although we saw no way to escape, we preferred to adhere firmly to tradition, and Champoon chose to suffer longing and pain rather than to take the easy way out.

"Taimuang was a small community, and nothing remained secret for long, especially a love affair like ours, with me the man and the daughter of Taokae Soon the girl. Talk swept the town like a forest fire, and soon reached the ears of Champoon's father.

"Our contacts and meetings were suddenly stopped. I could not see her. I knew that she was imprisoned in the house and had not been taken away because I had men placed so that they could tell me. Don't let me tell you of what I went through, all the agony and suspense. I tried by every means in my power to contact Champoon. It became an open secret that if anyone could succeed in taking my letter to her, there was a reward of three hundred baht, and if anyone could bring her letter to me there was a reward of five hundred baht. No one, however, succeeded, although several persons made attempts: most of them met with strange calamities. Taokae Soon had not ruled the region for decades for nothing.

"During the period of our underground hostilities, Taokae Soon and I had observed certain rules of civility. We were polite to each other on the surface. But now it was open enmity. We looked daggers at each other if we happened to meet, though we tried to avoid each other. As for Champoon, I got some news of her from some of my agents. She had been whipped and tortured, and was imprisoned in that long dark house of her father's. It sounded like an old Arabian tale.

"I had been kept away from Bhuket for a long time. This became a topic for talk in many circles in the region. A group of friends, therefore, hired a motor boat and came on a visit. The object wasn't only social in the ordinary way. They wanted to throw a wild party in order to console me.

"That party was a memorable one, in just the style that Bhuket was famous for. Food, drink, and women. I don't have to tell you about the quality of the food and the wine. It was what one would expect from a party where expense was no consideration. But there was something else which no amount of money could have bought. Every man there had a woman, chosen and assigned, and there was one brought especially for me. I was told that this special import from Penang usually cost two hundred dollars a week, but, on this occasion, it was a special invitation she had accepted.

"On a dark night, when the moon did not shine, a little resin torch was light enough for a darkened soul. So when one suffers because of a woman, it is appropriate that one should get consolation from a woman. My friends, after all, had some sense. That was how I rationalized and so I accepted the gift of the devil.

"She was called Anita. She was a Filipina with a dash of Portuguese blood. She looked exactly like a Thai. Her Caucasian blood only made her figure more elegant, and her movements more graceful. Her face was beautiful, her whole personality attractive. It was unbelievable that with her beauty she should be what she was. Or it might be because of that beauty she had become what she was, I don't know.

"My friends spent three days and three nights on the boat, and I was with them. They wanted to take me to Ranong but I had important business and could not go with them. They, therefore, went on their merry-making way, but left Anita with me. In five or six days they would be back to pick her up again, when she had to go back to Penang, or go to some other employer, as the case might be.

"I suggested to Anita that she should go on with my friends to Ranong. But surprisingly she chose to remain in that wild remote place with me. When I asked her the reason later she said she liked my youth, my looks, and my good manners!

"How destructive those attributes of mine were to

me! But how could I know what lay in store? How could I know what beautiful Anita's decision would do to my life and my soul?

"As soon as my friends left, Anita and I went to my house to enjoy the full delights of the flesh. Our newness to each other was still something exciting for us.

"My house was a wooden bungalow, roughly built. There were three rooms all open on to the verandah from which steps led down to the ground. One of these rooms, the first, I used as my bedroom; the center one was where I had my meals. From the center room there was a passage that took you to the kitchen and the bathroom. The last room I kept always under lock and key because it was there I kept my documents. I seldom locked my bedroom, even at night.

"My bungalow was a little way apart from other houses belonging to the company, about halfway from the river and the fringe of the jungle. It was quiet and usually deserted. I had a servant and a cook, who worked for me only in the daytime. In the evening, the workmen would gather at their own quarters, gambling or enjoying themselves some way. All this suited my purpose very well, and my bungalow became a veritable love nest for me and Anita.

"The evening before Anita was scheduled to be fetched away by my friends, I received an invitation to a dinner at the house of the company's engineers, which was near the sea. After dinner, we danced and the two engineers had a very good time.

"I knew that the reason for the invitation was Anita. The two engineers had been cut off from the society of women for a long time. The nearness of a beautiful woman was too much of an attraction for them to pretend indifference. But they knew proper limits and respected proprietorship. They danced with her and enjoyed touching her and flirting a little with her following Western customs. We had a pleasant time till it was almost dawn.

"I am usually a light sleeper and it always takes some time for me to go to sleep. That night, however, I dropped off to sleep almost as soon as my head touched the pillow. It must have been because I was very tired, due to the orgies that I had gone through for several consecutive nights. I felt that I dropped off only for a while, really, before I heard the creaking of the front door; the hinge was never properly oiled. I woke up immediately. I was sure that I had closed the door before I went to bed.

"I opened my eyes. The morning sun shone into my face from the open door. I could see a vague outline of someone moving in the middle of the doorway. I was not sure if I was seeing right. I raised my head from my pillow and rubbed my eyes.

"God! Was I dreaming! Was I gone stark crazy! That vision is still before me every time I close my eyes. It was the vision of Champoon all nude, without a single piece of clothing on her Her rich black hair fell all over her shoulders, wet. The sight was made more grotesque by the presence of an iron chain, about half an inch thick, one end of which was wound round one of her ankles, the other tied round her waist.

"The vision stood in front of me and we gazed at each other. We kept quite still for a little while, then I saw its eyes move slowly away from my face and I followed them as if hypnotized.

"Then we both held our breath, our eyes riveted on

the same sight. It was Anita sleeping, breathing softly, her body pressed against mine, in that fine, gauze-like, expensive mosquito net.

"I don't know why the naked form of Champoon did not stir up any shameful feeling, but that of Anita sleeping lightly clad so shamed me that I quickly piled a coverlet on top of her body.

"I could not look up to meet Champoon's eyes. I waited for her to say something. All that went on in my head was: Was I crazy? Was I dreaming? Was it a dream or reality? In the end, the silence seemed too long for me. I collected my presence of mind, pressed both my hands on my eyes and looked up.

"Champoon was gone!"

Champoon had confessed to her father that she was in love with Nai Amnuey, and that she had met him secretly several times, but assured him that her lover had respected her woman's honor, and that she had never thought of doing anything that would bring shame on herself or her family. But it was something beyond the understanding of a man like Soon. In his way of thinking, women could only suffer one consequence from secret meetings. Soon had six concubines in his home, and he believed Nai Amnuey to be a quite normal young man. And Nai Amnuey was his enemy, the only man who had dared to stand up against his will in that part of the country over which he had ruled for decades. His daughter had been a traitor to him. She had allowed herself to love that very man whom her father hated bitterly. He could not bring himself to listen to her.

When both father and daughter are so obstinate, and when they are determined not to meet each other halfway, the result is obvious. Soon became violent.

He snatched up a big piece of firewood and aimed a blow at Champoon. She dodged and he missed. He succeeded in giving her a severe beating, however.

Champoon was afraid the noise would attract the attention of neighbours. So she uttered only faint moans when the pain was too great for her to bear. But she asked for no quarter. And when Taokae Soon had finished beating her, she raised herself from the floor.

"I told you I am still innocent, and you won't believe me. You cursed and beat me. I will now do everything in my power to go to Amnuey and give myself to him. Heaven be my witness."

Everyone knew that Champoon would keep her word, because she had never said anything that she did not intend to carry out. One week later, she walked out of the house while her father was absent from it.

The word of the head of a Chinese family was law unto his house. Especially in the case of Taokae Soon, it was known that his power was absolute. Soon had threatened to whip everyone, wives, sons, and servants, if Champoon should ever get away. Champoon therefore could not escape. The whole household literally dragged her back, while some ran for the master of the house. Champoon's first attempt at escape was followed by severe punishment.

She tried again several times, but failed. In the end, Taokae Soon, who would brook no opposition, gave an order for her to be chained to a post in her bedroom. At night, to permit her some freedom, he allowed the chain to be loosened from the post, but it had to be kept on her ankles. Finding that Champoon tried to escape in spite of the chain, he ordered one of her stepmothers to go in every night and remove every piece of clothing from her before she went to sleep. This last measure, he felt certain, would be more effective than any other. He had sworn, too, that he would not give in to Champoon even if the conflict between them destroyed one of them.

But one morning when he unlocked the door of Champoon's bedroom, he found it empty. The roof was open and the glass that had covered the opening was pushed to one side. Taokae Soon had not realized that Champoon could have used her bedsheet to help haul herself up. He had relied too much on the chain. No one knew why or how he reasoned he would carry out his orders regarding his daughter's escape. The fact, however, remained that Champoon was gone.

Champoon had escaped to Nai Amnuey, the man of her love. It was never known what pains and dangers she went through to reach him. The local authorities could only guess.

"Champoon must have pulled up her chain from one of her ankles and tied the loose end round her waist somehow. She must have climbed on to the top of her wardrobe and hauled herself up on to the roof. She most probably used her foot to push open the roof, and succeeded in getting out through the opening. She was a strong and healthy girl, and it shouldn't have been too difficult for her to escape the way it was guessed.

"But it was miraculous how she found her way to my house. How did she cross the crocodile-infested river? No one could answer these two questions. It was believed, of course, that the bedsheet which Champoon must have used to clothe herself in had been washed away from her by the currents in the river.

"So it was really Champoon that I saw in the doorway of my bedroom. I knew that she had really been there when I found that she had disappeared. The opened door assured me that it was not an illusion. I jumped out and was on the verandah in a flash, but I saw no trace of her. I found my voice and called her name. I ran calling her all the way to the river bank. I ran back and forth until the sun was high in the sky. I realized then that she had intentionally hidden from me, because it was impossible for her to go far enough in those few minutes that it took me to get out of my bed for her not to hear me calling her.

"I ran to the workmen's quarters and collected about twenty men. I made them spread out in a long line, one end of which touched the river. I made them march upstream until dark. We failed to find anything and at sunset we returned home.

"I set out for Taimuang without going back to my bungalow. I would grovel at Taokae Soon's feet just to hear him tell me that Champoon was safe at home.

"When I reached Taimuang I learned from one of my secret agents that Champoon had not been home. Even then I humbled myself and went to Champoon's father. After all Champoon was his daughter and though Soon and I hated each other, Champoon had been dear to both of us. But the wretched Chinaman was a beast in human guise. He laughed and said that if Champoon were shameless enough to return he would beat her to death and send me her corpse in a coffin.

"So I went back home and got together again about thirty men. I separated them into two groups, and ordered them to march again along both banks of the river, because I thought Champoon couldn't have gone in any direction without following its course. She might have crossed the river somewhere it was narrow. We started about nine o'clock. I followed both groups of men in a boat which I rowed upstream.

"I had been either walking or running for the past twenty-four hours. I do not remember eating anything, only taking four or five gulps of brandy. I must have dozed off, but I came to with a start when the bow of my boat was pushed hard against a place on the bank of the river. I asked what happened and one of the boatmen pointed to something. . . .

"Do you know how crocodiles make a meal of a human being?"

I told him no.

"However big a crocodile, it cannot swallow a human body. Even though its mouth is big it cannot bite pieces off, its legs are too short to help it tear. It must always take it on land to make a meal of it. It takes hold of a part of the body in its mouth, and beats the body against a tree. It eats whatever part falls off from the body. It eats one of those parts each time and goes on beating and beating until the whole body is in shreds."

The patient stopped talking at this point. He gazed away into the distance as if he saw a sight which no one could share with him. The silence made me nervous, so I blurted out :

"Did the boatman find Champoon?"

"No," the patient said. "What he saw was a piece of chain tied round a human leg that was torn away at the knee. It was on a low branch of a tree. . . .

"Sir, can you tell me? Did Champoon go into the river on purpose in order to be eaten by a crocodile? Or did she try to swim back to go home to her father and confess to him that she had loved the wrong man?"

—TRANS. BY THAILAND P.E.N. CLUB

My Milk Goes Dry

[VIETNAM]

by Minh-Quan

MILK HAS played such an important part in my life that it should be spelled in this story in capital letters: MILK. The idea sounds laughable at first: what should milk matter to a child bereaved of her mother since the earliest infancy, and fed dairy milk with a glass bottle and a rubber nipple? The dairy milk on which I was nurtured was the Bird brand very well known in this country. But—I want to make it clear—the milk with which my life has been concerned, and which I take so much to heart, is human milk produced by human mothers.

I didn't learn the distinction between the two kinds of milk at school. The days I went to school could be counted on one's fingers, since the many odd jobs a small child could do were more useful than education. As a matter of fact, I wasn't busy all the time. I had a lot of spare time during the summer holidays, when my uncle and his wife and all my cousins went on vacation. But of course the schools too were closed at that time, so I had no hope of studying. What a nonsensical situation: when I was busy, schools were open; when

I wasn't. . . . But leave it. I will tell more about it later.

To be frank, I must confess that until I became a mother for the first time, I didn't really realize the importance of nursing a baby with one's own milk. Had I brought my child up naturally and simply, as other women did, I would not have to spin a long yarn about it now. But my story is rather . . . well, I'll tell it in full.

My uncle now and then set forth ideas which sounded rather eccentric, but the small child I was then could only listen to what seemed beyond my powers of thinking and imagination.

My uncle was clearly a learned man (at least I presumed so), for he talked and talked of the East and the West, of the past and the present, with no intermission and without consulting any book. He usually opened with, "According to books," to give more emphasis to his speech and to show people that he was a man of letters and not a poor fellow.

I must point out again that my unsophisticated mind was then like a wilderness, which would have to be cleared with an axe. My uncle gave the first stroke—too hard a stroke, it seemed to me. But as I was the lowest person in the household, I could hardly protest against his judgments.

How petty and humble is the position of an infant orphan in a family! I realized it better than anyone, so I tried to make myself smaller—the smaller I could be, I thought, the better. But unfortunately, nobody would take the trouble to understand what I was doing. They took it for granted that I was disobedient, unfeeling, a liar, and had all the bad qualities possibly inherent in a naughty child.

But all the insults, and even some bloody floggings, were not so painful that they produced a sense of outrage at my uncle's half-pitying, half-depressing looks and his disheartening speeches:

"This small girl is done for!" he would exclaim to his wife. "And you still beat and scold her! What's the use of it? It only makes your hands and body tired. You see, I ..."

He looked at me and sighed, leaving his sentence unfinished, but I understood what he would have added: "There is no hope for you, and I'm sorry for you. You are an untamed child, unable to turn over a new leaf. Even a rag can be used to wipe up dust, but you are less useful than a rag! Rubbish—no more, no less. Not only that, you are a burden to me."

I understood everything. As I stood there, my eyes would be dry, but my heart was wounded, paralyzed. Youth is generally reckless, though; it wouldn't take long for my sorrow to fade away. The next time, I would feel only surprised when my uncle unexpectedly stared at me with the same discouraging look, and began again.

"If you are ... it's owing to those three Frenchmen," he might say.*

This comment struck me as strange indeed. What had the French to do with a helpless creature like me? How could they be responsible? Who knows ... (my active imagination would work on a lot of hypotheses), had they murdered my mother, burned or plundered my house? Such a riddle was too hard for a small child to solve. It only made my head ache. Since I had nobody

* A customary way of mentioning the French in South Vietnam.

to ask for advice, the riddle remained a heavy unanswered burden on my heart.

After some time, I noticed that whenever my uncle talked to his friends or relatives, he constantly referred to two topics: milk, and "those three Frenchmen." Milk and Frenchmen were two topics of which he never tired; I, too, found them rather attractive.

"Look," he would say, whenever he had an audience. "These three Frenchmen are liars, dishonest people, plundering, raping, seizing other people's land. They are merciless beyond imagination, and they never flinch from any cruelty. And do you know why? Why are they so barbarous?"

Here he would stop, clear his throat, and pause so as to excite the curiosity of his listeners and make them eager for the answer. If his listeners were young men who hadn't heard this speech before, they would press him eagerly to go on. Others, like Mr. Hinh, a night watchman, would only laugh and say, "We don't know, tell us." Some, like my aunt, remained unruffled as they always were.

But whatever the attitude of his audience, my uncle always knew how to treat them. His pause was never so long that the enthusiasts cooled down, nor was it so short that his subject could be treated as other than one of momentous import.

At exactly the right moment, he would continue, "No surprise at all, my friends. It's because none of those Frenchmen is allowed to suck the breast of his mother. White men are not human beings; they are all devils. If a child is fed with animal milk, he is deprived of all human sentiments when he grows up. Believe me, I'm telling the truth. Worse yet, these barbarous people are now planning to corrupt the Annamite* in the same way.''

He would give a distressing sigh, as though he were pitying the whole Annamite race thus on the road to ruin.

Once, after listening thus far to his discourse, I moved closer to him, plucked up all my courage, and asked, "Honorable uncle, may I ask you something? I did not feed on animal milk, did I? I sucked ... I drank bird milk, and bird is not an animal; bird is a ..."

"Oh! Blockhead! Who told you that? You fed on bird milk? A bird is just the brand-label stuck on the milk tin. It would take too long to say, for example, 'This cake is of dragon make,' so instead we say 'dragon-cake.' This does not mean the cake is made of dragon meat. It's the same with milk: the bird is merely a brand name, but the milk comes from cows. Birds never have any breast at all; even if they did, it would be too small to hold a reasonable amount of milk. And it's no easy matter to catch them, anyway. Really, I must salute your stupidity. Listen carefully (now he was stressing every word): you were drinking cow's milk. Do you understand—the milk of cows!"

I started as if struck by thunder, but before I could start to cry, my uncle began to shout. "But how dare you ask a question, you saucy girl? Children don't know anything. Really, you are too bold!"

His anger made my legs shake and my head swim, but he soon completely forget all about his unfortunate niece. He sipped some tea to wet his throat and soon, more eloquent than ever, he was citing evidence to make his argument more convincing. For instance, he said,

* Old name for the Vietnamese.

Emperor T'sin Tche Hwang never enjoyed the suck of his mother's breast, so he remained quite unmoved even by a "river of bloodshed" or a "mountain of corpses." But Mencius and Confucius, the celebrated philosophers, had sucked the milk of their mothers until four years of age. So had Jesus Christ. As for Buddha Shakya Muni, he was reared by his aunt since he lost his mother. (My uncle did not specify what Buddha's aunt did with her own baby while she nursed her nephew, or whether she had recourse to the dread animal milk. But I dared not voice my questions. And I heartily wished I had such an aunt.)

My uncle also cited western examples: Neron of ancient Rome, and Ulysses of Greece. The Roman emperor did not suck at his mother's breast, he said, but the Greek king did. So it was no surprise that Neron did not shrink from any cruelty, while Ulysses was a wise man.

In Annam, he added, we also had two illustrious men, genius Tran Hung and sage Trang Trinh. Both fed on their mother's milk until they could read. In short, all the wise men, outstanding philosophers, and gentlemen of this world had sucked at their mothers' breasts, and all the cruel men and merciless murderers had not.

I drank in all these words from such a wise mouth, and was almost lost in thought when suddenly my uncle looked straight at me and said:

"Furthermore, man is the highest of all living creatures. According to books, among all the beings—the flying-in-air and the running-on-earth, the four-legged are the lowest. 'As silly as an ox' is a phrase we use all the time. Yet these devil French have imported a lot of cow milk to our country, and we have been foolish

enough to use it in rearing our children. The extermina-
tion of the Annamite people is only a hair's-breadth
away!"

I shivered from head to toe and my hair stood on
end as I listened to these words. I understood every
word of his speech, even the Chinese names (although
I barely knew how to hold a writing-brush). I felt
overwhelmed with shame as I recalled how I had boasted
of myself to my friends. I told them that if I was cleverer
than all of them, it was because of the bird's milk I had
drunk as a baby. Birds, I proudly said, belonged to the
superior feathered creatures.

"Superior feathered creatures? What does that
mean?" the children had asked, staring at me with
wide eyes. I had explained as clearly as possible:
"Superior means high; feathered creatures means birds,
and superior feathered creatures means birds flying
high in the sky, dignified and noble."

Not content with stopping there, I had gone on:
"Opposite to superior feathered creatures, there are
inferior hairy beings such as oxen, buffaloes, pigs,
horses, etc. Inferior hairy beings are animals moving
basely about on four legs, almost crawling on the
ground, forever enslaved to human beings." I pointed
to the buffalo on which I was riding and said, "For
example, we use oxen and buffaloes for plowing, and
horses for riding, and pigs for meat."

The whole group of boys and girls had greatly admired
my eloquence, and I felt so delighted that I went on
lecturing, like a professor: "Superior feathered creatures
are also called 'flying feathered creatures'; flying means
moving in the air and feathered creatures means birds.
As for the inferior hairy beings, they may also be called

'running beasts'; running means moving rapidly on the ground.''

On and on I went; as my audience showed no sign of wearying, I talked nonstop. Now and then, I threw in an "According to books," to impress the listeners. All at once I realized that I sounded just like my uncle, and stopped, startled. But I had proved myself a fine speaker. Sitting up on the buffalo's back, I had felt very light—so light that I might almost have flown up to the sky like a bird.

But now, my speaking career seemed to be at an end. How could I face my friends? I felt like an animal who had once had a fine coat of fur, but who had been shorn and now showed nothing but an ugly skin infected with boils and itching. Until now, I had been looked down on as a beast; from now on, I was in danger of regarding myself as even lower than that. I felt as if the earth were sinking under my feet and the sky darkening over my head.

But my uncle did not perceive my terrible state of mind. He went on speaking volubly of outstanding men all over the world; he quoted other extraordinary names, told anecdotes about them, and offered many convincing proofs to strengthen his theory. But I took no more pleasure in hearing his words. I confusedly heard something about Mahatma Gandhi, and that was all. To the rest, I was deaf.

What did Ulysses matter to me? And Neron? And even Tran Hung Dao? Did those illustrious men pay the slightest attention to me? Did they realize that I wished only one small thing to comfort me—to have been reared on the milk of birds—but that my dream was not to come true?

Suddenly, in the midst of his discourse against "those three Frenchmen," my uncle stopped and put his finger on the forehead of one of his daughters standing near him (he had many daughters), and shouted in a severe voice: "Mind you! If ever in the time to come, you snobbishly follow this 'civilized way' and rear your children with cow's milk, I'll beat you to death!"

From that day on, whenever he looked at me with his deep, sharp eyes, I understood what he was thinking: "Oh, saucy girl, I take pity on you. If you become rough, unfeeling, incorrigible, it is because of your mother's early death. You had to feed at the expense of a foul, inferior, four-legged being. Now the beastly nature has infiltrated to the very core of your backbone and dominated your nature. I feel awfully sorry for you, but there is no way to save you, no way."

One day, as his talk proceeded to its vehement climax, he suddenly pointed his finger at one of his daughters and sternly shouted, "Take care of you ..." At this, my aunt smiled sourly and cut him short: "Don't worry, your teaching has had good effects. Your niece says she will suckle her children with her own milk."

My uncle turned to her, his face crimson with anger. I really feared for my aunt, for I was sure he would scold her for her ironical remark; at the same time, I hoped he would show me some affection and praise me for my response to his preaching. But alas! he expressed his anger another way.

"You're quite a fool, aren't you?" he said to his wife. "I never mention this saucy girl; it's quite useless to teach her. I give lessons and advice to *your* children only, do you understand? But this evil girl will probably ..."

I understood him, even though he did not finish his sentence. My face hardened and became as rough as stone. My uncle saw this, and was pleased to see his farsighted prophecy coming true so quickly. "You see?" his look of triumph seemed to say. "Look at her face right now. Nobody else could be worse than she is."

That night I wept, and I could hardly sleep. My tears, held back for the whole day, now flowed like rain. I cried until I felt relief from all my pain, and then I pondered my fate.

I regarded myself as a human being like other people; I knew I had not been transmuted into an animal. My circumstances, while unfortunate, were extraordinary, I thought: because my mother had died so early, I could hardly have done otherwise than drink bird's milk—or rather, Bird brand cow's milk. I could not deny my uncle's assertions (whatever he said had to be true), but I decided that he must have overlooked the special nature of my case. Only those who lived with their mothers but still did not suck their mothers' milk, surely, were turned into beasts by cow's milk.

Kneeling in the dark with my hands joined together, I prayed earnestly to God, Buddha, Christ, the Spirit of the Mountains, the Spirit of Rivers, and even Providence to have mercy on me and help me to safeguard my human nature. Afterwards, feeling much better, I fell into a sound sleep full of sweet dreams. I came across Ulysses and Gandhi, looking kind and noble and very much like the pictures of Sir Happiness and Sir Fortune on my uncle's Chinese calendar. One after the other, they caressed my head and said, "Don't worry, I will help you. . . ."

Suddenly a shouting voice rang in my ears and chased

away my sweet dream: "You! Still lying stiff like that? Look, the sun has risen nine masts up the sky!"

I crept out of my sleeping mat, but I wasn't too frightened; "nine masts up the sky" just meant that the fifth watch was over and it was close to daybreak. Quickly I washed my face and led the buffalo to the rice field. I had not felt so calm for a long time.

Since that time, I have always prayed to Ulysses and Gandhi, as well as to the other gods, when I ask for protection.

After that day, too, I kept my ideas to myself. I had made the mistake of telling my cousins that I wanted to breast-feed my children; my words had found their way to my aunt and—worst of all—to my uncle. From now on, I would tell them nothing. I also stopped bragging about my knowledge of "superior feathered creatures" and "inferior hairy beings" to the boys and girls who drove buffalo to the fields. Soon I had almost completely stopped talking to them, too.

Instead of talking to others, I began to examine myself over and over to make sure that my actions and ideas were still human. I often caught myself looking into my own being as if it were a stranger, to search and scrutinize. I watched over myself as vigilantly as if I were an enemy. If I caught myself wishing or wanting something, I immediately checked the thought and said to myself, "Beware; the cow milk may still be lingering in your body and poisoning you."

One day my aunt told me to take some pigs to the market to be sold. It promised to be an unpleasant job, since I should have to sit close to those grunting pigs, each one shut up in a separate bamboo crate, all the way to the market. But I was pleased to be going by myself, enjoying a little freedom. Besides, my aunt was trusting me to take the pigs safely to market and bring back the money; this must mean I was getting to be a responsible grown-up person.

As we waited on the platform for the train to leave, my aunt gave me a bright silver ten-piaster coin and said, "This is for you to buy some food on the train whenever you feel hungry. But don't be in too much of a hurry. Wait until the train stops, then look around and choose the nearest food hawker. And always get the food before paying. If you don't, the train may pull out and then you'll be without both food and money. Also, mind you don't . . ."

I stopped listening. I could only absorb so much advice at once, and wished fervently that the train would leave at once, so I could be by myself. "Mind this, mind that, what else yet?" I was muttering in a low voice, when suddenly the train rumbled and began to move. But my aunt still shouted advice from the platform: "Mind you, don't stand on the wagon steps when the train is about to start, or you'll fall. . . ."

I was rather moved by her worry, especially when she called me "my dear," as she never had before. I might have been carried away by emotion, had I not caught her next words on a last breeze: "If something happened to you, who would take care of the pigs?"

I was tempted to cry, but the giddiness of a freedom such as I had never enjoyed, and the scenery on both sides of the train, diverted me from my unhappiness. Only when the train came to periodic stops at small stations did I realize that it was quite unpleasant to ride in close quarters with pigs in a cattle car. The rest of the time, I was quite contented.

At one stop, an old woman appeared on the platform. With one hand she leaned on a stick; with the other, she begged alms from the passengers at the train windows. Muttering unintelligible words, she waved her quivering hand up and down, back and forth, in front of the passengers for a long time. Getting no response, she moved in the direction of the cattle car, where I was. She groped her way step by step, looking quite wretched and miserable. With her eyes showing but their white corneas kept stiffly open, and with her nostrils now swelling, now deflating, and vibrating all the time, she was a sight both funny and pitiful. I felt deeply sorry for her, and put my hand in my pocket for my silver coin. I was just about to hand it out the window when I heard giggles and voices from the passenger car.

"Ha! The old woman is going to ask for alms in the cattle car! She must be blind. Nobody is there but the pigs!" But I was there, half hidden inside, and I saw two smartly dressed girls about my age lean their heads out of their coach to get a better look at the beggar; they acted as though they were enjoying a circus. I stood dead still, lest they should see me. The old woman moved on down the platform, patiently waving her hand to and fro and muttering insistently.

After a long, shrieking whistle, the train started up again. Brusquely I sat down on the floor, close to the pigs, and cried. I felt deeply grieved at the scene I had just witnessed. At the same time, I was angry with myself for having missed a rare opportunity of doing good, just because I was ashamed of being seen. I was afraid I should never have another silver coin in all the rest of my life.

Later, when I recalled that incident, I was gnawed by

remorse for failing to do a good deed. But at the same time, I felt proud of myself for having acted more human than the other passengers. In fact, I later realized, the giddiness of liberty I had felt in the train had made me totally forget to keep my usual close watch on my thoughts and actions. If I had felt like doing a charitable thing, it was really and truly a natural impulse—a very noble human impulse. Having thus proved my humanity again to myself, I felt very cheerful. I wanted to shout, so that everyone could hear me, "Look! I still have a human nature in spite of having drunk cow's milk."

Of course, I didn't shout, or even speak of the incident to anyone. I had learned my lesson. If I couldn't even confide in my uncle, who was my closest relative, who could I talk to?

Even though I didn't hold a grudge against my uncle for his lack of sympathy and understanding, I was far from tolerant of everything and everybody. I hated "those three Frenchmen" terribly and relentlessly. If I was forsaken, despised, and morally tortured, who else but those French could have caused my misery? They were responsible, according to my uncle, for bringing tinned cow's milk to our country.

I was lucky enough to be gifted with a strong human nature, I told myself; otherwise, the "animal substance" of cow's milk would have supplanted it and spoiled my whole life. I vowed that if I ever had children, they would all drink only my milk. I would never let them live in such a miserable situation as I did. "Oh Lord the Mighty," I prayed. "I pray Thee not to let me suffer death so early as my mother did. Pity, pity!"

And there you are, my friends and readers. Now you know the reason for my determination to feed my children with my own milk. If I did not, they might grow silly, cruel, or inhuman, according to the wise preaching of my uncle. The story sounds very simple, but it was written with the tears of a child.

Until I had my fifth child, I kept my vow to the letter. All my first four children had drunk milk from my breasts until they were able to eat rice. Even the fifth one fed smoothly for six months, when suddenly my milk began to go dry. One morning, when I got up, my breasts felt less tight than the previous day; they remained unchanged even at feeding time, and the baby seemed unsatisfied even though it sucked longer than usual.

I tried not to think about it, but my brain worked feverishly at possible answers to the riddle. Had I wronged my breasts in any way? I had not: I abstained from wine, cigarettes, spicy dishes, even tea; ordinary rice, common sugar, peas, and kidney beans were my usual foods. At 9 p.m. I shut myself up in my room and carefully barred the door, lest my husband disturb my rest. With all that trouble just for the sake of my milk, how could I be having this trouble?

"Take it easy, my dear," said a friend of mine, who was also my midwife. "Why make a fuss over a trifle? It's natural to have less milk after several confinements. I've experienced it myself."

"Take it easy!" I retorted. "That's easy enough for you to say. You don't have my worry—I don't have enough milk to feed my child!"

She frowned. "Have you given him his bottle yet?" she asked.

"His bottle? Oh no, I don't bottle-feed him!"

"But I advised you to bottle-feed him when you were confined, didn't I?"

"Well, at first I was going to, but then I decided not to. I didn't think I needed to, since I usually have a lot of milk."

"Good heavens! Well, hats off to you, my dear, but do give him an extra bottle now. There's nothing to worry about; he's old enough to do without breast milk."

All right, since there was no better solution. But it was hard to accept her suggestion. If you gave birth to a child, I thought, it was your responsibility to feed it by yourself—otherwise what was the use of women's showy breasts?

Looking for the first time at a bottle filled with strange milk intended for one of my children, I felt vexed and angry. My hands shook and could hardly hold the bottle. The baby seemed to suck on the hard nipple unwillingly. Unaccustomed to the makeshift rubber, he tried now and then to push it out with his tongue.

As I struggled with the bottle and with my wounded pride, I suddenly remembered a time several years earlier, during the resistance fighting, when condensed milk had been as scarce as gold. While all the other mothers worried about where they would get milk, my mind was untroubled. From time to time, my husband would ask me, "Darling, won't you buy some tinned milk for the children? It may be impossible to get when we need it."

"Thanks a lot for your advice, comrade," I would teasingly reply. "But your humble companion can produce enough milk for them. Please don't worry about it; just mind your grand affairs."

Usually my jokes would make him laugh, but sometimes he continued to nag at me: "You are never serious, but the situation is, and you don't care a bit."

It wasn't that I didn't care, I thought, but what could I do about the world beyond my baby and my breast? In time of war, people had better get closer, love each other, and not fight among themselves. So I thought, but I said nothing, and gave my teat to the baby.

My husband seemed to regret his outburst; he came closer and started to talk, just as I was trying to reach a glass on a nearby table. "Do you want a drink?" he asked. "I'll make it for you." I shook my head gently and took the glass from his hand. I put it under the other nipple, and within a minute the glass was almost half full of milk. I put my head back and drank it before his amazed eyes.

"You certainly have plenty of milk, haven't you?" he said admiringly. Getting no answer, he went on, "But don't you find it unsavory?"

"Do you think I'm a fish?" I retorted. "It's my own milk!"

"Is it really good? Tell me frankly."

"Why not?" I vaguely said, adding to myself, Aha, he wants some himself! "Why do you want to know? Tell me. If you want some milk I'll buy it for you. But don't pretend to worry about the baby; you know he's never lacked enough milk. Tell me the truth."

Red-faced, he denied it: "You're joking all the time! I'm not a baby."

We both laughed. Then I said, "I lied; my milk isn't good at all; it's a bit creamy and sweet, and difficult to swallow. I was just teasing you."

"Then why did you drink it?"

"Because I didn't want to waste it. In order to recycle it for the baby, I had to drink it, and if I didn't finish it in one gulp, I might not have been able to finish it."

Remembering this conversation, I also recalled a friend's words about something called the law of compensation. I wondered whether this law applied to my present situation. When we had been poor and sometimes had to eat weeds instead of rice to ease our hunger, my milk was always plentiful; but now, when I could have anything I wanted, I was denied what I wanted most—milk.

I also thought about the other women with whom I had become acquainted in recent years. None of them breast-fed their babies. Some said it would be unhealthy, or spoil their complexions; others thought their own milk was unfit for a child's constitution. Many said it would take too much time (although they did not spend their time working, but rather strolling, shopping, or otherwise entertaining themselves). One woman said, "Whenever I let the baby feed at my breast, I feel so tired!" Another held her husband responsible: "A queer fellow, my husband. He is against my old way of nursing."

All these excuses sounded like a Greek poem to me. Although these women were my friends, I paid no attention to their ideas on breast-feeding. Instead, I took advice from women who suggested precautions for insuring a constant flow of milk.

One of my cousins told me, "Now, drink as much milk as you can. The more milk you drink, the more you produce; just as eating pork liver is beneficial to our own livers."

I asked everyone for advice: everyone prescribed differently. My neighbors from the North suggested:

"Cook some pork trotters with papaw; that kind of food will give you a lot of milk."

"Banana flowers are the best."

"Glutinous rice soup is excellent. Eat it and your milk will be flowing like a stream."

A grand lady from Hue suggested, "There is no better thing than nenuphar seeds cooked with deer's stomach."

A friend from Saigon urged me to drink beer. Guffawing, she said, "Believe me, gulp it down and you'll have as much milk as you like. I'm not joking."

When I first experienced a shortage and had recourse to tinned milk I followed all this advice indiscriminately. I ate everything my friends advised. I even asked some religious people, though they know nothing about milk; they gave me a recipe for a decoction of fried cotton seeds, which they said was very simple but would have good effects. Since I was nervous, I not only drank the decoction, but also crunched the seeds. At first I sensed a creamy good taste, but soon got a sore throat from the seeds.

I began going to doctors, and dosed myself with every French medicine having remotely to do with lactation: mammary extract, Galactogil, Galacta syrup.

I grew heavier by the day, losing little by little my good figure, but it didn't worry me. I knew many ways of losing weight quickly, and could very easily regain my figure. Besides, my figure wasn't my biggest concern. I only wanted to be able to say that all my children had been raised only on their mother's milk, and had never drunk even a drop of tinned milk.

A sympathetic friend sent me a preserved deer foot, still coated with dirt, with instructions to cook it with kidney beans. Even this I ate, loathsome as it was. More than once, as I tried all these remedies, I could not help throwing up what I struggled to swallow.

It must be said that I accepted any and all advice because I had no organized theory of child-rearing myself. I always relied on my female intuition and on my own experience; this practice, I felt, would keep my babies healthy, less susceptible to disease, and able to recover quickly from sickness. In later years, after reading many books and articles on child-rearing, I became even more firmly convinced that this method had been the right one.

If the baby had a temperature, I would sense it in my nipple as the baby sucked; I had no need of a medical thermometer. If it caught a fever, I would try to discover the cause: a draft, too-cool bath water, or a tooth coming in? If it belched, it might be sick, or it might just have sucked too hard. If it had diarrhea, it might be because we did not cover it warmly enough; but more often, it was because we ate too many vegetables.

My love of the child, and the tender attention I paid it, gave me the ability to feel beforehand what would happen to it next. Because I had lost my own mother so early, I threw myself totally into being a mother to my own children. I learned by myself what had to be done, while I brought them up.

At the beginning, after I brought my first child into the world, I took minute care of my breasts, and they were the source of my deepest joy. While the baby fed on my milk, our mutual love grew deeper and deeper. While the baby sucked at my breast, I was listening attentively with my heart, my brain, and my senses. Overwhelmed with pride and happiness, I watched my child, that innocent infant who knew nothing but the suction of that vital motherly fluid. My heart overflowed with joy; I felt myself transported and ready to fly.

I became much stronger and steadier, feeling as if I could move rivers and mountains. I felt like a soldier waiting eagerly for the battle hour because he had entire confidence in the victory. When I held my child in my arms, all my griefs receded, and my disappointments disappeared; all the sorrows which lay heavy in my heart seemed to float away. All the hard trials of the past, the present, and the future became unimportant; I was well armed to face and overcome them.

Then one day, the child who had sucked unconsciously became aware of me. It looked around; its brown limpid eyes, sparkling like drops of water, darted here and there. Then it turned up to stare at its mother and now and then loosed the nipple from its pretty mouth. Suddenly, it smiled, an angelic and miraculous smile. Time seemed to stand still; reclining on the bed frame, I refrained from smiling, speaking, or making the smallest movement, trying to prolong the moment, afraid that if I so much as breathed deeper, time might be startled and flap its wings more quickly.

What could be similar to that exalted state of mind? The feelings of a drunkard given a lot of wine, or of a military officer decorated for distinguished services? The immeasureable sensations of a countryman who returns home after long years abroad, or the rapture of a poet who uncovers some classical verse which has been lost for centuries?

None of these emotions seems analogous to that which I felt as I suckled my child. I cannot describe the sensation in words, but those who have experienced it will understand.

Because of the happiness it gave me—and also, perhaps, because of the lessons I learned from my uncle, I regarded milk as something of great value. When I wanted to throw out the surplus, I counted every drop. If, after a bath or before I suckled the baby, a few drops were squeezed out, I was annoyed.

I took pride in the fact that I had nursed all my children by myself—from the first one, whom I nursed in an unexperienced and awkward manner, to the fourth one, when I was better off and could hire a maid. The maid could do any of the housework except care for the children; that, I reserved for myself.

But now, with my fifth child, my record was being broken. I was rapidly growing fat from eating too much for the sake of my milk. People I met on the street began to address me in a playful manner:

"My dear Thu, you are really looking well."

"Milk has brought good effects on you as well as on your child."

"Both of you are getting equally rotund; as our saying goes, the mother grows round and the baby grows square."

These witty remarks at last aroused me, especially when I heard the giggles of my sisters-in-law. One afternoon I went surreptitiously to a weighing-machine, and watched in dismay as the needle climbed up, up—to 54 kilos. Nonsense! The machine must be out of order. I went to another druggist, and then another, but alas! every machine gave the same answer. I had become fat. All the food and remedies I had taken, instead of aiding my milk secretion, had merely stagnated in my body and made me fat.

Suddenly I was boiling with rage. According to my height, my normal weight was 48 kilos. I hadn't wanted to become fat, but only to increase my milk production. Back at home, I threw out all the remedies and foods, and returned to my normal diet.

In the seventh month after my confinement, my milk was providing only one suck a day. These were the most troublesome days yet. From dawn to dusk I spun around like a top, cleaning, boiling, and washing the bottles; heating the milk; boring holes in the rubber nipples. The holes had to be of moderate size, to pass milk through in just the right quantity. If they were too large, the suction might choke the baby; if they were too small, the bottle would be refused. I would trust no one else to make milk for the baby. I was afraid the milk might be too hot or too cold, or the water not cooked enough, or the bottle not clean, or the amount of milk over or under the ration. ... All day long I worked, sweating through my clothes.

One day, my husband remarked, "Darling, are you practicing the arts of the conjuror? What are you muttering about all day?"

In fact, I felt very anxious about the baby's constipation. Often I started and woke up in the middle of the night. At meal time, if the maid came and signalled me with a look, I immediately put down bowl and chopsticks and left the table. Voices followed me :

"What's so urgent?"

"My dear brother, our sister-in-law is going to investigate the baby's excrements."

"Even while eating?"

My eldest daughter said, "Mummy acts like a medical doctor, doesn't she, daddy?"

"Maybe your mother is practicing the part of Cau Tien."*

When I came back to the table, all the children would be holding their noses. My husband would jokingly ask me, "Well, Sir Cau Tien, how are the excrements?" I might laugh with them, or stay sober, according to the result of my investigations.

I became a serious scholar of constipation. Books and journals on pediatrics piled up on my bed. I even read foreign books, giving my husband another opportunity to make fun of me. "In which points do you think the Vietnamese books are not so good as the others?" he would ask. To this, I remained silent, as if I didn't hear him, and went on reading.

Once I shouted at my youngest daughter, "Mai! Bring me the dictionary!" The poor girl, who did not know what a dictionary was, stood in confusion before the disordered heap of books. Once more I ordered, "Hurry up!"

"Mummy, I can't make out which is which!"

"Oh, what a stupid girl!" I reproved her, quite unthinkingly, and she began to cry. "Why are you crying? Nobody is hurting you."

Only when, sobbing, she reminded me that she had not yet been sent to kindergarten did I realize my mistake. I burst into laughter, took her in my arms, and patted her on the head to soothe her.

"I am sorry," I said. "I thought ... Now please go

* According to Chinese history, a defeated king who tried to taste the fecal matter of the Emperor to show his fidelity.

quickly to my bed and pick up the biggest book. That is the dictionary."

At once I resumed my reading, standing near the stove where the kettle boiled with the milk bottle inside.

Worried as I was about constipation, nothing distressed me more than feeding with a bottle this baby who never seemed to grow accustomed to it. Now and then, he rebelled against it, twisting his body right and left, and sometimes even pushing the bottle onto the floor and spilling the milk. In the face of such a reaction, I could only helplessly cross my arms and weep. So both of us, mother and baby, cried together.

The baby was still sucking at my breast once a day, but it seemed to be no more pleasureable than bottle-feeding. Often he grumbled and grunted while eating, and sometimes, when he drew in unsuccessfully, he turned abruptly aside and gave me a smarting pain in my heart.

Finally, the day I was trying to delay arrived : the baby had nothing to suck; my milk had gone completely dry.

Seeing that I was as wretched as a chicken in heavy rain, my husband said, "You're really strange! Where did you get these ideas about breast-feeding, anyway? You treat the child as if he were a newborn, hugging and embracing him. ... Besides, is your milk still nutritive enough to warrant mourning over it?"

Words choked in my throat; I shivered angrily from head to toe. But my husband calmly went on :

"There are plenty of tins of the best quality milk in the markets, and we can certainly afford them. Listen to me, and buy them for the baby; they would be much more nourishing."

His voice rang deafeningly in my ears at first, then seemed to get further and further away until it echoed as if from a long distance. I turned away, hid my face on the baby's shoulder, and used its clothes to dry my tears. Hugging the baby to my breast, I mourned again for the "golden days" when I could feed a baby from one breast and fill a glass from the other.

At least, I told myself, I had nursed this baby for nearly eight months without recourse to cow's milk. Surely that was the major part of the job, and I had been up to it. Still, I decided that it was probably not a good idea to have any more children.

But my sixth child came into the world in spite of my intentions. This time I was not taking anything for granted, and in the second month I began mixed feeding with one bottle each day. But the reality was worse than I imagined : in the third month, my milk began to go alarmingly dry.

Frightened, I tried every possible remedy, though not so immoderately as the time before. But alas! the better care I took of my breasts, the less they responded. I felt displeased, restless, and haunted by my failure.

In order to pull myself together, I busied myself with sewing, cleaning, sweeping, washing the linen, and bathing the children. I even read books, if I had time. But God save me from childbirth books and reviews : I had read them over and over again, and learned all their instructions by heart; I was fed up with them.

I told myself, rather unconvincingly, that milk could not stream up adequately in the daytime because I was so busy, and concentrated on nighttime. I stayed awake during the afternoon siesta time so as to sleep more soundly at night. But when night came, though I was terribly tired, I would lie in bed staring nervously at the ceiling and listening to my heart throbbing. I strained with all my senses to feel the milk surge up into my breast, but could feel nothing. Perhaps at daybreak, I would tell myself, and wait apprehensively. Some nights I heard the "odo" in the sitting-room strike every quarter-hour until the sun rose.

Finally I did not sleep at all. Often during the night I would get up, tiptoe into the next room, put a blanket over one of the children, rearrange the mosquito net over another, open a window in my husband's room. Then I would go into the sitting-room, where a very sweet moonlight showed everything at rest except my anxious and agitated self. I would sit down on a chair in a corner of the room and try to calm my nerves as I waited for time to pass. But instead, my grief would grow larger and larger, like an oil stain spreading on a sheet of paper.

After long days of anxiety and sleeplessness, I was taken ill. Always before, when I became sick, I had thrown off the sickness with my own natural vitality, without recourse to doctors and medicine. I thought I could do the same this time, but it was a big mistake. I sweated constantly, and my nose and eyes ran all the time. I felt so dizzy that when I tried to sit up I fell back down on the bed, and everything in the room seemed to turn round and round. I vomited up everything I tried to eat. For the first time in my life, I had to be helped to walk.

My grievances still troubled me, but in different ways; they changed from acute pains to more distilled, deeper sorrows. As I recovered gradually from my illness, my milk went completely dry, though I tried desperately to conserve the last few drops.

Anyhow (I tried to console myself) this baby had fed

on my breast for four months. But what if there were more babies? Deprived of their mother's milk, they would lose their most effective protection.

In spite of myself, my mind kept returning to my "golden days" of milk in abundance. I shut my eyes, and saw circles of all colors dancing before me—now approaching, now receding, now very small, now growing bigger and bigger like the wavy surface of a pond where the wind blows.

Suddenly my husband's words rang in my ears: "Is your milk still nutritive enough to warrant mourning over it?"

Ah! Now your milk is. ... What? I felt my breast hanging somewhat heavy and tense. A gleam of hope: milk? Feverishly I tried to get up, but fell back again, tired. No, not milk: only my old affliction acting up.

—TRANS. BY LE VAN HOAN

An Unsound Sleep

[VIETNAM]

by Nhat-Tien

A MOTOR-CAR stopped just at the pagoda entrance.
Three or four ladies, old and young, got out, twittering
cheerfully. A woman beggar abruptly set her partly
broken bowl on the ground, hung one of her legs curved
to look crippled, and rushed toward them, wailing,
"Hail, noble ladies! A wretched humble creature begs
you for some charity."

A ten-piaster coin was thrown at the beggar's hand, but
she clumsily let it drop on the cement pavement; it
rolled and rolled until it dropped into the opening of a
gutter. The poor woman hastened to look in but found
it dark and deep like a chasm, and turned up distracted.

Old Phan, sitting close to the entrance wall, burst
out laughing, and the other fellows with him giggled.
The woman beggar kicked a pebble over the gutter
opening and discontentedly came back to sit at her
usual place. She took up the broken bowl full of rice
mixed with other waste, and with her filthy fingers
helped herself to the rancid-smelling food.

One of the beggars said, "We could drive straight to

Thien-Thai, Tra-Cu, if we owned such a modern car.
A lot of people go on a pilgrimage there."

Another retorted, "Oh, the devil with you and your
beggar's mind! We wouldn't have to go begging at
temples if we owned such a car."

A third joined the argument, then a fourth, and soon
the whole lot was disputing noisily. Old Phan got up
and twisted his body with a cracking sound. He dipped
his hand into his worn-out khaki waistcoat pocket and
groped for the coins chinking inside. Then he left the
group of beggars and headed for the marketplace.

At the poorest-looking eating place, he ordered a
small bottle of alcohol and a dish of dry shrimps. He
ate and drank slowly, looking at no one, and no one
in the noisy crowd paid any attention to him. Suddenly a
man shouted, "Fire! A big fire at Lo-Gom hamlet!"

Old Phan looked up wide-eyed. "What!" he exclaimed.
"A fire, really? Is it true, a big fire?"

The man stared at him intently, then nodded and
said, "Do you take me for a liar? I just came down from
there. The fire started at Three-Oak hamlet where the
married couple Chin-Nho were living. Both of them lost
their jobs; they quarreled with each other and burned
the house out of rancor. I know them very well."

Other men gathered round to question the speaker,
and Old Phan bent down to put a shrimp in his mouth.
He had the small liquor bottle refilled, and by nightfall
he was totally drunk. He paid the bill, opened his
waistcoat to bare his chest, and got up to go out. The
city was already lit up, and neon signs blinked on and
off atop some of the tallest buildings. A few stars were
out; the air was calm, and the sky was clear. Old Phan
staggered through the main streets; after some time he

found himself near a park. Seeing a stone bench, he stretched out on it on his back; lighting a home-rolled cigarette, he gazed at the sky through half-shut eyes. Through a microphone hanging on a nearby tree, a radio voice croaked loudly. But Old Phan, in his drowsy state, heard only dimly the familiar slogan repeated so often : "Revolution! Revolution!"

After a few minutes on the bench, he started for home, wondering if his daughter would be there.

Old Phan lived with his daughter in Lo-Gom hamlet. Miss Phan earned her living as a greengrocer at the city market; her father was a porter who usually carried loads from several storehouses in Cholon. Before the Buddhist demonstration, the old man and the girl were as punctual as two Swiss watches. He usually came home at six in the evening; after washing and changing, he was ready at 6:30 to sit on the doorstep and enjoy a leisurely drink and peanuts. About the time the bottle of liquor was half empty, Miss Phan came slowly down the street carrying two baskets of fruit at either end of a pole across her shoulders. It was always before seven—never later.

But after the demonstration, as the city was thrown into a turmoil of arrests and police investigations, Miss Phan's punctuality was greatly disrupted. The first day, she came home half an hour later than usual; the second day, nearly an hour later; and the third day, about one and a half hours later. The hot rice and other food left for her had grown cold on the table. As time went on, Old Phan lost more and more patience. He decided that his daughter must be off cooing with a lover, either hidden under a bridge or in some stall at the marketplace.

This evening he was more cross than usual; he had drunk more than his usual one bottle of liquor, and his face was red, his eyes were hot, and his hands were furrowed with sweltering veins. From his seat on the doorstep, he watched the alley and grumbled.

"Oh, the devil with the whore! She'd better beware the stick! What kind of ill-bred girl is it who runs astray looking for God knows what company?"

The old man was really out of temper. He even thought of beating her with the door-bar when she appeared in the doorway.

And she did not appear until a few minutes past seven. Old Phan was blazing; with one hand he threw his drinking glass on the floor, and with the other he snatched at his daughter's dress. But he had hardly opened his mouth when Miss Phan pushed him aside, muttering, "Don't be fussy, daddy! I just went to the pagoda."

Old Phan's rising choler all at once subsided. He screwed up his eyes and asked, frightened, "You! You went there yourself, did you?"

Miss Phan nodded, but the old man kept staring at her. As he started, he seemed to see her as he never had before. Her eyes were big, black, and glittering; her round-oval face was fair-complected; on her flushed cheeks, tiny beads of sweat were running from the hair ends.

Seeing her father's amazement, Miss Phan could not repress a sweet but proud smile. "You're surprised, are you?" she said. "A lot of people from the market took part in the struggle."

The old man seemed thoroughly awakened by this revelation. He started and exclaimed, "But you are risking your own life. What can you women and girls do?"

"We can do a lot. Since other people participated, why not me? I would not like to be a shirker, daddy."

Old Phan discontentedly made for the door. He could hardly advocate cowardice in front of his daughter, but at the same time he didn't want her meddling in the struggle. It was too risky, especially for a girl.

Having put her things away, Miss Phan got ready to wash. The old man resumed his place on the doorstep, musing about his daughter's activities. He began to suspect her behavior, and to reprove himself for believing what she said so easily. She might have just gone to the river bank to gossip with other talkative girls, or met some boy at a corner. Why, a girl as credulous as she was might have been seduced by some artful man to make love with him in his house! His heart throbbed and his mind whirled just to think of it. Confused, he looked at the back yard, where his daughter was washing.

A few moments later, Miss Phan came into the house and sat at the table. Her hair, which she had washed, was lustrous. Gently, she pulled at the hairs one by one, picking out the pieces of lemon pulp which she had used for cleaning and which stuck to the hair. Then she combed it very carefully in order to get a good parting.

Old Phan felt disgusted as he observed her silently from outside. It was obvious that she had fallen in love and was trying to make herself smarter than usual. To fan his indignation, he poured one more drink, curved himself backward, and gulped it at a stroke.

Then he asked her, "Why do you need to pay so much attention to your dress? Simplicity should be a maiden's best ornament."

Miss Phan raised her head and stared at her father. "I only washed my hair, daddy," she answered.

"Try to behave properly and don't let people laugh at me with contempt," Old Phan said.

"Don't worry, I won't make it a secret if I get a lover. I will introduce him correctly."

The old man was completely silenced by this response. He knew that his daughter always behaved correctly, and he usually treated her accordingly. Having no answer, he retreated outside to his doorstep.

Miss Phan began to look intently into her mirror. She plucked some unruly hairs twisted in her eyebrows and removed one or two pimples on her face. Then she looked at her white teeth and began rinsing them.

Old Phan snarled, "You have nothing more to worry about, do you? It really makes me sick to watch you."

Without raising her head, his daughter retorted, "Why, dad? You *do* look funny tonight."

The old man rushed inside.

"I can't help looking funny, my dear! You said you took part in the resistance, and I believed you. But I am rather suspicious when I see you taking so much trouble with your appearance."

Miss Phan got up, went over to her fruit baskets, poked her hand inside one, and picked up a roll of paper. Showing it to her father, she took him into the kitchen and whispered, "Now do you trust me? I have distributed bundles of these papers all afternoon."

Old Phan started and stammered.

"I am done for!" he exclaimed. "Really, do you want me thrown into prison to share all kinds of punishment and torture with the lot of you? You must be crazy to bring home those damned leaflets!"

Miss Phan smiled.

"You know nothing about what happened outside tonight because you were shut up in the house," she said. "At the pagoda, people were busy moving in and out all day, and no one noticed me. I'll read the leaflet to you, all right?"

The old man waved his hand and beseeched, "Please don't. I won't listen. It's of no use to me. After this, take these papers anywhere you like, but don't bring them here. It would mean death for both of us."

Miss Phan kept silent, put the leaflets back in the basket, went to the wardrobe, and prepared to go out.

The father asked, "You aren't going out again at this hour, are you?"

"Yes, I am," his daughter answered softly. "Please go to bed as early as you like."

The old man pointed to the baskets at the corner of the house and asked, "Are you leaving those damned things there? If they are discovered, I'll have to suffer the consequences alone!"

The girl smiled.

"Don't worry, dad," she reassured him. "We are perfectly safe here."

"You are working for my death," the old man groaned.

His daughter said nothing but pushed open the door and went out. Old Phan watched her from the doorway for a while, then suddenly turned back and shut the door tight. He imagined the whole neighborhood knew of his complicity with his daughter in this terrible plot!

From that day on, Old Phan stood aloof and left his daughter free to continue her dangerous activities.

Each evening, he sat on the doorstep, drinking and eating peanuts. He watched the narrow street, waiting for his daughter's return each night.

Miss Phan often tried to soothe his feelings.

"Take it easy, dad. It will soon be over. After that, we may go anywhere you like, we may talk freely without fear of being spied on. And . . . there are many other things we'll be able to do, that the young man Su speaks about, but I can't remember them all."

Old Phan at once sprang to his feet.

"Well! Who is this young man Su? Why does he interfere in your business?" he demanded.

Miss Phan blushed deeply, and said, "Oh well. . . . This young man . . . Su is working in a garage downtown."

"You love him, don't you?" her father inquired urgently. "And he is also a member like you, isn't he? Good heavens! How can I bear such an offense?"

"Don't be fussy, dad," Miss Phan said, disappointed. "Su is a proper young man, and I think he would be a good match."

"Yes, I understand. There's a shortage of young men, so anybody can be a good match to you. But it's no use talking so long as I have not met your man."

A few days later, Miss Phan introduced Su to her father. The boy was healthy and tall, with bright eyes, a high forehead, and a jolly smiling face. The old man was pleased, but he pretended to be stern and difficult.

"You must be well aware," he told Su, "that my daughter is from a good family and has had a good education."

Su hesitated, then answered, "Yes, I know."

Old Phan muttered, "It must be so. I am just telling you the plain truth."

Still gazing at the young man, he went out to the doorstep with a small bottle of alcohol in his hand. After a while, he forgot all about the lovers whispering to each other at the table inside the house. He held up the bottle to check the contents, muttering to himself, "What a beast of a drink! Nothing but water, quite unsavory, not a smell of alcohol at all."

After that, Su visited now and then. He brought good news of the underground struggles against the government. Old Phan only listened and abstained from asking questions. He did not want to degrade himself before the man who was courting his daughter. But to himself, he could not help admiring Su for his ability and broad knowledge. The boy gave a careful analysis of the situation in Central and South Vietnam. He summarized the war news, and fully explained what was happening in Europe and in China. Old Phan decided that Su had had a university education. He himself, of course, could scarcely read the alphabet.

Miss Phan often interrupted her lover's speeches to ask a lot of questions. The most common was, "After our rebellion has been successful, we will enjoy all kinds of freedom, won't we?"

"Of course, all kinds," Su would answer. "Freedom of religious faith, freedom of press, freedom of speech. . . . And that's only the beginning."

"And black markets and illegal goods storing will be all over, won't they?"

"No doubt about it; all that will no longer worry us. All the profiteers will be ruthlessly exterminated. In the new era, whoever tries to impair the economy of the country—like fraudulent tradesmen or goods monopolizers—will be dealt with by the people in the streets."

Miss Phan smiled happily, and her eyes got brighter.

Even the old man unwittingly joined in the conversation : "I don't care whatever happens. I only want a secure job. They make fun of me and bully me like a dog because I have no other means of support than my porter job at the warehouse."

But then, lest the boy take notice of his deficiencies, Old Phan quickly added, "I must tell you that I don't trust in anybody. Just look out! Even in a new era, everything would soon come round to its former status. I've seen too much in my life."

Two weeks later, Su was arrested, and Miss Phan also disappeared. After waiting up for her until past midnight, the old man hunted for the leaflets and documents she had hidden in covered places. He burned them all and swept the ashes into the gutter. Then he went back to the doorstep and sat there smoking cigarettes until daybreak.

He stayed home from work for weeks, waiting for news. He could feel his cheeks getting hollow, and his hair and beard seemed to grow much faster. His eyes became duller and tired. He went to the prison for news, but saw only Su. The young man was no longer handsome; probably he had been tortured. But he smiled and said, "Don't worry, dad! Our troubles will soon be over, and we'll soon be home to help you."

The old man was deeply moved. For the first time, he grasped the boy's hands, and said very kindly, "I hope so. Pray God—pray Buddha—that Phan is safe!"

His eyes were wet with tears. He gave Su a bundle of bananas and a loaf of bread, and the two stood silently looking at each other. A few minutes later, a prison-guard sent him away. He walked away unsteadily, stopping now and then to look back at his future son-in-law. The boy smiled; Old Phan was very much tempted to smile back, but his throat was choked up.

That night, he drank at least three times as much as usual; dead drunk, he slept right on the doorstep.

Miss Phan was not released until after the revolution broke out. She was strikingly pale and thin, with dark circles around her eyes and a strained smile on her face.

She immediately wrote Su a letter. "I beg you to forget me, as I shall forget you, for the obvious reason you are well aware of," the letter said. But she wept bitterly after signing this missive. Seeing his daughter's unhappy face, the old man had a premonition that her life was going to take an even more unfortunate turn. He felt petrified; his face turned livid and his eyes grew hot. Sitting at his usual place, he watched her in the dark. His head was reeling; he had emptied glass after glass of alcohol. He wanted to shout insults and persecute everybody.

The next day Su came to the house, but the girl avoided meeting him; he left sullenly. The day after, he returned, early in the morning, and sat waiting until past noon. At last Miss Phan had to see him, even though she was still weeping.

"I would be a beast to give you up," Su said to her. "In this period of struggling, everyone has been a little offended; it couldn't be helped. We must think of ourselves as very fortunate; both of us are still alive."

Several months later, Miss Phan gave in to her persistent lover. They planned to be married at home, quietly, for they could hardly conceal Miss Phan's pregnancy.

Su had lost his job when he went to prison, and had

no way of renting his own house. Miss Phan was still
too weak to go back to her old job as greengrocer.
So the two of them had to depend on the old man for
their sustenance. Old Phan was obliged to work more
and drink less to meet all their needs. But he stayed
cheerful; now and then he even tried to cheer up the
young couple.

"Soon there will be a revolution, and then lusty young
people like you will never be unemployed," he would
say. And laughing, "As for me, as old as I am, the
government will probably put me in an asylum for the
aged where I could play chess and drink all the time.
But I would probably die of doing nothing in such a
house!"

Su was also confident in the new regime. He ran to and
fro like a shuttlecock, looking for a job. At last, a friend
recommended Su to the owner of a new garage; but the
job was far away from the city, in the highland of
Banmethuot.

Su told the news to the family. "I don't want to work so
far away from daddy," he said. "There are probably
plenty of jobs right here in Saigon; we mustn't lose our
patience waiting."

But the old man had already lost his patience.

"Ah, the devil with your fear of working far from
me," he said angrily. "What do you take me for—a
small child? Now that you have found a job, you must
consider it as good luck for both of you. Remember
this: a bird in the hand is worth two in the bush."

"Then you must come with us!" Miss Phan said.

Old Phan pouted. "My dear," he said, "try first to
cope with your child before you wish to cope with your
father too! When a newly married couple is burdened

with a child, the work quadruples. Believe me, I know only too well!"

Su looked from father to daughter with concern. "Well," he said finally, "we'll go, because we can't do otherwise. Whatever course we took, we would be failing somehow in our duty to daddy."

Old Phan tried to force a smile and answered, "You would be much less dutiful if I had to work harder just to support you."

A moment later he added, "I am just joking; but, to be serious, I think we must be practical for the time being. We would die of hunger if we let ourselves be softened by our feelings. My guess is, your fortune will get worse and worse if you stay here. As the saying goes, there's 'a little molasses for too many flies.'"

A few days later, Su and his wife left for Banmethuot. Old Phan felt lonely and forlorn; for several days he stayed home from work and drank and played chess with some loafers in the vicinity. He grew visibly thinner; his hair turned more silvery and his beard more luxuriant. His arms quivered; they were streaked with dull-colored veins betraying a sickly state.

One afternoon, he received a letter from his daughter, and had someone read it to him.

"My dear father," his daughter wrote, "we are very unlucky indeed. The job promised to my husband was taken by someone else; worse still, I became sick. But don't worry. Su has managed to find work at the bus parking lot. He seems to have a talent for getting out of difficulties; he has even been recommended by the garage manager. But his salary is rather poor, and I don't know how we'll manage when I am in confinement. I hope I will recover soon; then I'll be able to work myself, carrying materials for buildings. Do you know, dad, they are building a lot of new houses here?"

After hearing the letter, Old Phan left his chess game, locked up his house, and went to town. He thought of the baby coming into the world soon; it was his duty to send its mother a bit of money to relieve her sorry plight.

He drank some alcohol to recover his strength, then went quickly to the nearest warehouse. Since he was a regular porter, he could ask to be registered there for carrying goods. Someone put a package of imported fabric on his back. It was a heavy burden; he could feel his back sinking, his legs staggering. Even his sight became confused. He tried to pull himself together, but only sweated more heavily from every pore.

Some passers-by tapped on the package, urging him to "go ahead, old man!" "Why are you standing there, for fun?"

Old Phan tightened his lips, shifted the package on his back, and started to walk. But his feet were unsteady, and when another porter bumped against his load, Old Phan fell flat on the ground. The warehouse owner, a plump Chinese woman, rushed up, removed the package, and sent Phan away.

"It's just because I'm drunk today," he protested in a hoarse voice. "But tomorrow I'll stay sober, and you'll see.... I'll carry three times as much and carry it running! I'll bet nobody can compete with me in a race."

Everyone stared at him and then burst out laughing. He wanted to join in the fun, but was unable to slacken his lips.

That night Old Phan slept deliriously on his doorstep.

He dreamed of Su becoming the owner of a garage and of himself driven into the asylum where he did nothing but drink and play chess.

When he awoke the following morning, he was seriously ill. He realized that his vital energy had brutally left him. During the past few active months, he had been draining the last bit of strength before he collapsed, like an oil lamp blazing before going out.

He thought of his daughter, of Su, of the talks the two of them had had about their glorious past deeds. He felt no regret; nor did he bemoan his fate. He murmured to himself, "After all, this country sucks our blood. Why can't we suck on it for a while? No, no need to worry."

Old Phan's logic proved to be wrong: a few days later, he was thrown out of his house because he couldn't pay the rent. He sold the furniture to pay off the landlord, and walked out of the house with only a knapsack on his shoulder. He asked a neighbor to write a last letter for him to Su, then left Lo-Gom hamlet for Saigon city.

Now he saw that he had been right in his reasoning. He hung on the city like a greedy leech. In the daytime he threaded his way through parking lots, markets, busy streets, or pagoda entrances, picking pockets; at night, he sat by himself with alcohol. Most of the time, he slept in the park, but now and then he made do with the doorstep of some shop. He rested his head on the knapsack and his back on a piece of packing-paper which, after long use, became as tattered and threadbare as his waistcoat.

Everything about him was worn out and tattered except one small packet he jealously kept almost untouched: it contained the Sus' letters and the photo taken on their wedding day. He wrapped these valuables in a strip of newspaper; its front page had an advertising picture of "tiger balm," the back page, a political editorial. Old Phan took pains to try to spell out the editorial's contents, and perceived confusedly that the major subject was revolution.

—TRANS. BY LE VAN HOAN

Notes on the Authors

Peter Cowan teaches English at Scots College and the University of Perth, Western Australia. He has published three collections of short stories and two novels.

Hal Porter, who lives in Melbourne, Australia, has published two novels, two volumes of autobiography, two plays, and two collections of short stories.

Peng Ko is deputy director of *Hsin Sheng Pao* newspaper in Taipei, Taiwan, and a part-time associate professor at Taiwan Normal University. He is the author of numerous novels and short stories.

Lao She collaborated with Clement Egerton on the translation into English of China's famous novel *Chin P'ing Mei* (The Golden Lotus). His novels and short stories are noted for their humor and for their capturing of the vernacular Chinese of Lao She's native Peking.

Yasunari Kawabata, Japan's Nobel Prize laureate, died by his own hand in 1972. Many of his novels and stories have been translated into Western languages. He served for eighteen years as president of Japan's P.E.N. Club.

Yoichi Nakagawa, who in the years before World War II was a member of Japan's *Shinkankaku-ha,* or New Sensibility school of writers, is author of a number of popular novels.

O Yong-su, a former editor of the *Hyundai Moonhak* (Modern Literature) magazine in Seoul, Korea, is author of a number of novels and short stories.

Hahn Moo-sook, author of novels and short stories, was awarded the Asian Free Literature Prize in 1957. She is an active member of the Korea P.E.N. Club.

Lim Beng Hap works as a health inspector in Sarawak, Malaysia.

Mary Frances Chong is a recent graduate of the University of Malaya, with a degree in English.

Maurice Duggan, who lives in Auckland, New Zeland, has published four collections of short stories and is a contributor to several literary magazines and anthologies.

Roderick Finlayson, who lives in Maukau City, New Zealand, has published a number of short stories.

N.V.M. Gonzalez, whose fiction has appeared in a number of short story anthologies and has been translated into both Asian and Western languages, is a former associate professor at the University of the Philippines. He is presently acting director of the Writing Program at California State University at Hayward.

Bienvenido N. Santos has been awarded numerous prizes and study fellowships for his writing. He is on leave as president of the University of Nueva Caceres in the Philippines, and is a Fulbright visiting lecturer at the Writers Workshop at the University of Iowa.

K. Surangkhanang is best known in Thailand as a novelist, but she often writes short stories on a favorite theme : the plight of society's poor and weak.

Dhep Maha-Paoraya was highly acclaimed for "Champoon"

when it was first published in a Thai journal. He died shortly after writing it.

Minh-Quan was born in central Vietnam. She writes poetry and essays, as well as short stories.

Nhat-Tien, a journalist, teacher, and writer, is author of four novels as well as numerous short stories.